ASH RAVEN

The Librarian of Souls

Sins of The Flesh

Copyright © 2023 by Ash Raven

All rights reserved. No part of this publication may be reproduced, stored or transmitted in any form or by any means, electronic, mechanical, photocopying, recording, scanning, or otherwise without written permission from the publisher. It is illegal to copy this book, post it to a website, or distribute it by any other means without permission.

This novel is entirely a work of fiction. The names, characters and incidents portrayed in it are the work of the author's imagination. Any resemblance to actual persons, living or dead, events or localities is entirely coincidental.

Ash Raven asserts the moral right to be identified as the author of this work.

Ash Raven has no responsibility for the persistence or accuracy of URLs for external or third-party Internet Websites referred to in this publication and does not guarantee that any content on such Websites is, or will remain, accurate or appropriate.

Designations used by companies to distinguish their products are often claimed as trademarks. All brand names and product names used in this book and on its cover are trade names, service marks, trademarks and registered trademarks of their respective owners. The publishers and the book are not associated with any product or vendor mentioned in this book. None of the companies referenced within the book have endorsed the book.

Book cover designed with assets from freepik.com

Map designed using Inkarnate

First edition

ISBN: 9798390170250

*This book was professionally typeset on Reedsy.
Find out more at reedsy.com*

To Maggie, my ultimate enabler

"Man must be disciplined, for he is by nature raw and wild."

— Immanuel Kant, Critique of Pure Reason

Contents

Within these pages...   iii
Founding and notable members   v
1   Augustine   1
2   Joanna   10
3   Joanna   24
4   Joanna   37
5   Augustine   48
6   Augustine   61
7   Joanna   80
8   Augustine   89
9   Joanna   97
10   Joanna   111
11   Augustine   124
12   Augustine   136
13   Joanna   151
14   Joanna   163
15   Joanna   182
16   Augustine   197
17   Augustine   211
18   Augustine   221
19   Joanna   234
20   Joanna   245
21   Joanna   260
22   Augustine   268

23 Joanna	282
Epilogue	294
Thank you for reading!	299
About the Author	300

Within these pages…

Thank you for picking up the first book in my soft, dark Monster Romance series, Sins of The Flesh. This is an adult romance featuring a posh boogeyman and his human love. Please read through the warning below to prepare yourself, and know that this is not an exhaustive list.

CONTENT WARNINGS:

White coded characters, plus size female lead, blond moustachioed male lead, accidental mating, fuck or die situation, touch her and die, you touched her so you are dead, sand everywhere but make it romantic and sexy, spines and quills

TRIGGER WARNINGS:

Dubious consent (while both leads are very interested in one another, the dream state and lack of knowledge surrounding their initial coupling is a bit sketchy), blood/fluid play and consumption, age gap (immortal vs. 29), workplace bullying and gaslighting, poor mental health, confronting death, physical assault (on page), assault aftermath, parental death (historical), mention of foster care system, violence and gore (on page, graphic), gun violence, blood rituals (on page, semi-graphic), murder (on page), suicide by overdose (mentioned, historical), vomiting, implied homophobia for background character, discussion and descriptions around hunger, eating, and addiction that may be uncomfortable, humans as a food source

SEX RELATED KINKS:

Power exchange dynamic, consensual non-consent, chasing, collaring, pet play adjacent behaviours, ownership, worshipping, bondage, orgasm denial, aphrodisiac adjacent, monster genitals, oral sex, masturbation, p in v sex, minor ass play, spanking/impact play, sand play

If you think a warning was missing here, please send me an email at authorashraven@gmail.com

Founding and notable members

Augustine Ravenscroft (he/they)
Deg'Doriel 'Father Doug' (he/him)
Ramón Lagarto (he/him)
Orthia Moore (she/her)
Kragnash 'Nash' Hawthorn (he/him)
Nora Birch (she/her)
Arlo O'Shea (he/it)

GWENMORE
FOUND 1667

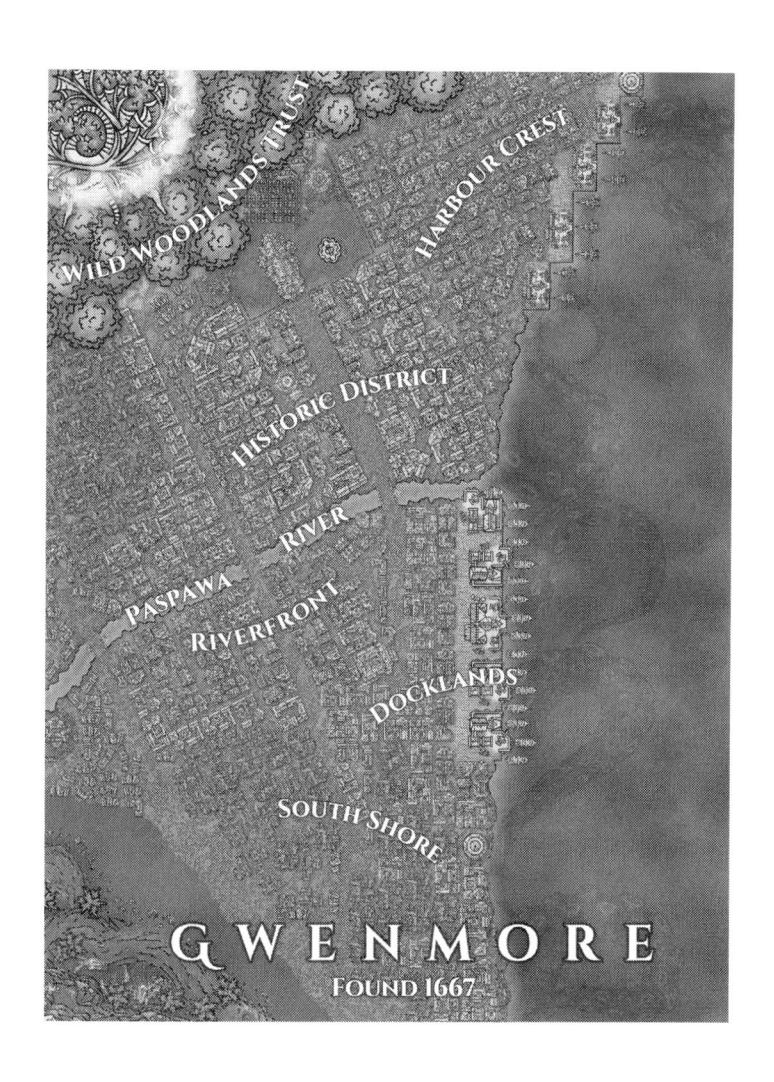

- Wild Woodlands Trust
- Harbour Crest
- Historic District
- Paspawa River
- Riverfront
- Docklands
- South Shore

1

Augustine

2752 days

The seventies were a disgusting era of interior design. The 1970s, that is. I am quite fond of the 1870s design choices. The grandeur of it all, how the decor could overwhelm the senses in such a deliciously satisfying way. Haughty socialites would gawk and squawk about the distance that piece had travelled or how much Lord Barrington had paid for that particularly risqué statue in his study. The era was rife with jealousy and greed and such glorious indulgence. They had their faults as well, but the Maximalist style is much better suited to my tastes.

Yellowing linoleum and buzzing fluorescent lights do not, however, suit me. The parish centre basement for Our Lady of Mercy was last renovated in 1976 and truly, it shows. Orange, faux wood panelling lines one wall and against the adjacent is a faded, tobacco-stained wallpaper that used to be a garish floral design. The rest of the walls are cluttered with filing cabinets and children's artwork of Christian iconography.

Honestly, I can barely recall how this all used to look before that. The years have started to blur together. My age is catching up with me, slowing me down, and making me set in my ways. Centuries of existence weigh down upon my back as I slog through the monotony of living in this modern world. While everything is constantly changing, I remain the same because humans will always sleep, and they will always dream. It has made my existence stagnant and predictable.

A human's waking hours are when their emotions are the most deeply buried. You can only catch the slightest tang of their tempting feelings in the air as they scurry about. Even those who try to hide their emotions cannot, from my observant eye. The auras around them are dull. They could not even draw the eye away from a boring book.

When they dream, they are fresh. Fear, anger, envy, lust. The scent of human emotions in the dream realm, in my realm, is like walking into a bakery after the first loaves of bread have been removed from the oven. Their auras overwhelm the senses, surround, encapsulate and vibrate with the very soul of their beings.

But all I can smell and taste in this foul basement is the stench of the creatures around me.

I pour boiled water into my mug, the cheap tea bag expanding and floating to the top. Lapsang Souchong is smokey and bold but still not the sort of tea I would serve for gatherings like this. The pine resin notes assault my senses with a harsh chemical quality that tells me this blend was done with profits in mind before the actual taste. But then again, as I take my usual seat in one of the only wooden chairs left amongst a sea of plastic, I look around at the other beings and think this is exactly the sort of drink they would find fancy.

Orthia, the sea witch, sits with her usual scowl and smells of the docks. A tattered scarf is tied around her throat, an accessory I have never seen her without. Her hideous fishing waders are stained with grease and years of defilement. The only time Orthia leaves that decrepit old ship of hers is for these weekly meetings. Her Love, that foul slime ball of an almost god, seems to force her here. They seem to be the voice of reason in whatever storm brews within the witch. Occasionally, her eyes gloss over. A milky white hue distorts her dull brown eyes, but when she blinks again, she is less petulant. Since the golden age of piracy, we have dealt with Orthia and her Love's tidal demands and, still, so much of her is a mystery to me. I cannot say I know her truly, just that her aura is a dangerous black that reeks of rage.

Next to her is our resident sewer rat, or lizard, to be more precise. Ramón is the only male stupid enough to sit near the sea witch. The beast believes himself to be some sort of mafioso, or whatever term for the leader of an organised crime group the humans use now. The green scales that cover his skin are a beautiful, deep shade that looks horrendous amongst all this orange. As he smokes his cigar, the long and heavy tail at his back swishes back and forth as he eyes our other members. Ash falls on his trousers, and I sneer at the reminder that we use the same tailor, that we have the same tastes yet are completely different in regards to our needs.

Off to the side, one of our newer members, an awkward ghoul of sorts, speaks with the woodland fae leader. I do not know his name, but I can tell Nora is trying to scam him, get him to agree to some bargain he cannot possibly commit to. She knows she is not supposed to work her asinine fae magic during these meetings, but the shy ghoul does not know. And what he does not know *will* hurt him, eventually. Especially if he cannot prove himself to be useful to our group.

That does not mean I can shirk my duties to our community, to our network of creatures trying to do more than subsist on humanity. If we are to continue to thrive in this environment and enjoy the pleasures of modernity, it is of utmost importance to have control of our appetites. We each have a role to play to maintain the balance with the mortals, a connection to a different section of humanity that benefits us and protects our existence. Mine is to be the note taker, the history keeper, an account of all who have lived in Gwenmore and what they have done. Arlo will be given his role, or he will be forced out.

A few more of the lesser beasts trickle into the seats; werewolves, vampires, lesser demons, sprites, and the lot. The crowd is not too extensive tonight, which is nice for me. I would much rather be at the library than listen to these beasts moan on and on about hunger and self-control. They do not know true hunger.

The craving, the desire, the gnawing feeling in your stomach and teeth that demands nourishment. They have not truly felt the ache that comes from decades of starving themselves simply for the pleasure of continuing to exist on this pathetic rock. They do not know what it is like to subsist off the barest amount, just enough to remain in control without alerting our prey of our existence. Out of habit and irritation, I take a sip of my tea and grimace at the artificial taste.

Where is that well-fed leader of ours on this fine evening?

"Auggie, what's got your knickers in a bunch tonight?" Ramón hisses with an amount of cheer that grates my ears. I adjust my glasses and remind myself that killing him will get me exiled from the city, which I helped build all those centuries ago, into this hellish utopia before me today. No amount of history will allow the rules to bend for even me.

"I have a lot of work to do, and we are running behind schedule."

"Books, books, books." His long, forked tongue slithers out between his fanged teeth. "Why not enjoy your old age? What is it this year? Millennia?"

I want to lash out. I want to let the wispy veins of sand running through me sink into his body and turn his brain into pudding. My gums ache as my teeth sharpen and my sands try to surface. Unfortunately, the reptile feels no fear, and I already know his brain is more blood clots than not. He would be an extremely unsatisfactory meal, awake or asleep. There would be no satisfaction in gorging on whatever soul the rat possessed. The others watch; their little tricklings of fear and anticipation are a breath of fresh air to keep my cool and collected.

Before I can retort, he arrives with his mobile phone pressed against his ruddy cheek. His form for the past few years has been a shorter, portly man with a nearly white beard. As are men of the cloth, I suppose. Through the ages, they have consistently been the men that society deems least attractive. Third, fourth, and fifth sons with no skills or good enough looks to snag a useful position for their families. They are also always the ones most likely to make a deal.

"Yes, Margie, yes, yes, I know the parish council-"

How he puts up with Margie Lawson, president of the parish council, astonishes me. I have seen him suck the soul from a child for crying too loudly. For all his heartlessness, Deg'Doriel is a fantastic actor.

"Of course, god bless." With a shiver and a smell of singed flesh, the priest skin suit disappears. "Dumb bitch."

A crown of sharp, short horns surrounded by falsely angelic curls and a good two extra feet bring our little spiritual guide, still dressed as a priest, back to his true power. The demon who first decided we would live under this new world order alongside the humans, decided also starving ourselves for the sake of actually living longer, towers over the room. Sharp, bright teeth glint under the fluorescents, and his thin tail whips angrily behind him as he heads to the central seat.

"I'd apologize, but I'm about to rip the heads off anyone that speaks to me directly, so please, someone fucking start this meeting."

Slowly, the usual twenty or so of us go through our last week. I transcribe all the meetings and make a note of who needs to be watched for this reason or that in a dark leather-bound notebook with a fountain pen I have had since the 1920s. It is ivory etched with a fluttering of feathers, a work of art itself. A gift from a dear friend during my short stint as a dancer when she first opened up her exclusive club in the city. It's a priceless piece of history and it belongs to me.

The notes allow me a certain level of control over the lives of others that attend our weekly club. I crave knowledge like this when I cannot truly feed on the emotions that envelop humanity. To know someone is to know their joys, their goals, and their fears. And oh, is that a tempting morsel. I suppose my role is one that I have always been suited to, but even so, the monotony, the same problem presented over and over again, has begun to tarnish my existence.

There are some unsurprising changes in controlled days. A vampire drank a human dry after three weeks of controlled usage, and another wolf killed a hiker because it is spring and the humans are venturing out further into the Trust despite clear signage. The sea witch's number of days is about to have its annual shift, and with spring comes the reawakening of her Love's hunger. The Fae are preparing for the midsummer sacrifice; Nora anticipates ten will do this year as long as the wolves can keep to themselves. The rest of us all hold steady with our appetites and do not succumb to the gluttony of humanity.

"As you all fucking saw, I am still in the same fucking skin bag and that bitch is alive, so I am up to 130 days." Deg'Doriel swipes a clawed hand over his face and to the back of his neck in a human show of exhaustion. He unclips his white collar. "Some housekeeping, Kragnash and Buster send their regards. As you can guess, he's very busy with the re-election so we won't be seeing much of him for a while. I expect to see you all out supporting him in November. There are planned police checkpoints in the Docklands and South Shores for the next few weeks, so stay clear."

He goes on to list a few more details that mean nothing to me. None of these really affect how I will go about my time. I do not have to hunt like most of the drivel here. My food comes to me. The library, for as long as the concept has existed, has always been a beacon for the curious, foolish, and weary parts of humanity. Humans have always been the type to congregate, and I found my sleepy hunting grounds in their place of study. Scholars and upper echelons of society used to gather amongst the hallowed halls, and it was so easy to prey upon their deepest emotions.

The crowd has not changed drastically from century to century, but my hunting ground has a way of bringing forth a rare and exquisite delicacy. A soul, a scrap of a meal so filling, they consume me in a way I want to solely consume them. They are a once-in-a-lifetime meal, one that threatens the grasp I have on my control.

My sands trembled at the memory of my first taste of the morsel who came to the library eighteen months ago. If I had known then what an addiction she would become, I still would have dabbled in her dreams. In her luxurious golden aura and the savouriness of her fear, the sweetness of her arousal, it is easy to forget myself and the monotonous drag of our existence. She is simply too delicious to ignore.

Her dreams are scattered and few between, even as exhaustion seeps from my new obsession's every pore. But when she does slip and fall truly into my realm, it is nothing short of glorious how she frees herself to *every* possibility.

But my old friend says something surprising that brings me back from my ruminations.

"And we will be hosting a monk for the Franciscan seminary in three months' time for a year. He isn't to be scammed, possessed, or eaten during his sabbatical here. Apparently, the idiot thinks he wants to be a priest, and with any luck, he will be my new skin bag. So do not fuck this up for me."

"Oh, so possessive already, Padre," Ramón teases, heavy tail swaying behind him.

The demon growls but says nothing more. Doug, as the current priest he wears is called, is maybe 40 years old. Definitely not at the current retirement age for humans. Something else about this skin suit must be bothering him. Another time I will ask when we are both feeling more patient.

All in all, a short meeting I am happy to be done with. I pack away my journal and tuck my pen into its inner pocket.

Before Ramón can annoy me further and before the ghoul, Arlo, can introduce himself to me properly, I leave Our Lady for work. The library and, if my luck persists, *she* waits for no one but me.

And I am so very hungry this evening.

2

Joanna

I'm here again. My body is exhausted, but my mind is restless. That's been the pattern lately, my thoughts refusing to settle, so I lay awake in bed for hours until the sun crests over the horizon and light filters through my thin curtains. I've tried all the usual methods of sleep aids- soothing teas, sleep casts, meditation, weed, masturbation. None of them stops the tidal wave of anxieties and stress, making guilt churn in my stomach and making my eyes burn from exhaustion.

Sleep should be an escape from the nightmare of my everyday life, but I can't find it.

My life isn't really a nightmare, by any means. For a short time, after my moms died, I got lost in the go-between of foster homes and university. That was a nightmare. Nobody knew what to do with me, so I did everything I could to prove to them I was fine. No matter how my situation changed, when I was moved on to the next placement because one person didn't want me, I always told the social worker I was fine. I've always been a people pleaser, a trait my mimi instilled in me at a young age. When I was sixteen, I latched on to it to try and keep her with me, even if it hurt me.

As I got older, I realised that everyone is holding onto something they shouldn't and mine really isn't that bad in the grand scheme of life. I went through a phase of reading self-help books, so I try to frame my situation in a positive light when I can.

My flat on the south side of the river is a bit damp and I can't keep it warm. But the bus can get me to work every day, and I can afford the rare fancy barista coffee or new shoes if I am indeed desperate. Work is shit, but who doesn't have a shit job these days? I'm not starving, and I've got a roof over my head. My life shouldn't feel like such a nightmare.

Yet when I slog home from work day in and day out, the monotony of it all is a hellish nightmare I can't escape. The boring routine has made me feel like a drone, a worker bee slaving away for its queen. There are times I want to believe it is because of the industry I work in, but I am even more frightened of the idea that every job will be like this one. I am belittled and ignored, but at least I know the enemy here.

There is comfort in knowing that every day will be the same shit. I don't have excitement or an adventure to look forward to, but I'm sure I wouldn't have the energy for that anyway. I don't feel anything except tired these days.

Except I can't sleep. My mind is constantly abuzz with a need to do... something, anything that could make me feel alive again. A shackle around my ankles that I slowly drag behind me each and every day.

So on nights like these, I throw on some clothes, whatever is soft and doesn't smell like the laundry I haven't done in weeks, and I go to the library. There is a sense of safety at these ungodly hours on the north side of the river that I don't always feel in South Shores. The security guard is stoic but always polite. The handful of homeless people seeking refuge and the internet are near the newly renovated front addition that holds the tech area and community resources.

I wander further into the building, leaving the shiny extension and into the real majesty of the library. Antique fixtures, low yellow lighting, and the slightly musty smell of dust and old books all transport me back in time. Built in the late 1600s, the Ravenscroft Somnium Library is one of the oldest buildings in town, at the centre of the historic district and open all night long. It takes me an hour on the bus to get here, but it is always worth the fare.

The interior is almost overstimulating. While the exterior of the building is just like every other Neo-Classic building in the district and blends in with the terraced shops and houses, the inside is like something from *The Picture of Dorian Gray*. Dark wood bookshelves are crammed from floor to high ceilings with books and tomes. Where there isn't a bookshelf, there are frames and frames of art pieces, each with a small brass plaque next to it. The curtains on the wall are a lush, ruby-red colour. The fixtures are ornate. All the little wires and modern essentials are painstakingly hidden away within the designs of the wallpaper or moulding.

A beautiful space for a beautiful librarian.

He is at his usual station, *the librarian*. He ardently works, reviewing books and taking notes of the damage behind a grand, tall desk. I can't tell if he is old or young, happy or tired. He is as resolute as the stone columns outside the library.

Maybe that is what I like about him. He doesn't change, and he's always working, like me. I've turned him into some sort of fixture of comfort and security in my mind because even when I feel like I am losing my grip on reality he's right there at that desk. A beacon I can rely on.

For a moment, I watch him from a nearby stack stuffed full of cracked leather-bound books. He's tall– long and lean, with sharp features that make the shadows dance across his olive skin. Well-groomed, his button-downs are neatly ironed and tucked into pleated trousers, a tie knotted perfectly around his neck and clipped to his shirt. He dresses like a professor from a different age, right down to his wire-frame glasses. Tonight, he is even wearing a hunter's green tweed vest that makes him stand out more against the curtains. His dark golden hair catches the light when he looks up.

He's spotted me.

Does he recognize me as a regular? I've never spoken to him before, because I have never needed to in the months of nights I have spent here. This is where I go to feel anything, to hopefully catch some sleep before I have to rush home and prepare for work.

"Can I help you find something?"

It's like honey and hot tea when you have a sore throat. His low, soothing voice washes over me for a second and warms my insides. For a moment, I savour it and let it soothe an ache I can't name inside of me.

My apology is slow and a bit slurred, punctuated by a healthy yawn. He almost smiles, as the corners of his mouth tilt upward, but like the muscles aren't used to being worked that way. I probably look like a hopeless grad student trying to get a paper finished. Something about the way his eyes move at that gesture is unsettling, though. I've seen him plenty of times before, but this is the first time I've heard the librarian speak. He's probably just asking to get me to move along or to make sure I don't make a mess of his space.

Fair enough, I wouldn't want people making a mess at my job, either. I smile, a bit tight-lipped, and pick up the first book I can find, *Critique of Pure Reason*.

I hustle over to my usual area, the cliche dusty stacks and worn leather wingback empty as ever. I'm not sure why this part of the library is outfitted with these instead of more hot desks or study tables, but I'm grateful. The chair creaks a little under my weight, and my hips barely fit into it, but it's my spot. I cross my ankles and settle into the worn cushion. Carefully, I open up the book, the leather spine protesting as it comes to lie on my lap. The philosophical words of Emmanuel Kant float through my mind whimsically but are easily pushed aside by more irrational thoughts. Like how surprisingly deep the librarian's voice was, how his tone dripped with something secret. He doesn't look old enough to have that much wisdom, but what did I know? He could be thirty or he could be fifty years old. My brain could be making all of this up in some sleep-deprived hallucination. I rub my tired eyes, blinking away the few tears that spring up from the pressure, and try to refocus.

Silence surrounds me. It's easy to get lost in the transcendental aesthetic Kant sets forward. Sentences are strung along and merge into a blur of black and stained white lines. I don't even realise how heavy my eyelids feel until I'm not in the library at all any more.

JOANNA

Warm, wet sand collapses beneath my feet as I walk along the beach. The waves lap at my ankles, making me shriek from the chill and giggle all the same. Behind me, there is more laughter, deep and different than what I remember.

My friends' laughter was high-pitched and filled with squeals of delight as we drunkenly ran along the beach. That summer holiday with friends had been the trip of a lifetime. Renting a cottage outside of the city along the shore for a week. I remember it being blissful. Sunrises and sunsets merging into one, games in the sand, splashing in the salty water, it had felt like a dream even then.

Up ahead, the cottage lights are on, and the shadows of my friends stand out against the window. A smile spreads across my lips. I'm exhausted from all the chatting and in need of a moment of quiet. The sun is setting now, golden streaks turning to lush purples and reds. My feet stop, my heart telling me to slow down and enjoy the wonder around me. It's not every day you see such beauty. The sun warms my skin, bathes me in comfort, and wraps its arms around me. A deep sigh passes over my lips, and I close my eyes.

Real, warm arms wrap around me, hands caressing my waist and soft stomach. They sweep up to my chest, long fingers guiding my head to the side so soft lips can pepper my skin in gentle kisses. My thoughts and memories are muddled. This definitely didn't happen on that holiday, but I am going to let it happen now. The person behind me presses into my back. My body turns heavy, limbs unwilling to leave this embrace to head inside.

"Just lie back, darling, I'll take care of you now."

The words wash over me like a wave, holding me down, drowning me in that warm feeling. My heart quakes at the promise of those words, of letting another have control as if it is natural for me. I do as I'm told with an eagerness to please. My body sinks into the lush bed below me until I am surrounded by rich fabrics and scents. The arms hold me close, pulling me deeper into the warmth of this dream. The lips on my neck are more insistent, sucking and biting at my flesh. They pull sounds from deep in my throat, desperate and hungry ones that I didn't even think I was capable of.

There are no inhibitions here.

My mind reels, fighting for awareness, but my body lets go. I can't control how it craves these things when I am in bed with my lover. With anyone else, I would hold back, but everything here pulls and tugs until giving over all of me is as easy as breathing, and my mind is at peace.

I'm not tired, I'm alive in this delicious fantasy. A tongue lashes at my pulse point, a frantic feeling settling in my belly. It's achy, needy, my hips bucking up to find any sort of friction. I can't form a single thought, form a coherent word, but my body screams and demands pleasure from the person toying with my body.

"Hush," my dream lover breathes against my ear. "There is no rush. We have all night, darling."

My fingers crush the velvet beneath me. A wet gasp leaves my lips at the feeling of sharp teeth dragging over the column of my throat. My back arches up, seeking the sensation even as my mind tells me something isn't right. I've had dreams close to this, with the teasing and touches, but never this demanding and fierce. Maybe it should scare me, but it just makes me crave more. My lover's voice in my ear is familiar, but there is an edge to it, a longing that makes my insides flutter and buzz with new excitement.

JOANNA

Fingers play with my body like they own it, like they've known me and my secrets for an eternity, drowning out everything but my desire, my need to truly be seen. I can't shake the aching feeling that pools in my belly. It grows the more he teases me, unable to grab hold of the person, the man, punishing me with his mouth.

His hands are no different. They soothe and taunt me with every sweeping touch. They glide up my sides, caressing the soft rolls that usually make me squirm, until they reach my breasts. They grab, massage, and pinch until my nipples ache from the attention. They wrap around my throat, giving me the softest squeeze, asserting their control over my body as if I needed reminding.

Fingers tease my lips and pull at my bottom lip until I can capture one of them. He vibrates against me, purring deep within his chest as I suckle, stroking him teasingly with my tongue.

"Is this what you need tonight, darling? Something to fill you up and make you focus while I finally take you apart piece by piece?"

I think I nod, but it's difficult when he presses that finger deeper into my mouth.

He slides it out, my mouth following the motion. His soft laugh rumbles through the air, echoes around walls I can't see. Two fingers are stuffed into my mouth next, pushing my tongue down until I feel his skin break against my teeth. He shudders above me, a deep groan leaving his lips as my mouth floods with a sweet honey. It mixes with my drool and seeps from the seam of my lips as I try to swallow it down, too addicted to the taste on my tongue to think about what he has just given me.

The hand that isn't fucking my slack mouth moves between my legs to spread my thighs until the stretch burns. Finally, *finally*, his fingers move to my soaked pussy, teasing my folds and slit but purposefully avoiding my throbbing clit. It makes me delirious, the need to be filled driving my hips against his palm. Anything to make the ache go away, the burning desire rolling through my belly while the fingers in my mouth mimic what I really need. His hand traces a path back up the hills and valleys of my body until he is holding my nape.

"You're so responsive, darling, like you were made for this." His teeth scrape the shell of my ear, sending a shiver down my spine. "Such a devious imagination as well, so many dark desires trembling just beneath the surface. I may just have to keep you."

Moaning. It takes all my focus to even do that as a response to him. Though he probably didn't expect anything from me in this state except begging. Something I am more than willing to do if it makes the ache go away. His fingers slide from my mouth, a line of spit still connecting me to him. That first free breath of air is choked by the whine that comes from my lips when his spit-slick fingers thrust into me. They glide in easily, my pussy swallowing them up like they will save me from the needy, achy syrup I'm drowning in.

I want to see him, to open my eyes and gaze into the face of the man ruining me so effortlessly, but my eyelids are heavy. It's so much effort to grip the velvet beneath me, to even close my mouth. My muscles are loose and warm, my pulse thrumming in my ears as every breath I drag into my lungs takes all my energy. The only thing keeping me moving, begging for more through panted moans and whimpers, is the burning need to be filled. It's all my brain can latch on to, when words are failing and my pussy is weeping for release.

"Are you ready for me, darling? I can feel how much you want it, how your body aches for me. Say you want it. Tell me you want me as much as I want you, darling."

Fingers around the back of my neck squeeze, move my head until I feel a nose brush against mine. Soft lips press against my jaw and cheek, but never my mouth. My tongue glides across my lips, wetting the dry skin just for my laboured breaths to make them chapped again. The saccharin taste of him dances across my taste buds again as I try to do as he requests. I repeat the action to force my lips, my tongue, my jaw, any part of me, to move on my command so I can answer him.

"Please," I pant, "need… you."

He groans into my neck, and sucks the skin between his teeth until I'm certain he's left a permanent mark on me. His cock slides through my folds, hot and heavy, coating him in my juices before I feel the blunt tip of it pressed against my slit. My hips jerk, wordlessly trying to make him move faster, to fill me up, to fuck me hard like my body craves. It's so close, the thing I've been solely focused on for what feels like years. Anything, I'd give anything so long as he is buried in my pussy.

He steals whatever breath I have as he surges forward, thrusting his cock into me. I feel him all the way to my throat; I'm so full of him. If it weren't for his hand holding me up, I'm sure I would have drowned in these sheets and honey. My back arches up as he draws his hips back. The smooth motion of his cock slipping from my pussy makes me clench. He can't leave me so soon when we've only just begun.

"Beg for me, darling," he commands, his lips bumping against mine, his deep voice sending a shudder up my spine to give me enough energy.

"Fuck, please," I moan. "Fuck me, need you, jus' needta be full, please."

My words slur together, my voice sounding like it belongs to someone else as it echoes around the room we're in. He doesn't make me beg for long, as the ragged breath he draws makes it sound like he's losing control as well. For a fleeting moment, I believe he is just as affected as I am, barely keeping his own head from swimming in the same syrup that coats my thoughts, and it pulls at the strings of my heart in such a way I would happily stay here forever if he were to ask, if he were real.

Hips snap forward, slick skin meeting and echoing around the room—a cacophony of sin vibrating through the syrup dripping over my mind. I can't think of anything else, just this connectedness and fullness overwhelming all other senses. While I can't find the strength to lift my arms, my legs wrap around his waist. A hand squeezes the meat of my thigh hard enough to ride the edge of pain. Sharp nails dig into my skin, sending shocks of pleasure through me.

He leaves wet, open-mouthed kisses against my throat and growls when my pussy tightens and clenches around his cock. Words in a language I can't comprehend, maybe French, maybe even English still, are poured over my skin like boiling sugar until I am burning under the feeling of his lips. I'm so close to cumming. The muscles in my thighs are beginning to shake with the effort of holding back. I just need a little more attention where I've been denied it thus far. A whimper escapes my lips when he grinds into me, my clit throbbing with need. The hand on my thigh moves, squeezing between my sweat-slick body so his thumb rests right over my clit.

"Let go for me," he breathes. "Cum all over my cock, darling. You are taking me so well, you deserve to cum. You deserve everything I am going to give you. I have you, darling, fall apart for me."

His words turn frantic as he begins to circle my clit. My pussy clenches and gushes over his cock. Stars burst behind my eyelids, and the feeling of his hips furiously slamming into me only prolongs the pleasure. As his movements stutter, I feel teeth against my skin again, sharp and wet.

They only pierce my throat when he cums. A scream rips through my throat, my head snapping back even as his fingers dig into my flesh, holding me against his hard body. The pain is nothing compared to the pleasure that floods through the hazy honey of my thoughts. My pussy spasms, it feels like too much. I'm slipping away from this reality.

"So delicious," he hums, licking at my neck. "You've done so well for me, such a sweet naughty thing you've been, but it's time to wake up, darling…"

A weight lifts off me, a light filtering past my closed eyes. I gasp when my eyes snap open, only to blink rapidly to adjust to the bright sunlight filtering through the windows overhead. This isn't the first time I've fallen asleep in the library. Never have I ever had a dream that explicit and vivid where I felt the choice of my actions. Most of my dreams involve me shouting at my boss or stomping on my high school math teacher's fingers, but I am just a watcher in those dreams. In this dream, I was there. I made the choices. Something about this dream was very different.

And I think I like it.

I shift slightly in the chair, grimacing at how wet I feel. Heat rises to my cheeks, embarrassment tightening in my chest, but it doesn't take away from the lightness I feel from the little bit of sleep and release I got from my public wet dream. I pick up the book that has fallen off my lap as my thoughts drift back to the dream. How different it was, how different *I* was. So willing to give my dream man every part of me when I try so hard to keep all those secret parts of myself buried. All those little things that I tell myself I don't need, I am willing to give to this man who has haunted my dreams for months.

As I stand up and stretch out the kinks from sleeping in the chair, a pain in my neck throbs. Instinctively, I rub away the feeling. The flesh is hot, tender to the touch, and slightly swollen. A quick shower when I'm home should get rid of all the aches and pains. I make my way back toward the philosophy section to replace the book.

For the first time in weeks, I feel rested. My headache is mostly gone, just a lingering dull feeling at the base of my neck. There is almost a feeling of elation that I haven't felt since I was a kid. The world is brighter, the colours richer. Is this all from a decent chunk of sleep? I stare down at the cover of the philosophy book and pull my phone from my pocket to check the time.

Shit.

I need to get going so I'm not late to work. The book slides back into its home, no one the wiser to my late-night reading except the dust bunnies.

When I turn this time I catch the librarian staring at me from his station. He glows in the early morning sunlight, his

JOANNA

lips spread into a lackadaisical smile, slow but closed. He adjusts his glasses, catching them in the sun and making it look like he is truly golden. I rub my eyes, distinctly aware of the mess between my thighs, as if he will be able to smell me or see a wet spot. Maybe I'm not as well rested as I thought. I raise my hand to wave goodbye, a sheepish smile on my face, feeling like I've been caught doing something I wasn't allowed.

"Have a good day, darling."

3

Joanna

I can't shake the guy's look out of my head as I rush through my morning routine. This is the most clear-headed I have been in weeks, but it's all I can think about. Maybe it's because I'm picturing two different versions of him in my head. The librarian from another time, who is stoic like a statue, and the librarian from this morning, who was golden and almost teasing. Was that the right word for it?

His words still haunt me as I triple-check that my front door is locked before heading to the bus stop. *Darling.* Goosebumps erupt on my arm, even just thinking about the dream again. Fuck, where had that come from? Definitely not from that boring philosophy book I had been trying to read. I can't even remember the last time I watched porn. The inspiration for that little incident is certainly just from my ill-placed crush on the librarian. *The librarian.* God I don't even know his name, yet I'm having pornographic dreams in which my mind casts him as the perfect man for me.

I'm nearly 30 years old. I shouldn't be having those kinds of dreams. I've known for a long time that those kinds of sexual encounters don't happen in real life. I've dated plenty of people who just want you around while you're giving them something to fuck, but when you need something? They leave. When you don't need anything from a partner, they can't hurt you. When you don't need people at all, they can't leave you when you least expect it.

The early April chill blasts my face and makes the hem of my wrap dress flap dangerously high. I shove it down, my purse sliding off my shoulders while I do it. Even with a few hours of sleep under my belt, I feel like a hot mess. A shower and a touch of lip gloss can't fix everything, I guess. The weather is humid but cool, the clouds burning up as the sun gets higher in the sky. My phone's news bar said today would be the first hot day of the year. I hate it.

Summer brings its own challenges. It's hot and sticky. I sweat through whatever I'm wearing the moment I step out of my door. The city is triple-packed with tourists, making the pavement even more crowded. I like the dark and cold of winter. Hot drinks and soft sweaters are what I crave, but when it's a billion degrees and humidity is at 115%, that's not exactly easy.

And let's not forget the return of the contract worker.

"Joanna, you know the drill. Make sure all the new guys are trained up and have their May schedules." Patrick ends the video call without another word.

I hold in my sigh. Patrick Concord doesn't seem to understand what my job role really is or what I was first hired to do. I am supposed to be the marketing and office admin. I am supposed to keep our small office tidy, make sure our project announcements are professional, and make the occasional post on social media about how we are helping conserve historic buildings in Gwenmore. That was before Janet, his ex-wife, left him and before he started his three-year-long midlife crisis on the Spanish coast.

Patrick is permanently tan with a drink in his hand now, while I am permanently his girl Friday. It started out simple enough, a few extra spreadsheets to help keep everything organised and suddenly all of Janet's old emails and documents were in my possession because I couldn't say no to my first boss. Janet knew my moms from university, and Patrick gave me a chance when I'd failed interview after interview. When Janet left, I couldn't abandon Patrick, even when he ran away to the other side of the world leaving me to pick up the slack.

And while the job is shit, and the seasonal hires shitter, the job market is the shittest. Here my old dresses and busted shoes go unnoticed in the sea of hard hats and hi-vis. Out in the interview world, I'm not sure I would ever be able to sell myself enough to get something better. I know this role now, these people, how to manage the expectations of me here. Out there, the world is unknown. I'm much happier with the devil I know.

My day dribbles on after that late-morning call. Purchase orders, invoices, customer complaints, compliance forms, project bids, and so much more paperwork pass over my desk, I don't even get a chance to stop for lunch. I don't even think I've stood up from my desk until our compliance manager knocks on my open door to remind me about the introduction meeting I'm leading.

Lance Jameson has been at the company longer than even I have. He's in his early fifties, has been married for twenty years, and has two grown kids who are out of the house now. He still has all his dark brown hair and, by anyone's standard, is very attractive. His constant guidance and kindness when I first started cemented an easy relationship for us during my first years when I was trying to prove to myself, to Patrick and Janet, that I was more than a pity hire.

Since the divorce and my sideways promotion that I'm not sure was actually a promotion, our relationship has been strained. I don't see myself as his boss, even though I'm in charge of the office rota and passing around payslips. I want to believe I can still come to him with problems if I have them. His opinions matter to me, but recently there has been something off with him that I can't exactly place.

He's distant. There is something about the way he looks at me, looks over my shoulder when I am working in one of the billion spreadsheets I have open all the time. Lance is trying to assess what I am doing, and it only makes me more concerned about my productivity levels. I find myself trying to prove to Lance now that I am worth my seat in this office.

I don't know how to broach the topic with him. Is he observing what I am doing to report back to Patrick? Or is he looking for a new job, thinking maybe he wants to switch to what I do in operations? Either way, I don't want to rock the boat. Lance weathered every storm, every fight between Janet and Patrick, the nightmare of divorce, all of it, with me. I don't think I could handle it if he got a new job. He is my daytime constant.

"You got everything?" he asks, a small bag slung over one of his shoulders.

I toss a backup, empty file folder into my purse so I can collect all the papers I will need to put away tonight. My eyes sweep over my desk, and I click sleep on my computer. "Yep, let's get this over with."

Lance leads the way as we start walking away from the office and over to the job site. This is my chance to ask him what he has been up to outside of the office, away from the prying ears of everyone else. I swallow down the nerves, tucking my purse tighter under my arms as we turn on to the busy sidewalk.

"So, how have you been? I miss our morning gossip." If there is one thing I miss the most about Lance, it is knowing everything that is happening about anything. Whether it was in the office or at a job site, he would have the best stories to tell. He has been in the business for so long, he can get you just about anything you need in the construction world as well. Now, between my workload and his distance, these little meetings are all I get with him.

"Ah, well, you know Toni and I are separated right now," he starts.

"What?" I stop right there in the middle of the pavement and look at Lance. Is that why he has been so weird? "Are you okay?"

"It was a long time coming, ya know, but I am working on it. I'm going to make sure we spend the rest of our lives together." He keeps walking, hands shoved into the pocket of his jacket. "C'mon, tell me more about this job, kid. I want all the nitty-gritty of it."

The armoury. Built in 1675, the building is one of several along this main strip of the historic district that was constructed when Gwenmore was founded. Unlike a lot of the buildings here, which were rebuilt after the revolution, it still retains its Colonial style of architecture. The contract is pretty basic. We are replacing the narrow windows and doing some structural maintenance around the building to keep it in tip-top tourist shape.

Concord is a small construction company in the grand scheme of the industry. We don't have the full-time manpower or connections to build new housing suburbs cropping up west of Gwenmore for commuters or the redevelopment happening around Dunst Overpass. We specialise in smaller projects and historic preservation. This contract is a much bigger win for us than the general sort of work we do for smaller commercial businesses and homes.

The armoury is a listed building, meaning it's partially owned and funded by taxpayers, even though now it holds a variety of different privately owned companies. It's leased by the city to some mega-conglomerate, who didn't really have a choice in the matter when the mayor and city council announced they were accepting bids on the project eighteen months ago.

I couldn't stop myself from jumping at this opportunity eighteen months ago. At being able to keep this little pocket of Gwenmore history alive. Patrick was sceptical, still is, that I am in way over my head and that the project will fall apart, but when I told him the city was underwriting the whole thing, he stopped fighting me on it so hard. Sometimes my stomach still does a dip when I think about how this project is going to look for Concord, for me.

But no matter how many times I do this introduction meeting, standing up in front of a large group of people never gets easier. But the contract we are starting construction on today is a big deal; it's my deal. It is my labour of love to show that I have done something for this business. Some of the guys today will be seasoned veterans who have worked for us before. They know me, know the deal. Their bored expressions and casual disregard for what I have to say will be annoying, but it's nothing new. The new hires will stare and pass judgement, because I am a woman working in construction, but I am used to that look.

Plenty of people have passed judgement on me. The difference here is these contract hires don't hold any power. It will irritate my skin, but when I leave for the day, it won't come home with me.

It has never occurred to me that this job is right next to the library until we walk past it to cross the road to the armoury. Up until recently, it didn't matter to me because I wasn't carrying any sort of schoolgirl crush on any individuals who worked there. This thing for the librarian is new to me, a few months old and I haven't had to visit the armoury site in months, so I have only confronted these feelings in the dark when I am alone.

Now, I am transported inside. I can't remember the last time I was here in the daylight, but my brain fills in the blank. The librarian is there, golden and shining in the afternoon sun. His jacket is off, and his shirt sleeves are rolled up as he carries an impressive stack of books to a shelf. I wonder briefly if he enjoys the sun or if he chooses to work the night shifts because like me, he hates the heat and baking sunshine.

Any thoughts of sexy librarians are dashed when I'm hit by the overpowering smell of dampness and underground. While the main entrance of the armoury is new and has security, the basement has obviously been neglected. Fluorescent lights hang from the low ceiling and cast an eerie light down the hallway that leads to the site office. A "Concord Construction" paper sign is taped to a windowless door that is wedged open with an old brick.

Further down the hall, there is a right and left turn that leads to the workmen entrance. That was one thing the leaseholders demanded, no construction crews in the lobby. Office staff like Lance and I were given temporary passes so we could talk with the security team when necessary, but otherwise they don't want the increased risk. In my opinion, allowing about a hundred contractors, and sub-contractors, and site hires basement access with no visible security is a bigger risk. But the aesthetics are worth more to them, I suppose.

The walls of the site office are lined with metal shelves stuffed full of plastic filing boxes, but just behind them, you can see the old brickwork. Massive stones backed deep into the ground centuries ago. It's dark and damp with narrow, bar-covered windows. A stink trap with fans that push the smells around rather than removing it. This space is obviously used for storage, and once we are done with our job and packed up, they will move everything else back. Like we were never here, little drones come to fix the hive who don't matter when the job is done.

And as a head drone, it's my job to control the other drones.

"Hey everyone!" I shout, my voice echoing around makeshift desks and folding chairs. "Please, quiet down. I know it's late, and you've had a long day of paperwork."

The room with about forty contract hires doesn't settle down; the roaring chatter of men continues on while I try again to get them to shut up.

"Gents, c'mon, we all want to go home."

Lance saves the day and blows his whistle. Everyone turns to face us and I swallow my embarrassment before I have to start speaking with authority.

"Okay, hello, I am Joanna Cole. I am the administrator for

Concord Construction. Payroll, work requests, scheduling changes, PTO, anything relating to your job this season is run through me." I pause to catch my breath, sweat beading across my forehead. There is a murmur in the crowd, but I ignore it. "For on-site requests or complaints, you have all been introduced to your manager, Gary, so please contact him first."

I run through a list of general safety information, explain overtime pay, collect all their papers, and hand out my business card. This is the one time of year I ever really need those stupid things. On a final note, I remind them that we are guests here and that we need to be quiet and respectful of the people in the offices above trying to do their jobs.

"Any questions?"

A burly guy with his hair pulled back raises his hand. "Do they still have canons and shit here?"

"I don't think that is relevant to the job," I say, really confused about why this guy thinks I would know this anyway. From the basement, you could probably think that. A quick scan of the walls around here and I can see hooks and stains where stuff used to be kept here. But there is definitely nothing dangerous in the basement.

"Ya know, 'cause back in the day, this used to be where they kept all the weapons and stuff. Heard it was all haunted."

"There is no-"

"It's not haunted," a sour-faced-looking man shouts over me. I think I remember him from last summer, but there is a newish scar on his face that I don't recall. "It's cursed because of some Fae magic to keep soldiers from dying."

I don't know how or why this topic came up, but I have completely lost control of the discussion. Several of the men are shouting about not wanting to work on a haunted site, more of them are arguing about the existence of fairy people. Gwenmore doesn't have Salem levels of fame, but there is a rich history of founding families, secrets, and other horrors that run deeper than the Paspawa River that splits it in two. It brings the community together and separates them all at the same time, as the ensuing argument before me shows.

Personally, I don't really care either way. If they aren't hurting anyone with their belief in magic, it's none of my business. Life is hard enough as it is, if decorating a random tree in the park or keeping salt by the front door makes you happy? I say do it.

But never have I had an introduction meeting like this go so off the rails. It isn't until Lance blows his whistle again that they finally stop talking and pointing fingers.

"Please leave anything in this room that isn't labelled with a CC or Concord Construction alone. We are just here to do our job and leave," I tell the group, already feeling the weight of the paperwork this crew is going to give me on my shoulders.

There are more murmurs, a few pertinent questions about being paid by check rather than bank deposit, another few about site stuff that Gary answers. At some point, I zone out while Lance goes into his safety training. Before I know it, the meeting is done. It's quitting time. I shake hands mindlessly with a few of the older guys I recognise. There is still a stirring of people talking about Fae magic, about what it would be like to live forever and not get old. I catch Lance talking to the sour-faced man who first brought it up. He actually seems seriously interested in it and I don't know why, but it rubs me the wrong way. He never seemed the type of person to believe in that kind of stuff, but maybe I don't really know

Lance.

I have never been one to believe in the mystical or spiritual. My mom was a science teacher and my mimi was an accountant, both of them only believing in cold hard facts. The one time we stepped into a church was to take a tour of the bell tower at Our Lady of Mercy, the catholic church at the top of the historic district. The only thing I remember about that trip was Mimi letting me get extra hot fudge on my sundae afterwards for not complaining about all the stairs.

I wave goodbye to Gary and leave the armoury. Outside, the air is fresh and brisk. The sun is starting to set, but the street lamps haven't turned on yet. Splashes of burnished gold sunlight illuminate the library across from me. A breeze at my back pushes me forward and before I know it I am standing in front of the doors again. My fingers dance up to my throat as I stare at the heavy glass doors that have replaced the old wooden ones. I could go in. The thought makes my pulse jump under my fingertips and I feel a heat radiating from the base of my neck.

Then someone knocks into me on the sidewalk, and I'm suddenly very aware that I am standing here looking lost when I should have been heading back to the office. The rest of the walk back to the office is hazy, spending most of my time thinking about my reaction to standing outside the library. It's all cleared up when I see my desk. In the short two hours we were away, a mass of emails and papers appeared. For all the effort I put in early, it hasn't made a dent in my workload.

My stomach grumbles, and I think about the leftovers I stashed in the fridge when I arrived. I could take those home, eat them for dinner while watching reruns on TV, and try to make my brain turn off for a little bit so I could sleep. Or I could eat at my desk and catch up on emails for a few hours *and then* go home to try and turn my brain off.

The office microwave dings three minutes later, and the shepherd's pie I made two nights ago burns my fingers. I shake my hand out while I rummage for a fork. There is just enough space on my desk to set the Tupperware down to cool while I buckle in for some work. Minutes and a few emails turn into hours, but at least scheduling is done, and everyone is now registered into the payroll system.

I rub my eyes, tears forming to try and rehydrate them. They ache from the strain of staring at my computer for too long. It's late, the sun is well past set, and I should be exhausted. My body should be ready to collapse into my lumpy mattress and drift off to dreamland, but I know if I get the bus home, that hour of sitting around will only make my thoughts louder. I think about contacting my weed girl but decide against it. I don't need my sweat to reek of skunk for weeks.

There are options, I have options. Pay checks go out next week. I have a bit of spare cash, so I could go and get a drink. Maybe even venture out of my comfort zone and find some stranger to take me home for a quick fuck. As the thought enters my head, it almost instantly curdles. It brings a gross taste to my mouth I can't place. My nails tap against my keyboard for a bit longer as I send off one final email to a supplier about something trivial while I contemplate what to do. The ache in my neck from this morning is still there when I stretch. A rush of feelings hit me like a truck when I rub on the spot. Ones that make my eyes close and my tummy flutter.

I know what I want to do. But I shouldn't.

I know I shouldn't because that will lead to me doing it

every night, and I can't do that. I can't make a habit of falling asleep in the library. No matter how appealing a few hours of sleep are. No matter how comfortable *my* chair, tucked away in the quiet, cosy nook is, it is not a public sleeping area. No matter how attractive certain inspiring librarians are, I will not get my hopes up about seeing them again because that is just ridiculous. You can't repeat dreams, anyway.

4

Joanna

I wish I had called in sick to work. My stomach has done nothing but roll, flip, and cramp for a week now. I feel feverish, but when I take my temperature, it's perfectly normal. I'm more tired than usual and ready to snap- whether in anger or a fit of hysterical sobbing is yet to be decided. This is some of the worst PMS of my entire life.

And my neck still fucking hurts.

I've rubbed my skin raw trying to massage out the ache. Icing and heating the spot where it hurts the most for the past week has just made it worse. Even wearing a necklace at this point irritates my skin. I called my doctor, but with no skin irritation, swelling, or fever, he told me to just try to de-stress and get some more rest.

"Drink something other than coffee."

I would rather cut my head off at this point than give up coffee.

This armoury site is proving to be the biggest pain in my ass. I've gotten more complaints from this site manager than I ever have in the past. If it isn't him, it's someone in the main office coming to complain about PTO or interoffice politics that I don't think I'm really qualified to handle. Every morning when Patrick has called me this week, I swear he's been half drunk. The jug of sangria is right there, off to the side of his phone. I want to throttle him, but the more work he piles onto my plate, the more I just smile and nod.

There is something wrong with me. Obviously. When it comes to pleasing people, nothing will stop me. It has never mattered what I've got on my schedule or what I have prioritised. If Patrick asks me to do something, I tell him it will be done immediately. When I first started at Concord Construction, it was easy requests. Can you update the copy on the website? Joanna, can you put together this presentation bid today? Would you mind staying late to rework the budget you requested? Joanna, Joanna, Joanna.

A part of me has always known that it isn't the requests that are bad but the timeline for them. They are needed right now, by the end of the day. *If I don't have it on my desk for my meeting at 8 AM, you can kiss any sort of pay rise or security goodbye.* The voice in my head keeps telling me if I work just that extra bit harder, prove how valuable I am, Patrick will see it and tell me what good work I have been doing.

He never does, though.

I cried in the bathroom for 15 minutes this morning. It's Tuesday, the work week has really only just started, but after spending all of my weekend working on three different contract bids on new refurbishments in the Docklands, I couldn't keep the tears in. It's not the first time I have cracked like this under pressure, but I wasn't ready to be yelled at by Patrick so early in the day.

The new legal assistant was just trying to do their job and

had submitted the form as they were supposed to. Except, it was missing one of the accreditations we needed to attach to it. The business relies on numerous certifications and credits when applying for jobs with the city. It is an easy mistake that we should have caught, would have caught if a second pair of eyes had reviewed the submission portal.

An angry call from Patrick demanding to know why we have been fined ten grand was the snapping point at 9:30 this morning.

Thank god for Lance, honestly. That man pulls me up when I need him most. His calm presence stopped the flood of tears when he found me coming out of the bathroom, still sniffling. He magically smoothed things over with legal and Patrick in the short time I was panicking. Apparently, all we needed to do was call the accreditation office and ask for Debbie Forts, and she'd get us sorted. I can do that.

I did that. And lo and behold, problem sorted. She reduced our fine to a measly two grand, sending over the receipt and proof of refund before I had even ended the call. Patrick is still going to be angry about the two thousand dollars, but I can sort that out with accounts and there won't be any real shortfall.

If I ever have a free moment again, I need to buy Lance a drink or ten.

"Hey, Jo." Andrea from marketing's head pops around my door. "Did you have a chance to go over the budget proposal I sent you?"

Shit.

"No, I'll do it before I head home today so I can discuss any issues with Patrick in the call tomorrow so we can get approved before the end of the week."

"Thanks, you're a star."

She's gone before I can say anything else, and I slump into my desk chair. This is too much. I rub my eyes until all the little fuzzy bits appear and I think I've removed all my eyelashes. My fingers travel up to my nest of greasy hair I've piled on top of my head. I need a shot, a shower, and a short coma to feel like a person again. I look at my phone, only a few more hours until everyone will go home and there will be no more distractions.

A knock on my door makes me jump.

"Thought you could use this."

Lance places a mug on the corner of my desk and swirls of black coffee catch my attention. Not my usual way of taking the drink, but the gesture is kind and warms something in me after the day I have had. He remains at my door for a moment, and I wait for him to ask me for something. When he doesn't, the anxious urge to fill the silence overcomes me and I blurt out the first thing that comes to mind.

"Do you want a raise?" I joke, but already making a mental note to ask Patrick about it. He deserves it.

"A raise, more vacation days, corner office," he laughs, his eyes crinkling up at the side to show his age more than usual. As he looks around my office, Patrick's old office, I catch him making assessments as if he is sizing the room up to be his own. This doesn't look like a space I have been in for almost three years. The only bit of me in this box is a half-alive houseplant that I found on the side of the road one morning.

Lance looks tired. Where there usually aren't any signs of stress, there are now. The bags under his eyes are the biggest giveaway that something is keeping him up at night. Are things with Toni getting worse? Maybe he really does need that raise if they are trying to rinse him. I know he said he was working on it, but I hope he knows to take care of himself too.

"You doing alright?"

I smile a little, about to ask him the same thing.

I'm not sure if I should give Lance the real answer. We aren't *friends*, having only spoken to each other in the office, about safe for work things. But there is a camaraderie between us. When I was fresh out of college, and completely new to working a full-time office job, Lance had been a mentor to me. My desk was shoved next to his for nearly six years, and he seemed to understand that I needed guidance. I think he liked having a young person around as well, to keep him from really acting his age.

He certainly doesn't want or need to know that I am on the verge of PMS insanity.

"I'm alright, just exhausted."

"I hear you, but at least things should calm down again since all the new people have settled in."

If only he knew.

All I do is nod a little, my eyes flicking to the coffee mug placed precariously on the stack of employee files on my desk. I really need to organise those. It isn't safe to keep them out like this. Knowing me, I'll just end up knocking that mug over and ruining them all.

"Well, I'll let you get back to it. You need me to take those off your hand?" He points down at the files like the mind reader he is.

"Yes, please," I say, picking up the mug with both hands.

"Don't forget, Gary over at the armoury site wants to have a call before we leave for the day. Something about some of the guys not being up to snuff." He tucks the files under his arm.

I want to roll my eyes, but I'm scared that if I do, they will just roll back into my skull and stay there. *Lance is doing me a solid*, I remind myself. He doesn't actually have to be on this call. It isn't in his job description to handle these sorts of problems. He is only supposed to be dealing with our safety compliances and making sure the labourers are trained and wear their PPE. Gary just listens when Lance repeats what I'm saying. I am used to it with these guys.

"Does five work for you?" I ask, already setting up the calendar invite so neither of us, mainly me, can forget it.

"Sure, but I need to be out the door by 5:30. I've got tickets to the theatre tonight."

Even though he says theatre in a silly, fake aristocratic voice, my gut still twists up with guilt. If the calls I got last week were anything to go by, Lance is going to be late for his show. It will be my fault, too, if it has to do with how screening these new hires has been done. If they aren't up for the job, that's on me for being negligent, spending too many evenings in the library. Hiring the contracted staff has been solely my job for two years. I don't normally have any issues, but it seems like whatever lucky streak I had in that regard has vanished.

"You know what?" I force a confident smile. "I'm sure I can handle Gary on my own. I don't want to risk you being late, but I want to hear all about it, okay?"

"You're really sure, Joanna?" When he asks me this, he looks at me like he is gauging something more about me. Like my answer will tell him something more than a simple confirmation.

"Absolutely."

"Okay, well, if I don't see you again before I head out, have a good night."

Lance points at my coffee before turning on his heels and leaving. I look over at my computer screen, the pink sticky notes littering the frame with reminders and requests. Three more hours until I have to call Gary, and by the time I am done with that call, the office will be empty. Then I will be able to make some real headway on my to-do list. I promise myself I will only stay a couple of hours late, and then I will go home and treat myself to a bubble bath. I'm not even going to bring any work home with me tonight.

I slump into my chair, the security lights on the main floor already flicked on. Only the light in my office is left to illuminate my work. The call with Gary did not go well. Beyond not being able to get a word in edgewise, he had already gone over my head and fired two guys. More paperwork to do, files to find and reorganise. That also means I need to find two people to fill their spots, which means calling eight different people from the backlist to ask if they are still available and could start tomorrow.

I hate making these calls. It feels skeezy to say, 'oh you didn't get the job the first time, but hey look for reasons I can't disclose, we now have two positions open'. I did it though, because this contract means a lot to the company, to me. This is the first big win I have worked on as the lead. I created the bid proposal, negotiated and worked and lost countless hours of sleep for this job. If this goes well, it means I am good at my job. It's tangible proof to Patrick that I am loyal and know what I am doing and deserve more– praise, recognition, money. It'll show him that I belong in this role that he has somehow shoehorned me into.

I am too deep into it to let it fail because someone didn't meet Gary's standard.

It is well after the time I said I would leave. Even though I knock a couple of big items off of my to-do list, I add a half a dozen more tasks for myself to do tomorrow. The biggest of those being finding the fired employee files to hand over to accounts so they can be taken off the payroll. The work is never-ending.

For a second, I think about my bath at home, the warm water easing the ache in my body and soul. Even if my body is too big for the tub and the water gets cold too quickly, for a brief, blissful moment I can be weightless. The world almost fades away, and I can almost forget about work and the pathetic amount of money in my bank account that has to last me another week.

Sometimes in those moments, I think about what life would be like with a new job. If I got a position at a different construction company, would I still get the odd glances and disrespect? Am I the reason those things happen to me in the first place? I don't dream of labour, but I think really hard about being in a new job and everything just clicking into place. My boss is present and appreciates me, co-workers who go out for drinks on Thursday night, a shorter commute to the office– all of these things fill my head with flights of fancy that I don't ever foresee coming my way.

I am scared to leave, to abandon the first thing in a long time that has been a constant in my life. Since my moms died, I have been moved from one place to another over and over again. In college, that didn't bother me so much, with roommates constantly fighting and burying myself in my studies. Even when I was looking for full-time work after graduation, I bounced or other people bounced from flatshare to flatshare. Getting the job at Concord meant having a form of stability in my life that I missed.

That I still miss.

The bath won't help me fall asleep anyway. Taking a bath relieves some tension in my bones, but by the time I drag myself out of the icy water, my muscles have locked up again. Any relief I felt has gone down the drain with the lavender and honey bath salts I sparingly use. I can't remember the last time I was relaxed, my mind not tormented with paperwork and deadlines and anxiety.

That's a lie.

I can remember, but I've been forcing myself to not think about what caused it. The pulsing hot pain in my neck, the hot flashes, the cramps, the *horniness*, those are all things I can't ignore. My fingers have fumbled around in my sweatpants at least once a night since that dream. The aching in my neck will lessen for a while when the pulse moves between my legs. I've gotten short intervals of sleep that don't allow for dreams, but I'm almost grateful for that. If I could dream, they would be about that night in the library, about *him*.

My fingers skitter over the open neckline of my shirt, the cheap material chafing against my skin as I pluck at it to fan myself. Almost instinctively, they reach up for the sore spot on my neck. It throbs as I swallow, trying to wet my dry mouth and throat. The gentlest touch makes goosebumps erupt across my heated skin. I close my eyes, slowly counting to ten before pressing on the spot, hard. Digging my fingers into the tendons connecting my neck and shoulder until tears prick in my eyes and my pulse throbbing between my legs makes me feel almost alive.

This pain feels good.

I close my eyes and focus on the feeling, the burning sensation coursing through my system. My thumb teases a line down my throat and, for a moment, I can imagine it's his soft finger on my heated skin. I squeeze my thighs together, squirming in my seat until I can't take it any more. Even though my back aches and the waistband on my trousers digs into my stomach, my hips roll forward.

My imagination takes over.

Clear as the day we were there, as the dream, I am on the beach. Sea foam bubbles up around my ankles and the setting sun paints a watercolour sky that I can't take my eyes off. Hands caress my bare skin like I am fragile and breakable, a fine treasure that should only be touched with the utmost care, but I long to be grabbed, gripped, controlled with force. I want that more than anything. To be owned and used with purpose.

I inhale sharply, licking my lips before adjusting myself in my chair again. The metal frame creaks and I am reminded once again that love, carnal or emotional, like that doesn't exist. Or if it does, the person is a walking red flag. I remove my hand from my throat and look at my computer again. It's almost ten o'clock.

I want to say I can't believe I did this again. Stayed too late, forgetting to eat and drink for most of the day, but I am not surprised. This is a classic Joanna move, which is always followed by a cheap kebab from the chippy around the corner from my flat. I know I shouldn't. I can't afford new clothes if I grow out of these ones, but god the thought of cooking anything right now feels like too much.

Before I sign off officially, I send one final email to Patrick

JOANNA

telling him I want to have a call tomorrow about Lance. Work is staying at work tonight, the worn out, oversized purse on my shoulder lighter than it has been in months. I wave goodbye to the building security officer, as he offers a kind and tired smile that I try to match.

With all my good intentions this past week, I can't bring myself to go home. The sidewalks are near empty. A few other business-dressed people move with speed down the pavement, and a couple drunkenly giggle on their way home. Turning left takes me to my bus stop, where I'll get home in an hour, where my bath is. But if I turn right, it will take me to the library.

For the first time in a week, I turn right.

5

Augustine

2759 days

It has been a week of this incessant ache.

Seven days since I have tasted the sweet nectar of my darling. My library is barren without her and her emotions perfuming the stacks and shelves that surround it. For over a century, that scent has brought me comfort, but now without it coating my very existence, there's nothing but pain. My teeth, my sands, all of me aches for a woman whose name I do not even know but so desperately want to bind to my eternity to.

It is not even the physical, primal call of the bond that pulses in my sands. The desire that urges me, fights with all of my time-learned sensibilities to hunt her down, that makes me crave her. It is not the lack of a delicious morsel, for the weary who enter the library are sustenance enough.

It is the freedom of my darling's dreams that I so dearly miss. The wildness that runs through her when she believes no one is watching. In her dreams, I catch glimpses of it. Short bursts that revive a part of me I did not know was dying. The last dream, where I lost my control, convinced myself I could stay a while longer with her and feed and enjoy her dream, was eye-opening.

As if observing Renaissance and Baroque masters converge into an exquisite and beautiful work of art, my morsel came alive in luxurious shades of gold. Some of them were a soft honey, others a deep amber, and even the palest of yellows like the dried petals of chamomile tea. I can still taste her, feel my teeth sinking into the skin of her throat, my talons digging into the soft flesh of her thighs when I can no longer control myself.

Denying the bond is foolish. I was a fool to allow her out of my sight after that moment, so here I remain where she last left me, like a discarded puppy. I know she will return to me, to this library, because the bond must be burning through her the way it does me.

Does she dream of me even though we have not been near?

I daydream of her. As dusk begins to settle over the city and the usual crowd of the library thins to the odd being using the computers, when I slip into my office with the intention to read something from my private collection, my thoughts wander until I envision a beach. The dark waves crash into black sands not unlike my own and my human lies among them, surrounded by them, writhing in the smooth grains that cling to her. Her golden aura is blindingly bright and shines against her naked skin. An animalistic urge takes over me, driving me into a sprint so I may catch her and possess her soul and body for eternity.

Gods, her body.

My jaw clenches, and my hand moves to swipe across my moustache and bottom lip to make sure I have not drooled over my first edition French volumes of *Les Misérables.* The delicate pages and hand-marbled paper show enough signs of age, the last thing they need is evidence of my lacklustre control of my urges. I place them carefully back into their box and set them aside on my desk. The analogue clock above my office door claims it is only a quarter to seven. Arlo shall not be arriving for our introduction for another thirty minutes.

Another baser urge.

The mere thought of my darling's existence, the memory of her joy and her racing heartbeat as she ran down that beach, make my cock harden beyond comprehension. The seam of my trousers is permanently indented into the skin of my shaft after the week it has spent hard and unsatisfied. It is a matter of principle more than anything that I have left it, forcing myself to ignore the rush of heat through my sands that makes my skin tingle. There is nothing abhorrent about self-pleasure, and I have spent plenty of nights discovering the sins of the flesh as they are so called with myself, but under that surface-level urge, there is a deeper one.

It is even more dastardly, one that racks through my sands and makes my cock leak at the images it conjures. My darling, *my mate*, covered in my essence until she shines with only me, until her own golden aura is obscured by *me*. I want to cover her in it, bathe her in me until she knows that it is me she truly belongs to. I will be the only being who owns her.

I remove my lenses and toss them aside as my other hand presses into the front of my trousers to soothe my aching cock. Truly today is an example of my weak will, a miracle as to how I have survived this long when I cannot remain celibate for even seven days. Even as I berate myself, the hand on my trousers undoes the buttons, and my head falls back against my chair in relief. I will not be stopped from gaining this ounce of gratification, not now when I can almost clearly see her.

The image of my human that my mind paints is skewed by the way she perceives herself. All dreams are a perception of how one sees the world and their own interactions with it. My darling has a very pragmatic view of herself, an honest one that does not do her glory justice. It means my vision of her obscures the closer I get to her on that beach. Her body has a clear outline, a form that would ruin weaker humans. One made purely for me. The rest of her is a blur, like seeing a painting too close and losing the finer details. I do not know the shape of her breasts or the formation of her stretch marks. I have felt them beneath my hands, traced them with my sands, yet I cannot follow them like a map. I will not truly know her body until she is mine.

My cock jerks at the simple thought. *Until she is mine.* I stroke myself from the base of my shaft to the tip, pressing my thumb into the soft black quills that cover this side. My sands tremble at the pressure as they flex with resistance. I fist my palm tighter, adding pressure to the quills on the side and bottom of my cock. The pull of my flesh is barely eased by the precum that leaks from my slit. My quills fight against my grip, pushing and expanding as I imagine the wet heat of my darling surrounding me entirely.

How I will coat my sands in her cum, until she is lost in pleasure and cannot think. The only emotions she will feed to me are her desire and satisfaction. I crave them as much as I crave her joy and fear. My fist moves faster, pulling at the short quills with each downward stroke until they are leaking molten gold ichor through my grip. The talons of my fingers dig into the leather arm of my chair and more of my sands release from my body. A band of them tighten around my balls and more of them gather around my asshole. The flat graze against my skin has my mouth opening, sharp teeth on display as I work myself into a frenzy.

My thoughts become more disjointed, frantically jumping from images of my human pinned beneath me with her ass on display, to her stroking my cock with her soft wet tongue pressed to my hole, to how her thighs will wrap around my head and shake as I devour her pussy. There are so many ways I want to feast upon my human, but the one that is my undoing is the dream memory of my teeth pressed into her neck. She is soft and giving and free. Somehow, by the will of the fates or my length of stay in her dream cycle, she was able to get a bit of control and chose to wrap herself around me.

It is the memory of her plush thighs around my hips, her heels digging into my backside, that is my undoing. Her fingers gripping the velvet sheets beneath her, how I long to feel their grip on me. Every part of my body tenses and my sands vibrate under my skin, on my skin, until I am cumming across the surface of my desk. Thick ropes of pearlescent golden fluid dribble down my once-clean desk. If my human was here, I would have her lick my essence clean until it shined anew. Not a drop of me would be wasted.

My cock jerks at the thought of her submission, but a stroke of my talon between my quills sends them quivering with an amount of overstimulation that cools me down. The burning, primal urge of the bond is sedated for now, but I feel I have only opened the floodgates to more and more devious actions.

If my darling does not seek me out soon, I will have to enlist the help of Ramón to find her. The tension in my body eases and I stare at the high ceilings above me, ready to get lost in thoughts that will hopefully be more useful to obtaining my human.

A knock on my door makes my sands lash out. My body jerks to sit up straighter, any relief from my manual massage decimated by the intrusion.

"One moment," I call out, quickly tucking myself away and pulling the spare handkerchief from my top desk drawer. I swipe the mess away and discard the thin cotton material into the trash. A waste, but a necessary one. I toss today's Gwenmore Guardian over the main surface of my desk to cover up any other evidence of what remains of my slip in control. As I stand, a pleasing rawness rubs between my cheeks, and I have to clear my throat to keep my head on straight. As a final precaution, I run my hands over my tie and put my jacket back on before I open the door to my office.

Looking squarely at the space between his battered boots, stands Arlo O'Shea, ghoul and newest congregation member of Our Lady of Mercy. While tithing at the church has never been a requirement of the monsters in our group, I am sure it adds a mark in Arlo's favour with Deg'Doriel. The mouse-like ghoul eventually looks up at me, only long enough for his lips to part and then snap shut, his eyes widening. The taste of his fear is like rotted meat and it hits my senses when I realise I haven't fully righted my appearance. I blink, and the sands that still kept my eyes dark retreat.

I move aside and allow him into my office. He shuffles to sit in front of my desk, his head never turning to look and observe his surroundings. His sallow, sunken skin has no colour, no doubt from lack of a meal. Perhaps he is just exhausted, perhaps he is hiding something. Either way, I will find out.

"Tea?" I ask, closing the door firmly. I watch the subtle movements he makes as I work behind him. Arlo swallows and nods.

The process of making tea takes no time at all. The fragrant Darjeeling leaves float in their strainer for a few moments before I place it aside and pour the steaming liquid into cups that already have their splash of milk. I set the sugar pot on the tray and arrange some digestives onto a plate as well. Arlo is quiet the whole time, barely breathing as if that will cover up the anxious tart flavour he is adding to the room.

I set the tray down over the newspaper and take my seat. For some time, I stare at him while he simply stares at the tray. His clothes are very well worn, the jeans dirty and his threadbare flannel shirt is stained in multiple places. He has clearly been 'roughing it' before coming to Gwenmore. The tart scent of his anxiety is tinged with that rotting taste again. The show must go on, as they say.

Tea in one hand and my pen in the other, poised above a new archival manila file folder, I speak again.

"Arlo O'Shea. Is that your full name?"

"Arlo Christopher Matthew O'Shea," he responds quickly, like he has practised saying his full name.

"Pronouns?"

"What do you mean?" He looks up at me as he asks the questions, and I squint for a moment.

"For example, I use the pronouns He and They to refer to my gender," I explain cautiously. There is still his fear trying to overtake my senses, but no malice.

"Oh, oh, I catch your meaning, Mr. Ravenscroft." He takes a digestive off the plate and then I scent it. Like a moulded cheese, his embarrassment coats my tongue just as I take a sip of my own tea. I hold in my grimace. "I, well, I was born a boy, though I guess now I'm an It."

I don't hold back on my expression then, utter bewilderment running through me, trying to determine what exactly that means and how exactly to handle this now very delicate situation. My intentions were not to throw open the doors to the great spectrum of gender identity, but here I am. Arlo stuffs the biscuit into his mouth as well as if that will cover up what he's said.

"I will mark He/It in your file, but I am going to recommend some books you check out before we leave today. If you ever feel like these no longer fit you or you would simply like to update them, please let me know and I will do so." I take a sip of my tea, ready to move on with this interview. "Date of birth?"

"November 19th, 1929."

"And when did you become a ghoul?"

"May 1960," he answers. "I don't know the exact date."

"Can you give me a brief summary of what occurred?"

"It really ain't polite."

"Tell me anyway," I say, observing the way he fidgets. His fingers tremble around the hot cup of tea and his knee starts to jump. He is ashamed of what he has done and what he did to survive.

"I was a miner, and there was a cave-in. A few of the other guys and I were trapped for days. To stay alive, we ate somebody." Arlo's words are quiet, his emotions an overpowering scent that makes me want to open the door for fresh air.

"Survival is what we are about, Arlo, no shame in that." I am surprised to find myself trying to comfort this creature, especially when he poses a potential threat to my darling, who could easily be his next meal if she doesn't return to me soon. Or any monster's meal, for that matter. I clear my throat as my sands threaten to expose themselves. To show that I am a threat despite my manners. "Now, I am going to ask some more personal questions. My only request is honesty."

The ghoul and I chat for another hour, and my file on one Arlo C. M. O'Shea becomes full knowledge. His unwanted immortal life has been of penance and hunger. He is self-aware enough to realise when his hunger is getting too strong, yet so consumed by the guilt he will let himself suffer, creating his own hell since he seemingly cannot send himself there. After the tea has long since been finished and I have whisked away into the small staff kitchen to clean and replace back amongst its set, Arlo is almost relaxed.

I give him a short tour of the library. Pointing out community resources, the tech stations, and lavatories before taking him back to the front desk so he can obtain his library card. While one of the random humans on staff manages that, I head through the new metallic shelves to collect the book on gender identity I want Arlo to read. It was written by a harpy who I had the pleasure of hosting during their book tour, truly a fascinating creature. But this book is an excellent aperitif for Arlo and his journey of self.

Book in hand, I see that he is still getting his photo taken, so I turn back towards my office to collect my belongings for tonight's meeting. We might as well walk there together at this rate. I pick up my satchel, make sure the inkwell in my pen is full, and lock my office door. There is hesitation to slide my keys into my bag. I will attend the meeting, even though there is very little choice on the matter. Except what if she comes to the library and I am not here?

I cannot miss my darling.

"Fuck, finally, another human being."

The voice is too loud for the library and too annoying for me. The person marching towards me is older for a human, dressed in some casual workwear that came from a department store. He is all and all average at best.

"Jesus, you need to talk to your staff. Two hours ago, I tried to get some skinny punk who was loitering back here to help me, and he ran away from me."

Arlo. "With an attitude like this, I would not wish to speak to you either," I say, derision slipping through my tone. "What book are you looking for?"

"I'm doing research on city history because a buddy of mine found this thing and..."

Oh. He is one of those people. There is a special breed of humans, usually older men like this one, obsessed with history and conspiracy theories. The theories are usually right, but telling the humans that would reveal the darker side of the world to them that they aren't ready for. Gwenmore, in particular, being a city built as a haven for all monsters, is rife with folklore and carefully hidden away secrets.

"... and I can't find this book by Milson Bushwhipper. It's about the armoury across the street."

Milson. Thank the gods, that loathsome druid is dead, but his terror still knows no end. That book he wrote is a beacon to all those determined to prove the tunnels under the city are real and that there really is a secret treasure hidden in the hills south of the city. It has caused nothing but drama amongst these quack historians, but it brings them to me. Food is food at the end of the day.

"This way." I direct the man to follow me until we are at the full shelf dedicated to Gwenmore history.

"I've looked here," he claims, having the gall to smell annoyed with me. I cock my head in his direction and raise an eyebrow. "The lady up front said it was in, but I can't find it."

"Yes, but as this book is rather old and a part of city history itself," I move around the side of the shelf and roll the ladder across the circular rail to be in position. Still holding my keys in my palm, I select the one I need and begin to climb. "We keep it under lock and key. To review it, you must sit in one of the front rooms that the other librarian will unlock for you." I pull the book from the glass case at the very top of the shelf and then relock it.

"It's just a book."

"It is one of a kind, *sir*. Do not damage it, or the city will press charges." I stare at the man for a long moment before stepping down.

"No need for that," he placates easily enough, although I do carry the book as we headed to the front.

"What is the reason for your interest in the armoury?" I ask, the worn leather-bound book heavy in my hand.

The man walking next to me muses on my question, like he is weighing his options. I am merely trying to protect my property from someone who cannot control himself. His faint aura is a plain red colour and his emotions are being held in tightly. This man is doing everything he can to not appear suspicious of something. By the time we are at the front, Arlo has finished up and is standing off in the corner waiting.

"That's the freak that ran away," the man tells me in barely hushed tones, clearly loud enough for Arlo and everyone near us to hear.

"Mr. O'Shea is a guest of mine. Treat him with respect if you wish to keep using the Ravenscroft Somnium Library. We are a safe space for all beings," I practically hiss.

That is one thing I will not tolerate. For as much as I see everyone below my attention, humans are the lowest. They are lucky to have the peace that they do with beings such as Arlo and me so close to their vicinity. I can smell the sudden rotted spike of fear from the ghoul from here. His emotions are on display for everyone to see now.

"Mx. Meadows, please check out study room one for…"

"Jameson," the man says.

I hand the book to the librarian and quickly step behind their station to check out the book for Arlo. The picture on his library card shows a young man who is lost. The grainy black-and-white image doesn't give away much else. His eyes are a little wide, his mouth set in a firm line like he is trying to hide it completely. Checking my watch, I scan the card. His scent is doing something to my sands, as I fight down the urge to lash out at him for tainting the air. He has not done anything, but something about tonight is drawing lines through all of myself.

When the librarian returns, I instruct them to make sure that book is locked in the safe in the front office if the man leaves before I return. I trust them to make sure it is done and follow Arlo out into the night. A shiver rushes through my sands as we leave. The wind is cold against my back, but this is something different. Mistrust makes my sands agitated, making me want to do something that would completely break my control.

But I keep the floodgates pressed firmly closed. My slip-up in my office is nothing I am ashamed of, yet I know my control is slipping. What little it eased me still cannot stop me from turning back and looking at the armoury, wondering what that man thinks he will find in that building.

6

Augustine

2759 days

I refuse to tap my pen nib against the open page of my notebook. If I do that, it means admitting that I am twitchy and in a rush to be done with this dull meeting so I can run like a fool back to the library. My lapse of control this afternoon may have sedated the bond for a few hours, but now my sands are threatening to seep from my pores like sweat just to be back at the library. It is taking all of my control to simply keep them inside of me. I need to stay in control.

I am not even thinking about that conspiracy quack. How can I when every part of me is screaming for her?

I do not want to miss the plump, lusty morsel that has yet to return to my domain. My little darling has consumed my every thought since that night. It was a mistake to bite her, to bond her, to feed so gluttonously from her, but the emotions wafting off of her were too intoxicating to resist any longer.

The fates, or genetics for all I truly know, kept drawing me back to her just like it had before. It taunts me with shining auras and emotions that make my sands palpitate beneath my flesh until my control snaps.

The first stage of the bond is a feral one, driven by instinct that I have spent centuries burying inside myself for the simple fact that I must coexist amongst my food to stay alive. I do not know what will happen if it is ever completed because I have never done such a thing. When the darkness fades and the light of day reveals who I truly am to my fated prey, they have all run. I know, instinctually, what I must do to complete the process, but that is it.

Yet something about this one is different. From the moment I met her and entered her dreams, everything felt different. There are desires that lurk deep within her that seem to crave a darkness that calls to me, signals to the more monstrous beast I keep locked deep within my sands.

But more than that, she craves.

The longer I picked and nibbled at the emotions of her subconscious, the more entranced with her I became. To know her anger, her joy, her doubts, her fear– with every crumb of feeling I gathered from my sweet indulgence, my desire to know the causes of all her strife and emotions, and to possess her, grew until my control snapped.

"I only ate his arm, so ya know, progress and shit," Ramón says, a chuckle if that is what you can call the noise he makes after that vexing debrief of his past week. Around us the circle nods, but all I can think about is that there is a witness to his antics, to his existence, that will need to be taken care of in some form or another. Ramón should have just eaten the poor chap and saved us the trouble.

Deg'Doriel checks the time, something I have been avoiding doing since I sat down with my low-quality tea. What if she has come and gone while I have been here?

"Augustine," he grins, menacing and taunting. "You haven't shared yet."

"That is because I have nothing new to share. My week has been the same as it has been for over seven years." Under no circumstances will I admit to mating a human in a dream. I feel no shame in my bondmate, but our rules dictate that humans are strictly a source of power, a controlled one that is used sparingly to sustain our way of life.

Rules that I helped draft and create, rules that I agreed to when our city was born.

"Really, Ravenscroft?" Nora leans over into my personal space. This will be the last time I allow her to sit next to me. "You look different, smell different."

Ramón's tongue flicks between his lips and everyone else in the room shifts in their seats. If there could be a glint in his cold reptilian eyes, I am sure there would be. Orthia does not move an inch from her perch on the chair, her eyes closed and obviously no longer amongst us, but lost with her Love in whatever realm it resides. Arlo twitches, his throat moving as his fingers curl into the worn denim of his trousers.

Tension in the room rises, as do the emotions. Dull auras shifting and rising until my sands are crawling under my flesh. The unfinished bond makes them more beastly, makes my own animalistic desires hard to control. Perhaps a half truth would be best. Admitting my bond with my darling, but letting her origins remain my secret. Something to calm the raging desire to claim her publicly so everyone knows she belongs to me.

I stare the demon down until the sands emerge from my skin. My pores seep the black grains until my claws are fisted around my notebook and pen. A swirl of the sand snaps out at Nora before recoiling back into my neck. The room shifts again, their fear bringing out more of my sands. I suck on the sharp teeth in my mouth, cracking my unhinged jaw. The skin around my cheeks stretches unnaturally tight. My eyes will look even more unnatural as the black sand takes over my scleras. I cannot recall a time when I exposed myself in such a way in front of the whole group.

My true form threatens to break free, to be the monster that stories say that I am. The darkness, the nightmare, the boogeyman that will hide under your bed and snatch you away. I have not been that monster since the time of the Romans and during the middle ages when the world had turned upside down for silly Christendom, since the need for my true form had waned. It is only an antique now, much like myself.

Its shock value is all that it is good for now.

Deg'Doriel is unmoved by my threat. My old friend has been to hell and back after all. He certainly will not budge from my little show.

"I have," I pause to let the tension and emotions around the room rise, my sands vibrating with glee, "begun the mating process with someone. She is still alive, but unaware of it."

"Knew it looked like you got laid." Ramón claps me on the back, though his scaly palm does not make it through the sand.

Orthia surges to her feet suddenly, a dangerous sneer on her face, but the milky white glaze coats her eyes. The lights flicker before *they* speak, "what do you mean unaware?"

Her Love's voice reverberates deep in my being and makes my ears ring. Our usual group of lessers scatter at the otherworldly voice, the terror they leave in their wake is delicious. My sand pulses, attempting to absorb it, to feed me, but it will not quench my ever-expanding thirst. Arlo is frozen on the spot while the others lean in waiting to see what I will do, what I will say to explain away this unheard-of slip in my regulated existence.

"The first stage of bonding is a sex ritual in your chosen's dreams, isn't it?" Deg'Doriel asks, even as he knows the answer. We have known each other long enough, have been through enough, that I trust Deg'Doriel with my secrets. He knows how volatile this state makes me. The demon wants to toy with me because he is bored. A bored demon can only cause suffering, and it would seem that Orthia and I are his targets tonight.

Control slips through my clawed fingers. Those around me have tasted blood in the water, and I will not be shown as weak. If the priest wants a confession, then a confession he shall have.

"Unaware because she can only control so much until the bond is in place. It is easy for me to bend the subconscious mind as I please. It is a grey area." I concede to the witch, but her eyes are still lost in that other realm, and I cannot be certain she understands my meaning. So I continue on with my sordid confession, a swell of possessive hunger rising in me. "She has tasted my ichor and I have consumed her in my realm. We must only seal it in the mortal one for her to be locked to me forever."

Silence settles over the group. Orthia is the first to react, storming out of the room and taking all her rage and saltwater smell with her. It is probably best that she leaves, hides away from our meetings until I am through with this unfortunate ailment. The allegiance between us and them is shaky at the best of times. I'm not sure who would win in a battle, the sea witch and her Love or the rest of us. Fate has never worked in our favour, but for Orthia especially. Her wrath has fuelled her for centuries. There is no telling what would happen if she were to truly unleash her potential.

The odds of winning against an unknown beast and its vessel are slim, but I cannot think about that now, not when the thoughts of ample flesh and honey-sweetened desires are just out of my reach.

I should have hunted her down.

I should not have let her leave the library, but I was too high and sated for the first time in decades to think straight. The vision of her glorious backside walking away from me is forever burned in my retinas. The scent of her is a ghost that haunts me. Her honey, sweet lust still tastes fresh on my tongue. I burn for her to be mine, to own and keep that delicate soul to be my plaything for the rest of eternity.

My fingers flex with contradictory urges. I want to leave and hunt down the human, to complete the mating bond. In equal measures, I want to peel the skin off Deg'Doriel's smug face for forcing my hand.

"Wait, wait, wait, you gave some rando a wet dream?"

Ramón's crass question breaks the silence and my control. The sands snap. They strike without my command. Spikes form and pierce Ramón's chest with precision, easily slicing through his shirt and the toughened scales of his body. He grunts, shaking and fighting to force them out, but it only makes them burrow deeper. They seek out his fears, his worst nightmares that sink deep into his bones and soul. They want to feed.

AUGUSTINE

"Augustine," Deg'Doriel's hellish voice rumbles and shakes the ceiling tiles.

A grimace winds its way across my full mouth, skin stretched and sharp teeth exposed. I take a deep breath, and suck the sands back to me with the inhale. I blink slowly, clearing my eyes. Ramón looks ready to strike the fearless buffoon, but Nora wraps a hand around his bicep. She has always had a weak spot for stupid animals.

"Speak of her again like that, and I will kill you."

My words drip with an icy venom, potent and deadly. It is a threat that I will enact should I even hear anyone has spoken of my human. Before any of them can utter a word to me, I leave. I need her. I need my mate. I do not care what she wants. I will make her mine tonight.

The spring rain must be an omen of misfortune. Even as I attempt to convince myself otherwise, if I did not have to make the walk from the church to the library, I would not venture out in this weather. The tunnels would have been easier, but the thought of missing my darling is too great. The air is brisk, the rain pelting down in sheets. My sands thrum under my skin with need. Need, desire, thirst, and feelings that I have been holding in check with the barest hint that something is out of place are rushing through me. Drops of water spatter against my glasses and soak through my wool suit jacket.

A realisation that I left my bag in the parish centre only darkens my mood the closer I get to the library. She will not be there, she has not returned. Whatever brought that delicious being to my domain for so many late nights has not arisen in her again. Yet I know, I know, she is feeling this.

Her body will ache with a need that only I can satisfy. Just as quickly as the thought of her with another rises, I squash it. She will not want for another. Even if she seeks it out, her body will revolt against their touch. She is mine now.

Mine. Mine. Mine.

The human is mine. The word echoes around my sand-filled being as if it could possibly sate the thirst I feel for her. How I have planned on feasting upon this woman, devouring her lush body until she is nothing but sweetness and her soul burns brightly for me alone. Every rational thread holding my body together is being snipped. My thoughts turn desperate. If I do not have her, surely this time, I will finally die. If I do not complete our bond, I will die without knowing what it means to be full, to be truly sated and to want for nothing.

She won't run from me. I won't let her. And if she does, I will chase her. This time I will have my mate.

The lights on Main Street are reminiscent of the gas lamps that once lined the street, the warm yellow glow just breaking up the darkness of the stormy night. They glow so faintly; the beasts of the night can so easily slip from a building to an alley to a secret alcove in this district. Yet another reason why I needed to find my human. She does not fear the dark, but she does not know what goes bump in the night. She cannot protect herself from man or monster.

I walk beneath the scaffolding that is being constructed across the street from the library at the armoury. It is ghastly but necessary to keep the historic district in working order for the wealthy and for the tourists, even if it is an eyesore. I push my soaked hair back and take a moment to calm myself before I turn to cross the street.

My composure breaks.

She is here. Standing out in the rain, in the white glow of the new Ravenscroft Somnium Library sign, my mate stares into the abomination I was strong-armed into adding to my library by the city council. For as much as my name is on the building and my "families" history with it, it is still partially funded by Gwenmore taxes. Waves of need crash into me as I am pulled towards that light now, to her, like a moth to a flame. Decades of control slip through my fingers like my sands, and I stumble up the pavement next to her.

"Can I help you find something, darling?"

I echo my first real words to her. Then spoken with hints of missed derision at someone interrupting the quiet of my sanctuary, but now they almost sound hopeful. As my sands prickle against my skin, I remind myself I can't spook her. Not now that we are so close.

Say me, my thoughts plead, *say you are looking for me, my sweet little morsel.* She blinks slowly, coming back from whatever spell she is under. The lost expression on her pale features is replaced with a heated blush, her gaze caressing my features slowly. Soft, rosy cheeks that I can still picture flushed and hollowed as she sucked the ichor from my fingers.

"I-" My darling yawns, interrupting whatever she intended to say.

"Let's go inside."

Efficiently, I usher her to the back, away from the plainness of the new amenities and into the comfort of my space. My gaze is solely focused on her and getting her away from everyone. There could be a fire and I would only notice how the warmth of the flames makes her skin glow. She moves slowly but surely. My hand rests on her low back and the chill on her skin has me urging her a little faster. Everything in me is suddenly pushing me to care, protect, provide.

In the furthest corner of the library are my office and the stairs to the basement archives and tunnel system. Without thinking, I swiftly break the lock to my own office and guide my human to sit down in the plush chair in the corner I keep for myself. Her thighs squeeze between the rigid arms, and I cannot think of a time when I have been jealous of furniture, but I am. How I long to be the object holding her up, moulding her plush form to fit my desires yet easing her discomfort as if it were nothing. A few moments pass, but the air that was saturated with her desire, in the unfinished bond between us that begs to be made whole, is tinged now with something keen to shame.

As the sour taste hits my senses, my control snaps into place and I do what is proper.

"Would you like a cup of tea?"

I am already walking over to my kettle to fill it with filtered water. Every part of me, now that I have her so close, is driven to please her, this baser instinct to prove to her that I can provide, that I am the right choice.

"I-" My tongue-tied mate is flustered as well as tired. "Do you not need to work?"

"No," I state simply because while I technically work as a librarian, as I have on and off for centuries, there is no need for me at this late hour. Nothing is required of me.

Except what you require of me.

The thought nearly slips past my lips when my mate turns her head to the side. I put the kettle on to boil and begin the process of preparing the tea. There is proper etiquette for these things; no matter how my body burns, I will follow the unwritten rules. While I am not such a purist as some, I do believe in the importance of selection. On a wood tray, I place two cups from my 18th-century Italian set onto saucers and open a sealed canister of Chamomile blossoms.

She watches my every move. I do not need to look up from the side board near where she sits to know this. I can feel her eyes on my skin like they are caressing my hands, my chest, my jaw. It is muscle memory that guides me to add the correct amount of blossoms and the corresponding amount of water. While it steeps, I add chocolate-dipped Viennese biscuits to a separate plate. Delicately, I arrange them in a radial pattern so the chocolate is facing inward. This small action gives me a moment to think about how I am going to broach a real conversation with my human.

I pour the steaming, floral tea into our cups and present the tray to her like a proper host, even with these meagre offerings. My darling picks up the tea, both of her hands gripping the saucer. Visions of her gripping my lapels as she presses her full, soft body against mine fill my mind. My soaking wet lapel.

My jaw clenches. We are both soaked to the bone still. I should offer a towel, my handkerchief at the very least, but I now cannot think of anything but peeling off her transparent shirt and ill-fitting trousers to see all of her in the waking hours. Stiffly, I replace the tray and remove my wet outer layer to hang up on the hook by the door. An aroma stronger than the floral tea wafts through the air. Her cup rattles quietly against her saucer.

I look over my shoulder to see her staring at me again, the flush on her cheeks covering her soft jawline and throat. The hints of shame that I once tasted are fully replaced with lust now. I peer down at myself, trying to assess what has caused this reaction. Perhaps it is the suspenders I decided to wear today instead of a waistcoat.

This is good. I am learning more about what she desires in her mate.

"I am sorry I do not have more than this." I offer her my handkerchief before picking up my own tea.

It is only once I take a sip, does she. The apple tart notes dance across my tongue and I long to taste them on hers now. She dabs at her skin discreetly with one hand, but I watch the beads of water that decorate her features disappear in my handkerchief. Little droplets infused with her essence to carry with me. She pushes back loose strands of her dark hair as if they are not perfect where they lay framing her face already. I take another sip of tea, almost content to watch her for the rest of the night.

Almost.

The gnawing aches that twist and knot in my stomach like I have not been fed an ounce in years is ever present. My tongue is heavy in my mouth as saliva threatens to drip from my lips like a beast. I wonder how she would react if she saw my sharpened teeth, the way my maw can open to encase her throat. I feel my sands begging to reach out, to seep into the soft folds of my darling until we are one.

Her eyes catch mine, the beautiful hazel colour almost like honey itself. Her throat contracts as she swallows, our gaze never breaking. The emotions seeping from her pores so sweetly drive me, urge me, force my hand until I am taking the saucer from her and tossing aside any thought of conversation. The beautiful flush of red that coats her cheeks darkens to crimson. My wet hair slips in front of my eye as I lean into her space, crowding her into the recesses of my chair as I hold tightly onto my sands, my control.

"What's your name?" She asks.

It is a simple enough question, but as I watch her lips form the word, I am lost again in a vision of her. That supple mouth wrapped around my fingers again, slick with drool and ichor in such a debauched, gluttonous fashion my cock stiffens in my trousers just thinking about it. I want her to call me everything, to call me hers. I want her sweet lips to whisper for her god and for her to mean me.

But I will give her my chosen name for now.

"Augustine."

"Joanna," she whispers.

The six-letter word wraps around my tongue so beguiling, I repeat it.

"Joanna."

"Augustine."

Sparks burst in my chest, and my eyes flutter as I swallow the sweetness of my name on her lips. The light accent in her voice forces a shiver through my sands. Her hand shakes as it reaches up to my face. I hold my breath. Her finger caresses the damp curl on my forehead like she is mesmerised by its mere existence. I grab hold of her wrist and Joanna stops breathing. The still, warm air between vibrates with a potential energy, of the incomplete bond that threatens to override everything proper in this realm.

Doubt suddenly taints the air again, like she realises what she is doing. Does she not know the power she wields over me? Before the sickening taste of her emotion can ruin this spell any further, I surge forward. My lips crash into hers with barely there threads of sensibility. The kiss is unpractised, askew in my trajectory, and her hiccup of surprise expels between as we both breathe into it. Our lips work in tandem to right themselves so we may feast on each other's desires at last.

I pin the wrist I am holding to the top of the chair as desperation takes control of me. I have tasted the heavens, and I will not let Joanna take it away from me. Her lips part, fingers of her other hand grip my suspenders to keep me in place as well. I am happily bent to her will while she lets me plunder the sweet taste from her lips. Without hesitation, my hand goes to her throat. My palm settles right over my mark. It calls to me like sirens of old, while my fingers grip her nape. I have captured my mate. She is mine.

Mine. Mine. Mine.

The word rattles around in my head as joyous relief and unrepentant lust rush through me. A moan, soft and sweet, just like my darling, hums through the back of her throat when my tongue mates with hers. I am reminded of her dream, the dark taste of her lust as she let me know exactly what she wanted.

"Darling." I press slow kisses across her cheek until I can whisper directly into her ear, letting the monster slip out. "I am going to devour your sweet cunt until I can bathe in your release, until you are trembling and begging me to stop."

Her lips part against my cheek, in shock or delight. I do not care. All I can taste is her lust and desire. The memory of her taste is on the tip of my tongue, and I demand more. I drop to my knees before her, keeping hold of her neck and making her look down at me while my other hand goes to the leather belt at her waist. She does not say no, does not push me away, she tilts her hip up in offering to me. My darling watches me easily pull the strap from the buckle. Joanna's breath shudders past her lip the more I undress her. Spreading her thighs, I position myself between them, worshipful and direct.

"You do not know how much I have thought about this," I murmur, my voice softening as the hand I have around her neck slowly travels down her front, between the valley of her small breasts, until both of my hands are shaking with a need to rip off her trousers.

She hums her agreement, eyes fixated on me, dark with desire. Her hips do not lift when I tug, but I do not need them to. I pull the fabric down and out from under her with ease. The trousers pool around her ankles as I lift one of her soft thighs to my lips.

"Augustine," she gasps, and it is a sound I want to surround myself with forever. Her hand finally releases my suspender with a pleasurable zing of pain that sets my body alight. Joanna cups my cheek and stares into my eyes. There is so much there, so much she does not understand and cannot vocalise. Yes and no are still an option, are still thoughts we can both form, but I pray she does not deny me. "Please."

The hunger and thirst and craving that has been gnawing at my insides for over seven years roar with so much satisfaction my control slips. My lips stretch across my cheek as I bury my mouth in the cotton of my human's soaked undergarments. I drag my sharpened teeth across the damp fabric until I have what I want. The ambrosia of my darling. I lick the seam of her exposed cunt again and again like the starved beast I am.

Joanna's hands slap against the leather chair arms as my teeth toy with her flesh, leaving a ghost of her caress on my cheek. I need her touch, the dig of her nails into my scalp, forcing me further into the warm depths of her pussy until I might suffocate. My tongue circles her clit slowly, lavishly, until her tiny breaths turn to whimpers. Her thighs shake around me, but it only encourages me. Inhaling every drop of her desire I can, I trail my gaze up her sumptuous body until we lock eyes again. Can she see how she makes the monster inside of me rattle in its cage?

"Touch me, Joanna," I growl, the guttural sound coming from deep within the deserts of my being. "I shall not break."

Even as my cock aches to be buried inside her, my quills pulsating around my shaft tormenting me, I cannot think of anything but tasting her release. Like a drug my body has never known it needed to survive, I must have it. Timidly, her hand grips my wet hair and directs me back between her plush thighs. The smugness in my grin is almost sickening. She so easily follows my command, just like I knew she would, just like I know she wants to.

Joanna wants to be told what to do, when to do, and to not have an ounce of thought in her beautiful head. She wants to surrender to a higher power until the stresses of her life melt away and I intend to be that power. My lips wrap around her clit and the moan that erupts from her shakes me to my core. The sands in my veins thrum with renewed life. It is as though I have not even truly lived before I knew the taste of my darling Joanna. The fledgling bond between us is growing stronger, every grain of sand in my body demanding completion. I cannot get enough of her. My fingers, *my talons*, dig into the flesh of her thigh while my other hand moves between us. Her pussy weeps, her slick drenching my fingers as I spread her lips to tease and toy with her slit.

"Oh god," she cries out, those fingers pulling at my hair while her hips grind against my face. "Oh, fuck, please, fuck-"

She gasps again when at last I thrust a blunt finger into her slick heat. Her pussy pulses around me and my eyes close for a moment. I drink in the sounds, the feelings, the emotions rolling off her succulent body until I think I become one with her. I stroke my finger in and out, sucking and lapping at her clit while I do. Joanna's stomach contracts, shakes, as she breathes faster and harder. I watch her reactions, let dribbles of my sands feed off of them as I bring her to the precipice of her orgasm. Her beautiful features are flushed crimson, eyes closed in ecstasy, and my own body throbs. I slip a second finger into her cunt with ease and curl them up, calling for her orgasm to come to me like a trained pet. My darling opens her mouth as if to speak or shout, but all that can come out as her pussy convulses around my fingers and her juices flood my mouth is a shocked, bitten-off sound, like she cannot believe what has happened. I keep pace, drawing out her climax until she is whimpering again.

As I pull my mouth away, I see the tear slip down her cheek. I surge up to kiss it away, refusing to remove my fingers from her clutches, still stroking and coaxing the pleasure from her body. My own barely contained and practically glowing with so much life. The bond between us vibrates with need. We are so close to becoming bound, so close for her soul to be tied to mine for eternity. She pushes at the back of my head as if she is begging for my teeth in her neck.

Mine. Mine. Mine.

An insistent, ear-shattering ringing starts. Joanna's eyes open and she gasps again with shock. She rips her hand from my hair, and I almost yank it back. How dare she stop touching me? Be distracted during our final time together as two beings, I think not. As she reaches over the side of the chair for her purse, I take my opening and latch onto her throat, biting and sucking on her skin until I am certain there will be a mark. I am too distracted to realise she has not silenced the blasted thing but instead answered the phone with my fingers buried inside her.

"Hello." Her voice shakes as she answers her phone, reedy and breathless. Her aura shifts noticeably as she listens to the caller. "Are you sure this can't wait? No, no, I understand, it's just-"

"Hang up," I nip at her skin, tongue lashing against the spot I plan to mark her permanently. She squirms in my hold, rolling her hips into my palm, but continues talking.

"I'm sorry." I don't know if she is speaking to me or the caller, but the air begins to shift, the scent of my mate losing any of the honey sweetness it once had and being tainted with worry. "I can be there in five minutes, no, no trouble-"

"Yes, trouble," I growl, even as I am reigning myself in, hiding the nightmare back under my skin.

"Thank you, yes my code's set up. Bye."

I look at Joanna. The flush of her supple skin, the look of guilt that settles on her brow as I keep working my fingers in her slick cunt. She leans forward, her lips brushing against mine for a moment as if to say goodbye, but then without urgency, she kisses me again. Her tongue teases the seam of my lips only to pull back before she truly tastes herself on me.

"I'm sorry, it's work. I can't- It's just- I'm sorry- This-"

Not a full thought comes past her lips as I continue to work my fingers. If she believes she is going to leave me now, she is wrong. We will not be separated again. I will drag her body from this library to my home by force if I must. I press my thumb just above her swollen clit and start to circle it.

"Joanna," I say, speaking calmly, as if I do not feel whatever measly control I had over this illicit liaison slipping from my grasp. "Let me take care of you. *Nothing* is more important than right now, than you. Not while your greedy little pussy is making a mess over my leather chair and I still hunger for you."

She whimpers, and for a moment, I think I have won. Her eyes flutter close and she licks her lip. *That is it*, I think. *Give in to me, darling.*

"I- Look, I just need to go across the street and make sure everything is fine."

"What do you mean across the street?"

I do not stop moving my fingers. The sound of her pussy sucking me in deeper and deeper echoes around my quiet office. Just when I think she is going to cum again, forget her ridiculous job, Joanna grabs my wrist. Instantly, I stop, easing my fingers from her warmth.

"Fuck," she groans. "I have to go."

"I am going with you."

Before she can say another broken thought or complete sentence, I lean back and pull her to her feet. There is a tilt in her aura, in the scent of her emotion, that tells me she is shocked but hopeful. As if I would let her out into the night alone again, when our bond is so close. I slide her trousers back on over her shoes and do the belt up in the worn-on-out hole before rising to my own feet. I grab my damp jacket and drag Joanna back out into the night, ready to be done with this errand so we may finish what we started.

7

Joanna

I am going to die.

Slowly. Painfully. Emptily.

My brain is on fire, and my belly is twisting with a horrible, shameful lust I can't stop. If it weren't for that call, I would have let that librarian do anything he wanted to me. I can't believe I did answer the phone. What in god's name am I thinking? I don't even know this librarian.

Augustine.

I know his name. I know his voice is firm, scholarly even when he tells me things I have only fantasised about. I know exactly what his moustache feels like against my clit.

He is strong, kind, and so fucking hot.

And into me.

If it weren't for that call, I would have thought I had fallen asleep at my desk. Men like him don't exist outside of dreamland. The well-tailored, commanding, and respectable man is not interested in the overworked office drone. They have chic significant others with skincare routines and regular sleep schedules. Augustine is the kind of man I dream about;

JOANNA

he has been the man I dream about for months now, but I could have never dreamed of this.

I have had exes who won't take me on dinner dates but will text me at midnight for a booty call. I have had exes tell me I am too distant. I have had exes tell me I am too clingy. I am not enough and still too much all at the same time so why even try to form romantic attachments? I have grown to find that even with the rare one-night stand, I could work up the energy to find lacklustre and more work than the physical touch is worth.

But Augustine's grip on my hand, the way my cum slicks up my shredded panties, almost has me believing he wants more than tonight. His grip remains firm in my hand as we step out into the pouring rain. In the small space of his office, with his scorching body pressed between my thighs, I had forgotten I was soaked to the bone. Under the pelting rain, my hair plastered on my forehead once again, I am shivering and huddling closer. He wraps his arm around me and pulls me into his side. Just as the crosswalk signal starts to blare and traffic slows to a stop, he tilts my chin up and my heart stops. It's hard to see, but my pulse races and heats all of me at once at the look in his eyes. They are dark, uncanny, even though it must be a trick of the light, and so very hungry.

At the same time I am rising up on my tiptoes, Augustine bends down enough to meet me in the middle. Every bit of fire and sweetness I felt in the library comes soaring back to life inside me. I can't think of anything more right than kissing him in the rain. His lips are soft and supple and I can still taste the slightest bit of me on them. My head reels and my body melts, and I don't want to ever leave this moment. Augustine pulls back slowly like he has to drag himself from my embrace.

"It is time to cross," he whispers, and I have to blink to get some sense of reality back to me. Yes, crossing the road, doing my job, and handling the problem on-site. Not crossing the metaphorical line to having sex right here in the rain.

Well, once I am done handling this site situation, then I am going to beg the Adonis opening the door for me to take me home.

It goes completely against the company policy, and probably the law, to drag Augustine down into this sub-basement to check on the site office. But he isn't letting me go. With each door he opens, his hand returns to my waist– a guiding touch that makes my skin buzz with possibility.

He hasn't stopped touching me since he took that cup of tea out of my hand.

I don't even think about the lack of security guards around in the lobby until I am inputting my security code for the site office door. I am mentally exhausted from work and completely hazy from the mind-bending orgasm Augustine gave me. The look in his eyes when he tasted me, and licked my release from my pussy like it was honey makes me feel hot even now. My fingers shake as I put in the wrong code and have to do it again. I want this done and over with. That security guard better be back at his station when I am done.

"Breathe, darling," Augustine murmurs against my cheek. "The night is young and I still have yet to fulfil my promise to you."

Jesus Christ. My knees threaten to buckle. My cheeks explode with heat as a small, pathetic noise comes from the back of my throat. I can't stop it, and I don't want to. For whatever reason, I want him to know exactly how weak I feel in his presence. I trust Augustine like I have known him for a lifetime.

Finally, I push in the code correctly and shove the door open.

"Could you stay out here? Please? This is technically confidential and I really shouldn't have let you all the way down here to begin with. It'll be two seconds."

Augustine's fingers flex against the soft skin of my waist, like he doesn't want to let go of me. It should be weird, but my silly tired brain thinks it's kind of cute. I lean up and kiss him, the taste of rain and me on his lips. He pulls me in closer, our wet clothes clinging and uncomfortable even as he turns his head to deepen the kiss. It would be easy to forget myself, to drag this unbelievable man into the dark office and let him ruin me. I think I could do just that, but then the little alarm telling me the door has been open for too long starts to go off.

I break the kiss and he tries to follow me, a rumbling sound that is unnatural and delicious coming from his chest.

"Two seconds," I promise.

"Then I shall wait."

He takes a step back and I get lost in the entire look of him. Out of the warm lighting of the library, he looks sharp. The fluorescents burn a bright white and make his olive skin look washed out, like he hasn't spent much time in the sun. His deep, golden hair is dark and slicked back. Rainwater dots his temples and I want to lick it off of him. His shirt is buttoned all the way to the top and his leather boots look expensive. As I shut the door behind me, I am again struck by how different we are.

I flick the light switch on and flinch.

This place is a fucking disaster zone. *Fuck. Fuck. Oh fuck, I am so fired*. My stomach drops onto the floor as I look around. The security guard told me he thought he saw an employee entering the office, not that there had been a break-in. I mean, this is beyond my job description. Shouldn't he have just called the police? I grip my soaking wet purse to my chest and carefully step around the files on the floor. The wall of files that belong to the armoury appears untouched. The plastic boxes labelled CC are smashed and the files in them are tossed around like there was a party.

I can't believe this.

Gary is in charge of opening and closing the site office. I know him, and as much as he can be hard to work with, he is good at his job. He wouldn't leave the office like this and forget to lock the door and set the alarm. I pull out my phone and start taking pictures. *This is just what I want to have to deal with*, I think. The computer screens are all here, which I guess is good, but until this is all cleared up and I can go through all the information, I won't know what was taken... if anything. Copies of employee information for the seasonal workers are stored here. If anything from their files had been taken, I am going to have a much bigger problem on my hands.

I should send Augustine home, or really back to the library. He must have work to do. I can't just leave him hanging around outside and I don't want to have to explain him to security. No part of me wants to do that, though. For the first time in a week, I don't feel like I am going to combust into a pile of ash. When his hands are on me, I feel melty and soft and sweet and exactly like how I imagine people in movies feel.

I look down at my phone, the broken screen protector is cracked around the edges, and no service. I wonder if I should call Lance. He's at the theatre, though. He's living and I shouldn't stop him from doing that. Police, I need to call the police. I look around the room again. The undisturbed shelves look out of place amongst the mess of Concord files. Interesting how shit like this can mirror reality.

My fingers dig into my bag, crushing the lumpy material to my chest. What a way to end my night. At least it saved me the bus trip... and I got an orgasm out of it that I won't forget.

I turn around to leave, flicking off the light and resigned to a night of talking to the police and doing paperwork. The darkness is nice, the glow of the city lights and the thin line around the door frame is just enough for me to see. I take a deep breath, let the disappointment of reality settle back onto this plain of existence and off the dreamland I was in ten minutes ago. I practise what I am going to say to Augustine. I'm sorry. This is a total nightmare. I'm sorry. I have to call the police and a whole list of other people. It's going to be a huge mess. I'm sorry. Do you want my phone number?

The last part sounds desperate, even in my head. I grip the door handle and am suddenly yanked back by the throat.

"Don't move."

A hand is clamped over my mouth before I can think fast enough. What do you do in a situation like this? Am I supposed to fight? Oh my god, what if they have a knife?

"You aren't going anywhere, bitch." A gruff voice whispers in my ear. "At least not until we are done with you."

The babbling, panicked noises I make don't do anything for me. Tears prick at the corner of my eyes as a second hand wraps around my throat. Another masked figure moves to stand in front of me and my whole body begins to shake. As I try to free myself, they rip my purse from my hand and drop it to the ground. It barely makes a sound as it falls onto the papers. It's terrifyingly quiet in the room, the sound of harsh breathing echoing off the linoleum and plastic boxes.

I'm frozen in fear and every thought I have right now is about Augustine being just outside the door. He is so close, but it doesn't matter now. The man holding me drags me deeper into the room with a grunt, away from the light under the door and my one hope. I cover my arms over my chest, and as I move, I touch the arm of the man behind me.

His arm is too hot, freakishly hot. Even the brush of my skin against his suddenly has me jerking away. The hand around my mouth doesn't feel like this. I don't know. Alarm bells are screeching inside of me that if I don't get away I am going to burn. The ache in my neck feels like an open wound with every brush of his fingers against it.

"Sorry, darlin', you ain't my type." The masked figure, the man, doesn't sound at all apologetic as he shifts in front of me.

His fist lands squarely in my gut. My soft belly and organs concave around his fist. Air punches out of my lungs and chokes me. My throat seizes and I can't breathe. Tears fall down my cheek as another punch hits. I twist in the grip of the man holding me, claw at his scorching arms and stomp my feet where I think his own are, but all that does is make the grunting turn to a snarl. Spittle lands on my ear and I flinch like I have been cut, but it only makes everything worse.

"I said, don't move." The hand around my throat tightens until spots appear in my vision. I flail, my eyes bulging as everything blurs and darkens at the edges. Another punch lands on my stomach and the grip loosens.

I try to breathe, that lone survival instinct kicking in as

JOANNA

I take the beating, but it's getting harder and harder. Sobs rack through my body as my knees finally give out. The man holding me can't keep my weight and I fall to the ground. I breathe, pulling in a full breath of air that only makes me want to throw up. Everything hurts.

There is a knocking sound, I think, maybe. Maybe it's just my knees hitting the floor too hard. Maybe it's my heart breaking from my chest because it is pounding so hard I am scared it's going to run away and leave me behind with these monsters.

A kick lands on my back and I whimper. I am going to die. I am actually going to die. My knees draw up and my arms cover my face. The sounds of soft grunting and my choked whimpers are a cacophony of how much of a nightmare my life is. I have done nothing of value, nothing of interest. There won't be photos at my funeral, except maybe one from the seaside holiday three years ago. Would anyone even go to my funeral?

There's a flash, and then a hand is shoved into my damp hair.

"Smile for me, darlin'."

Another flash. I can barely see. I've taken at least one hit to the face and I am not sure if my vision is gone because my eyes are starting to swell or if it is because of something else. There is blood in my mouth and I am going to die alone.

"Remember, this is what happens when you go sticking your nose where it doesn't belong, darlin'. Leave, or he will keep reminding you again and again until you learn your lesson."

The whispered words send a chill down my aching spine. The knocking is still there. My heart is trying to escape. I am living someone else's life, their nightmare. I am a nobody.

I know I am nothing important. My life is the same grey pattern, day in and day out. Nothing about this makes sense. When they release my hair, I crumble back onto the floor with a whimper.

I can't move.

I can't see.

I am going to die, but I don't want it to be tonight.

The room suddenly floods with light. My head is split in two about what it believes. Is it the light at the end of the tunnel or simply the door opening? I don't know what I want it to be any more.

There is surprised noise, voices speaking, and then utter silence again. I guess it was just the door, then. I am going to live, at least for a few more minutes.

Something warm wraps around my trembling body and I try to shake it off. A whimper gets trapped in my throat. I can't take another hit. I can't. Please stop.

"Sleep now, Joanna."

The warmth lifts me and I am swimming in honey, floating into oblivion.

8

Augustine

0 days

I am going to burn these wasterals and dance upon their ashes until their ancestors feel the rage coursing through my body. The desecration of their mortal forms will be noted in history, and for eternity I will torment their stored souls until they feel nothing but fear so I can feast upon them again and again. The scene that unfolded before my eyes as they opened that door will haunt me. I had expected Joanna, thought maybe she had tripped in the dark or dropped something. The sweat on their brow and the bored expressions on their faces twisted to shock, anger, and terror. How I feasted on that terror as my sands sucked their souls from their bodies with a greedy hunger. Their lifeless husks discarded like trash in the hallway. There was no enjoyment when I saw my mate crumble on the floor.

Joanna's broken form lay there as if she were simply asleep. Her body curled up on papers and files that soaked up water and blood. Her laboured breath only made me wish I could kill those scoundrels all over again. That I could do unto them as they have done onto my darling. There was no aura around her, nothing I could sense to tell me she was alright. With clawed hands, I lifted her into my arms. My chest still aches with the weak sounds she made.

I am a fool for ever letting her out of my sight.

Forcing sleep upon her is the easiest option; it is the only thing I can think to do. She cannot see me yet, not when the bond is unfinished. I kick the husks of those men into the office and shut the door behind us. It is a problem for others to deal with them. I do not care what happens to anyone except for my darling, my human. She is in need, and I must get her out of here to safety. I race down the halls and head for the tunnel entrance. The room I found Joanna in, is not facing the street. We need to get to the front half of the building to gain access to the tunnels that run under the city.

The tunnel system is used mainly by the more unruly of us. Humans who enter these systems are never allowed out. They will have seen too much, heard too much. Their scent alone upsets the delicate balance of our coexisting ecosystems. But revealing Joanna to the monsters that lurk beneath the city is the least of my worries. Soon enough, she will be just as much a part of it as I am. Then, when our bond is solidified, I can tell her everything and anything she wishes to know.

I kick in the last door to my left, a grunt pressing through my lips as Joanna is jostled in my arms. I cannot bring myself to put her down. Not when we are so close to completing the bond, not when she is so vulnerable. I cannot feel anything from her, no emotions. Her dreams are empty and her subconscious is floating in an ocean of nothingness.

This room is an absolutely disgusting mess of shelves overflowing with broken computers, printers, and boxes. All things that could have been easily recycled and would not be blocking my way to the tunnel. It is ridiculous, but humans are disgusting, vile little creatures who deserve what they get, except mine.

Joanna does not make a sound when I set her down on a desk. It creaks under her but stays intact. I cannot recall if this silence from her is good or not. It has not mattered whether a physical injury could permanently damage them. My feeding does not cause physical damage usually. I never had the taste for blood or violence. It is a flavour I left to the lessers.

Except now. For her, I will tear anyone limb from limb.

Carelessly, I shove the useless machinery away until I can get to the wall I need. It appears the tunnel was bricked over, but it should still be fine. Forcing sand into my left fist, I punch the grey-painted stones again and again. The rage I had only just begun to feel in control of resurfaces. My body changes, growing, becoming the vicious beast I keep under lock and key at all times. Spines prick through my damp jacket, ruining the fine wool, but I cannot remove the taste of their fear from my senses, how good it felt to feed on it until there was nothing left. Their very souls were absorbed into my sands.

I am shaking by the time I have created a space ample enough for us to fit through. My movements are jerky, spines at my back rattling, sand pulsating throughout my being, tainting my veins and searching for more. I reach out for Joanna, needing her desperately back in my arms, but when I see the claws, the glittering black of my hands, moving toward her I have to stop. I cannot touch her like this. I cannot even feel her. She could be dead already.

I cannot do this.

I cannot save her if I cannot control myself. Sharp talons dig into my palms as I remember the last time I could not control my hunger. How it ruined me, how I was forced to disappear, how I was forced to suffer for my own incompetence. *This time is different*, I remind myself. This is not a frenzy fifty years in the making. This is my human who needs me. It will not happen again. I pull at every grain of sand, the softness running across my flesh until I am in my contained form. I take a deep breath, the scent of Joanna, her blood, keeping me on task.

Her throat contracts as I lift her and relief zips down my spine. She is cold from the rain, not death. But if she remains like this she might as well be chasing it. I enter the mouth of the tunnel, an itemised list of everything that must be done forming in my mind. Muscle memory guides me through the darkness.

Gwenmore is like any good city. The public transport system is funded just enough to be absolutely vital to the mortals that use it while being just unreliable enough that nobody questions when a station must be closed or a train diverted because of a signal failure. The tunnels came nearly a century before the subway system. The city had grown exponentially and we needed a way to move lurking creatures at any hour. Integrating the two just made sense.

As I wait for the subway cars to speed through its perpendicular tunnel, I feel the eyes on me in the darkness. Joanna's scent attracts those who would usually scuttle by, but I sense their curiosity, their hunger for fresh meat. My sands lash out like a whip as an imp attempts to touch her shoe.

"If you touch my mate, I will end you." My voice is cold and uninterested, but the sands that grip the creature squeeze so tight it squeals. The sands at my back bleed from my flesh to form spikes and spines, ready to lash out and defend my Joanna until we are safe again.

I walk through the wide, dark tunnel until I get to the safety of the library.

Now for the hard part. I must call my friends and truly explain what I have done.

My small office smells worse than a cheesemonger's on a hot summer day. The emotions of an orc, a demon, and a ghoul all merge with an absolute lack of scent from the one being that I called them here for. Deg'Doriel fumes as he leans against the buffet behind my desk. The moment he opened the hidden door to the archives, his scent turned sour. Arlo pumps out so much fear and hunger it is like a festering wound opening up over a beautiful roast dinner. Kragnash's mossy scent is mixed with that of his wet dog that is curled up under my desk, waiting to be called to his master.

"There's just the two of them?" Arlo asks, jostling from foot to foot as he waits to rush into the tunnels. In his left hand are the scribbled directions Deg gave him.

"Yes, they will not be overly filling, but consider it partial payment for a job done," I say, shoving him behind the open bookcase and down the stairs. I look over at Kragnash. "What do you need?"

"Well now," his voice trails off as he drags his murky eyes in the direction of Joanna's broken form.

Deg'Doriel brought most of the supplies we could need, along with my belongings. My darling lays on a plastic sheet, unmoving. Her chest barely rises as she breathes, a shuddering wet sound that has my sands roil and curl under my skin. I wiped most of the blood from her swollen face, but so much is still covering her clothes. I did not even know humans had so much blood in their bodies to lose.

"You want me to save a human?"

"She is my mate," I bristle under the accusation in his tone, but the orc is unmoved.

"Not if we just let her die," Deg huffs, crossing his arms over his chest. "That would solve our problem."

"What do you need to save her?" I demand. It takes everything in me to keep under control, to keep myself from telling my oldest friends to leave and that I will save her myself.

"May I?" He crouches next to her carefully, his hulking form casting a large shadow. He opens his palm to me.

Taking his hand, I guide it carefully to touch Joanna. The largeness of his palm against her cheek makes my teeth grind, but I remind myself I am the reason he is here. Kragnash is going to help my mate. This is what needs to be done. Even as my sands pour from my fingers and cradle her swollen face.

He swipes his thumb gently under her nose and pulls it away, a dribble of blood on his skin. Kragnash inhales, his eyes closing. Silent tension leaks into the scents mixing in the room. My sands wrap further around my mate until her head rests on a pool of black sand. Moisture, Joanna's blood, slowly leaks into them, and suddenly it is like my sands are on fire with hunger. I turn to Deg'Doriel and let his furious gaze ground me because if anyone is creative enough to find a way to kill me, it would be him.

I cannot turn into a frenzied beast, the bond between Joanna and I has turned unstable. It slips between us like sands through an hourglass, our time coming to an end if I do not do something, save her. My instincts riot with a need to feast, but there is no deciphering if that feasting will bond us or kill my Joanna.

Deg'Doriel's phone goes off and he answers sharply.

"What? One second." He snaps his fingers, and Kragnash opens his eyes, cocking his head in the direction of the demon. "You need a live one?"

"Yeah."

"Bring him here and then you finish up."

Arlo returns carrying an unconscious man over his shoulder. The ghoul has shed his flannel and his undershirt is untucked. His thin pale arms strain, but he does not seem to have a problem carrying the weight of a fully grown man. Carefully, he is laid down next to Joanna.

"Thank you, son. Now go on and finish up. We can do the rest of the clean up." Kragnash does not move to begin anything until he has gone, unwilling to share his secrets so soon with the new member. He turns back to me. "What happens if she has your blood?"

"Without the bite, I assume nothing." Already, I am pulling the sleeve of my half-dry shirt up. I genuinely do not believe anything will happen, but there is no certainty. This could complete the bond, or this could sever it.

Kragnash begins to move quickly. He pulls a pocket knife from his jeans and grabs the bucket I took from the janitor's closet. It is like we are orchestrating a murder from one of those ridiculous human crime shows. Deg'Doriel watches the whole time with a scowl on his face as Kragnash manoeuvres the man over the bucket and slits his throat. Blood pours quickly into it and the knife is handed to me.

"Your turn, as much as you can, then I can begin."

9

Joanna

This is the worst hangover I have ever had in my entire life. No homecoming or frat party could have ever prepared me for the way my body screams at me. My stomach rolls and my eyes are glued shut as I turn onto my side. The bed dips, but I can't find the edge. That doesn't stop how I heave. My gut riots against everything and anything.

As the first round of purging begins, hands and arms move my body. The antiseptic smell of bleached plastic fills my nose and I throw up. A voice washes over me, warm and firm, as my body expels all the horrible things inside it. Cool water is pressed to my lips when I am done, but it hurts to swallow.

A hand presses to my forehead and now there are more voices. I don't know what's going on. My eyes won't open. I'm scared. My heart pounds in my chest frantically, desperately trying to send a message to my heavy body. Run. Get out. Wake up.

"Sleep, Joanna," the warm voice whispers in my ear.

It tickles but slows my racing pulse. Sleep takes me quicker than it ever has.

The ocean waves crash into the sandbar. Behind me, I can hear the bass music from the cottage pumping. This vacation has been everything I could have ever asked for. Swimming, eating, and catching up with friends who I haven't gotten time with in ages. I should probably go back inside. The bottles of wine were piling up well before I needed some fresh air. It's also not the safest thing, being this close to the water with the amount I've drunk, but listening to the girls plan a shopping trip was starting to grate against my good mood.

I pull my knees up, my belly hindering them from getting too close to my chin. The action is still comfortable, it still feels like a hug. I wish someone would hug me. I can't think of a time when I have gotten more than a quick arm tossed around my shoulders. My heart craves more. My body craves the warmth of another, but I know I won't get it from the people I am with, my friends.

"Darlin-"

The sudden word sends a fierce shiver down my spine that it never has before. My hands clench around my linen trousers when I look up. Augustine stands on the beach in the clothes he wore in his office. His shirt is loose and stained with something, hanging out partially from his trousers. The metal clip that holds back his dark tie glints against the soft glow from the cottage at my back. The brown leather of his boots is coated in sand, and I feel like I am somehow at fault for that.

"Please don't say that," I whisper, trying to swallow the unease that twists in my belly.

JOANNA

"You called for me," he says, eyes looking down at my phone. I squint, trying to remember if I did that or how I got his phone number at all. "How are you feeling, my da-"

He cuts himself off before he says the word, but it was there on his tongue. My heart lodges in my throat. I feel exposed and vulnerable, and I don't know why. Tears pool in my eyes. Something is so horribly wrong, but I don't know what it is. My body feels like it is being wrenched in two all of a sudden, the peace of the beach slipping through my fingers like the sand. I turn away from him.

It's true, I wanted Augustine here. I want to feel his warmth and I want him to put me back together again. I don't know why, I just know he can. For whatever reason, he knows what I need. There is so much happening around me that I can't explain, the energy in my limbs and an awareness that this isn't the cottage from my memory. I am in control, but my emotions are rioting against what's right in front of me.

"I'm sorry," I choke on the words though I don't know why.

"Do you speak French?" He asks, his voice firm as he takes a seat next to me on the sand. He sits primly, if that is even possible, in the sand, back ramrod straight and ankles crossed.

"No." And for some reason, I feel ashamed of that. Augustine oozes wisdom and higher, private education from every ounce of his being and I feel unworthy of his attention. I am a dead end, a drone.

"*Mon abeille*," he breathes, the tone of the endearment worshipful and hungry. "I will always come when you need me."

He says more in French. The words sound sad and rushed in a way that is so unlike him.

The intensity of his promise does something to me, though.

My twisted stomach buzzes like a hive of bees is living inside it. My skin thrums with energy and lightness as I have never known. I feel like I have a sugar rush that won't ever end. Its sweetness coats my tongue, but there is a sickliness to it as well that only makes me crave more.

He reaches out for me and grips my chin so gently. "You are a queen to me, *mon abeille*, let me treat you as such. Give yourself to me, here, and in the mortal realm, and everything you have ever desired will be yours. I promise."

The words to question him are on the tip of my tongue, but my mind can't keep up with my body. My fingers wrap around his suspenders and pull him to me. His lips touch mine with such a softness, such tenderness, it makes my chest ache. I press harder, goad him with nips and licks at his full lips until his fingers are digging into my chin and holding me still. My body pulses and drips with warmth.

I want him, all of him. I am drowning in my need for a man I barely know, and I don't care. I'm alive for the first time since I was sixteen. Even at his office in the library, where the weight of exhaustion hadn't stopped me from letting Augustine eat my pussy like it was his last meal, it didn't compare to every sensation trying to burst from my body from this kiss. I chase the taste of honey on his lips, begging for this feeling to never end. Every stroke of his tongue against mine sweetens the thoughts in my head, making it hard to think of anything but what I need. A desperate ache that I know only he can fulfil.

Augustine breaks the kiss, his eyes blackened with glowing golden irises. My heart jumps in my throat at the sight, the *otherness* of his form slipping out from behind him in long tendrils and sharp spines. Dark veins appear in his arms until they are black, and the fingers that grip my chin become sharp-tipped. They press into my flesh with so much familiarity my cheeks heat.

My dream lover.

The thought stretches out before me, turning opaque and sticky like the taffy my mimi took me to see being made at the Harbour Crest Pier. The longer I think about the dream, the lover in them turns from a clear liquid imagination and solidifies into Augustine. It has always been him, whatever he is.

His lips spread in a lazy smile like the one that morning a week ago, except now it stretches across the whole expanse of his face. Sharp teeth glitter in the dim light from the cottage.

"What's happening?" I whisper, fear and arousal battling for control of my body. My fingers flex against his chest and warm black sand grips them in return.

"It's your dream, Joanna. Anything you want can happen here," he explains, tongue darting out to wet his bottom lip. My eyes watch it travel from ear to ear, his moustache still sitting right under his nose. "Your soul is ready to see the real me, *mon abeille*, and I cannot deny you that truth any more. Will you deny me?"

Black sand and golden bronzed skin radiate unnaturally in the moonlight. It glitters and glows and buzzes with something electric that I can't resist. There is a dark promise in Augustine's eyes. He knows my secrets, that dark fantasies that trample over everything I was taught about love, and he wants to give them all to me.

Fear surges in my lungs and I want to tell him no, even my blood pumps arousal right between my legs. The image in my mind is so beautifully tinted and clear that it has been caught in a piece of amber and preserved for millennia. I stare at the monster before me and he stares back. Augustine looks at me with desire and hunger and tenderness, just like he has all night. He has seen me falling apart from burnout in my old sweatpants when I don't have the energy to shower. For months, he was in my dreams learning every part of me. He knows what I deny myself, even in my dreams, because I think it will keep me hoping too much.

And yet he still wants me.

The beach shifts, the sands beneath me becoming a plush carpet and the sea salt in the air is replaced with the earthy smell of old books and stained wood.

"If you want me to be yours forever, Augustine." I start to rise, my feet bare, as the new silk shift feels smooth against my body. "Catch me."

I am not fast. I have never been a runner or one for exercise. But I am trying my hardest to escape the person I want most in the world. Sweat dots along my forehead as my feet pound through the endless, towering stacks of books. My breath pushes through my mouth, heavy and ragged as my heart tries to crack its way free of its cage. I don't look behind me, I can't without slowing down.

Augustine is silent, or I am simply too loud to hear him. He taunts me, the occasional book clattering to the ground making me jerk and my pussy slicken. My breath comes out in wheezes, and I slow down. I turn the corner, hoping for a hiding spot, but I am surrounded by sand. The blackness overtakes my vision and I scramble to turn around. I almost fall, but sands wrap around my middle and steady me.

"Let's play a game of hide and seek, Joanna." Augustine's voice echoes around the walls of this library and sends a shiver of warmth down my spine. "You are so keen to hide from yourself, but I want to find all of you."

A shiver rakes down my body as the sands tighten, and a hard chest presses into my back.

"If I cross the line, please tell me." He kisses my jaw. "This is for your dream."

"I'll say 'iris.'"

"A blossom that means trust, how fitting for us."

The moment his sands release me, I dash away in the opposite direction. Blood thumps in my ears as I creep through the stacks. If I run, he'll hear me or my heavy breathing. This game only works for me if I can be silent, move across the carpet carefully and remain calm. My heart jumps with every creak of the floorboards or rustling of paper. The fear that grips me is exhilarating and consuming. My body burns with need.

"I can taste it, you know." Augustine's voice is whisper soft in my ear and goosebumps erupt across my flesh. I dash from behind one bookcase to crouch behind another. "Your fear is tangy and smokey like tea, but your desire, *mon abeille*..."

The rumbling groan that echoes through the halls is impossible to place. He could be anywhere. My clit throbs at the depth in his voice.

"Your desire is the nectar of the gods, the sweet honey ambrosia. I have lived for as long as humans have existed, and nothing has done to me what you have. How I crave you, *mon abeille*. Every emotion, every thought in your head, I want to know it. How I am desperate to throw away everything that has held me together for a millennia just for the chance to devour your soul and keep it with me forever."

My breath falters. He can't mean that. This is just the game. This is my dream being unleashed and unhinged.

"Do not spoil yourself with doubt," he hisses, and a shiver rakes my spine. "When I find you, you will see."

At the risk of exposing my position I let the words flow from my mouth. "Prove it to me, Augustine."

"Rapturously." He materialises right in front of me in a wave of sand.

A shriek catches in my throat and I freeze at the sight of him. He leans over, hunches almost until we are face to face. His mouth is spread wide open and his teeth seem sharper than before. The spines at his back are razor sharp, just visible over his shoulders. Augustine's glasses seem to magnify his black eyes, his hazel irises a glowing golden hue that hypnotises me. My fingers reach up to touch him, to make sure he is really here, but my fingers stop just short of his jawline.

"You are forgetting the game," he murmurs. "You are to run from the nightmare, and I-"

"You are a dream come true," I whisper.

My fingers connect with his skin, and I am engulfed in a swirl of sand. He presses me into the bookcase with his body. Augustine's too-big mouth crashes into my lips and I feel the sharp teeth. My eyes flutter close when he pins my wrists above my head.

"Do you still dream of me even when I am not here?" He kisses my jaw, just below my ear.

"No," I deny it, stumbling back into the game and tugging at the sands around my wrist.

"You are a beautiful liar, Joanna." His teeth scrape against the column of my throat. I moan and thrash. I want him to own me, to fight me, to force me to be his because I can't admit how much I want it, *need* it like the breath in my lungs and blood racing through my body. I need him to prove he wants me so much he will force me.

Augustine makes me feel alive again. He is a high I will chase for as long as I can. He is indulgent and stoic at the same time. I want to know everything. I want to be his everything. An addiction we have for one another that will never end.

"One more time, *mon abeille*." He drags his body away from mine like it pains him. "Run."

It takes a moment for the command to set in, to force my feet to move, but I do it. I race down the stack again, pumping my arms and begging my lungs to work harder. No matter how much I want to get caught or how much I want Augustine, he has to prove to me he can do it. That he can own me.

I don't make it more than three rows before he crashes into me. I shriek as we fall. His sands carefully cushion our impact as I claw at the carpet to escape. He pins my wrists down with his sands, grinding his cock into my ass greedily. My shift disintegrates and all I feel is skin on skin. Augustine's body is burning hot and hard against my pliant one. The sands wrap around my throat in a thin line and yank my head back. He presses his cheek to mine, the split of his lip unnatural against my skin, but it doesn't stop the blood in my body from rushing further south.

"You are mine, Joanna. *Mine*. My queen and my pet."

My body shakes with fear and need. The ache between my legs that has been tormenting me for the past week takes over rational thought. I spread my legs wider even as I try to break free of the sands binding my wrist.

A grin stretches his lips and his tongue teases my heated cheek and jaw. Behind me, there is a delicate rattling sound as Augustine rises up onto his knees. Clawed fingers dig into the flesh of my ass and I whimper. Pinpricks of pain ripple up my spine and coat my thoughts in syrup. With the pain comes a drowning pleasure. He pulls his hand back only far enough to crack it across my ass cheek.

"For lying to me and yourself." He bites out the words, before striking me again. "For not returning to me sooner. For making us suffer seven long days without each other."

The next series of strikes happen in quick succession until tears stain my cheeks. I am weeping and pathetically wet. My pussy clenches around nothing when he grabs both globes of my ass and spreads me wide open. He tsks before tracing a clawed thumb through my slick flesh. Humiliation burns in my gut, but I want him all the more.

"I do not even think I need to finger open your little pussy, *mon abeille*. You are staining the carpet with your arousal."

I whimper, shaking my head, but he doesn't listen. Augustine moves until he cages me in with his long, lean body. His muscular arms bracket my head while his sand collar keeps my head up. I can't hide any more or escape what I want so desperately.

His cock slides between my folds, heavy and burning hot. The tip catches on my slit and I gasp. It's different this time. It isn't blunt. Instead, it's pointed and so much larger. Hard veins twist around his shaft and pulse with each teasing thrust. My hips buck up as my thoughts begin to swim and wade through the syrup coating them. What will it feel like inside me? Will it hurt so deliciously that even if I wake up I will still feel the stretch of it?

"Such a naughty thing you are," he purrs.

"No," I groan, even as my cheeks burn.

"Your pussy is crying for my cock, Joanna. You cannot deny this, or me, any longer."

JOANNA

"I can," I argue. My ass still burns from the spanking, but I told him he would have to make me. I want him to make me.

"I will just have to show you then, *mon abeille*."

Augustine plunges his cock into me. He pushes into my giving body until he has buried himself inside me. The stretch burns and pulses through my centre. My pussy convulses as he slowly grinds his hips into me, making sure I have taken all of him. Then the veins of his cock flare inside me and make fullness impossible to comprehend.

"A greedy pussy," he moans, "made for my taking. Do you feel how my quills mould to you, how hungry they are for your release already?"

My mouth hangs open, the drool slipping from my lips as the words ripple through my thoughts. *Quills*. As if they could sense my thoughts, they pulse inside me, pressing against that sweet spot inside of me that makes my skin buzz. Pressure leaks from the base of my skull in sweet relief. I can't think, my mind is thick with sweet nectar that slows me down. My fingers twitch and tremble until they are coated in sand and restrained. Another wave of arousal rushes through my body, my pussy clenching and causing my body to convulse with need.

"Beg me," he growls, but I am already shaking my head. "Beg the monster to ruin your cunt."

"Please," I whimper, my belly fluttering and embarrassment turning my insides to boiling sugar– sweet scorching temptation.

"Use your words, *mon abeille*."

I can't. Augustine's cock rubs up against my sweet spot again and my vision blurs as I cum. My pussy gushes and squeezes his cock until I am drowning in honey and desire.

The collar around my neck tightens, constricting my breath just enough to keep me aware. I want to drown in it though, the overwhelming reality of being with him heightening every touch. I am nearly lost for words and I never want to surface again.

"Beg me," he pants, and I can just make out how his clawed fingers dig into the carpet, how he is holding himself back.

"Ruin me, Augustine, I'm yours." My words are slurred, but their meaning is clear.

He pulls his hips back and pounds his cock back into me. I feel every soft quill and ridge of him now. How it stretches my sensitive pussy and electrifies my nerves. His mouth hangs open next to my ear, harmonising every moan I make with one of his own. Augustine fucks me like a wild animal, his hips slamming into my sore ass over and over again until the pain doesn't even register.

My world tilts, the axis of my existence shifting and moving the rougher Augustine is to me. My thoughts can't keep up with what I'm feeling. My body is buzzing and sinking, floating and falling. Everything about me feels good, heavy and impossible to lift. My neck falls to the side and he takes his opening. Augustine's teeth scrape across my flesh and send a jolt through my honey-coated thoughts. His grin is victorious against my sweat-slick skin.

"There you go, *mon abeille*. Taking me so well, like a good pet ought to."

He doesn't even sound tired. The whimper I make is weak and so needy. Augustine's cock squelches every time he buries inside my abused pussy. His quills massage, pulling and stimulating my insides until I have ruined this carpet forever with the arousal that pours from me. My body is begging for release yet it won't let go. It won't let the sweetness sugar coat the final part of my mind. I need more, but I don't know what it is.

"Please, please, please."

"Let go for me, Joanna."

Augustine's voice harder, his hips frantic as he chases his orgasm. His body moves with urgency. One of his hands disappears before reappearing in front of me. He presents his fingers to my lips, but they drip with something golden and thick. My heart skips at the sight. The sudden rush of hunger floods my mouth with saliva and turns needy, pleading sounds into the most desperate noises I've heard before.

"Drink my ichor, *mon abeille*, be with me forever, be my queen."

His body rocks and shakes my vision as my tongue reaches for his fingers. I want to lick and suck at them until they are more a part of me than they are Augustine. My lips press against his skin, and it smears the fluid across my cheek. I am making a mess of it, but I don't care. The sweet ambrosia hits my tongue and I am delirious with it.

"Augustine," I cry out.

"So perfect," he grunts. "Just need every hole stuffed full before you will behave?"

His fingers hook into my mouth. He presses them down onto my tongue. I slurp around them, tongue between them. I suck on the sweet ichor as he pounds me into the carpet. Heated kisses are pressed into my neck, into the spot that has been sore for a week and that every time I touched made my knees weak. Augustine slams into me one final time before his teeth sink into my neck. My scream is muffled by his fingers, but my throat aches from it. I cum so viciously, my pussy gushing and clenching around his swollen, twitching cock. Everything turns a deep golden hue and my muscles give out.

My eyes close as he pulls away, his teeth and fingers leaving my body. He doesn't pull out, shifting his weight just enough to press his body onto all of me like a weighted blanket. Comfort envelopes my shivering form. The sands release my hands with a gentle squeeze before slithering back to Augustine. The collar on my neck stays in place and I am silently grateful for it. The subtle weight of it, of working to draw in each laboured breath, keeps my head above the syrupy nothingness.

"Wh-y me?" My voice cracks, parched and exhausted. *Even in your dreams, you question your worthiness.* "You could have anyone. Why me?"

"I can't answer that," he sighs like it's a question he has asked himself before but has never found the answer. "Your soul calls to me in a way I have never felt before. I can't let you go now that I have tasted you. Please wake up, *mon abeille*."

"What if I don't want this to end? This dream is all I've wanted."

"Let me make it a reality, Joanna. Wake up for me."

10

Joanna

Peeling my eyes open is a chore. Every part of my body, from the tip of my hair to my toenails, aches. I am covered in something sticky and wet that makes my stomach roll with just the thought of what it could be. As my brain connects with my vision, a choked sound tumbles from my lips as the night rushes back to me. Above me Augustine stares down at me, his lap cushioning my head and stroking tears away from my cheek.

"Shh, *mon abeille*, I have you," he murmurs.

My gaze darts around me, the warm lights, the smell of books– this isn't the site office any more. We made it out. I'm still here. I take a shuddering breath that cools against the mess covering my chest. The awareness of my nudity is slow to come to me, like my brain is saying one traumatic realisation at a time.

"Look, she's awake, *finally*. Arlo has done his best to cover up the problem, and I have returned your shit." A purple demon, like from the fucking bible, grunts and looks at Augustine. "Can we end this now?"

"Mon abeille." Augustine sighs and speaks further to me in a language I don't know, but his eyes never leave me. He drinks me in even though I'm covered in muck.

"For fucks sake," the lavender-skinned beast groans. "You're speaking French?"

The being with bejewelled tusks and heavily scarred skin throws a blanket over me. He looks familiar, the grey streaks in his shoulder-length hair reminding me of a bus ad about something. His eyes are murky, and a deep scar streaks across his face like lightning in the dark. I don't know why, but I trust him more than the one with a crown of horns.

Both of them are terrifying, I should be frightened, but this is the most exciting thing to ever happen to me. Everything about this situation is surreal and a panic tries to lodge itself in my chest, but I can't get past the euphoria of being alive. I look down at my body, covered in red sludge but seemingly as whole as it was this morning. My only thoughts are about cleaning up, getting some ibuprofen, and questioning the man, *boogeyman*, massaging the base of my neck.

"Thanks," I croak, the fluff of the blanket sticking to my red-stained fingers.

Augustine's sands slip beneath me as he helps ease me into a seating position. It's comforting and disconcerting to feel their smooth warmth even when I am awake. Something new burns between the two of us, an openness I've never shared with another, a vulnerability and power that I am not sure it's safe to have given up. I look at my skin again and see the red sludge covering all of me, with strange marks smeared into it. My stomach rolls when I smell the coppery tang of it and I gag.

"The blood ritual will leave you woozy for a few days. I

recommend taking it easy."

"Holy shit," I mutter. "Mayor Hawthorn."

He taps the side of his nose and stands. A large dog that I do recognize from bus ads waddles around the side of Augustine's desk and noses at the mayor's hand until he takes the thick leather leash from his mouth. "Nash is fine for the mate of a friend."

"She isn't his mate, yet."

"But you can sense it, can't you? Just like I can taste it in her blood, *their ichor*, it's almost finished." Mayor Hawthorn, *Nash*, smirks at him before standing up. "It's about time he does something interesting."

He slides a thick signet ring onto his pinky and his visage changes. I blink, my eyes burning like I've been staring at the sun and I need to clear my vision of spots. Before me stands good old Nash Hawthorn, Mayor of Gwenmore, who is almost certified to be re-elected. He still looks a bit alternative, compared to what I used to think politicians look like. His salt and pepper hair is slicked back and, even human-looking, he towers over me and Augustine. The man is built like a brick fucking house.

"Deg'Doriel," Nash claps a hand on the lavender being's shoulder. "Maybe it's time to usher in a new age. Live a little."

"This will only cause problems."

"Deg, she is one human. What harm could possibly befall our union?" Augustine's gaze flicks to me and heat rises in my body at the lust in it. I wrap the flimsy blanket tighter around my chest. Embarrassment sets my skin abuzz, but I don't hate the feeling.

"Oh yeah, that is easy for you to say with your soul-melding bullshit, Ravenscroft." Deg'Doriel swipes a clawed hand over his massive face. "What about Ramón or one of the fucking vampires?"

"What do you mean melding?" I ask, my voice a little stronger than before. "I agreed to a relationship." *Give yourself to me, forever...*

"Oh, sweetheart." His tone drips with venom and condescension. "You agreed to so much more than that. Didn't she, Auggie? Worked your sands until they were soaked to get her to say yes, didn't you?"

"Stop," Augustine seethes at my side, but the words hit hard.

Normal sex that regular people have doesn't look like what I dreamt about. It doesn't involve chases, games, or saying no when you mean yes. It is boring and lacklustre and human. I know that much. The shame of my fantasies isn't something that gets thrown in my face usually, because I don't let people know them. But my heat-of-the-moment commitment to Augustine is just another item on my to-do list of shame.

One bit of affection, of indulgence to my dark desires, and I agreed to be his forever, in body and soul without even knowing what that meant because I thought it was just a part of the roleplay. What the fuck have I done? What has he done?

The soft sands that were supporting me grip harder, wrap around my arms and torso and drag me across the tarp I'm on. I flail at the abrupt shift and end up clutching Augustine's damp shirt. All three men look down at me quickly before looking at each other.

"Don't what? Tell the truth? That you manipulated her subconscious and bonded yourself to her?"

Augustine stands and my weak grip slides down his body. Blood from my arms smears down his side as my fingers dig into his trousers. My head rolls as I focus on the way it ruins the soft weave of his trousers.

"Like you have any room to talk, hellspawn. Why are you so against this?" A clawed hand settles on my head, petting me, shoving me like a scared dog back behind Augustine, but I am too dizzy to fight it.

"In my opinion, ignoring the bond at this point will kill the girl." Nash shrugs, like it might rain later.

"Then so be it! What is so odd about that? They die all the time."

Whether this week or in forty years, my inevitable death is simply a fact, like the sun rising or Patrick having sangria for breakfast. To him, to all of them, my death would mean nothing because it is barely a blip in their lives. What did Augustine say? That he has lived for as long as humanity? Has he done this before and watched his partner wither away to bones?

I am struck with a thought. Who do I have close enough for my death to cause a ripple in their own existence? I am replaceable at my job, and I haven't gotten more than a one-word text from my friends in a month. My moms have been dead since I was sixteen. There is no one in my life. My existence is one of monotony and slogging through days exhausted. I'm a number on a census, a Tuesday lunch you forget about because it barely even registered.

If I died because Augustine, the boogeyman, some ageless dark monster, decided he didn't care any more, it would matter to no one. And yet, that would be the most exciting thing that ever happened in my short life.

My breath falters in my chest, before trying to rise faster and faster while not actually leaving my mouth. Each time I try, it gets choked out by some invisible force. My existence doesn't matter. Nobody would notice I died because my life is a waste. I am worse than a drone because at least they served a purpose. I start to feel light-headed, panic making my limbs tingle and ache even more than before.

"Jesus Christ." Augustine drops to my level and takes my face in his hands, black veins appearing on his golden skin.

"Don't say that name to me," Deg'Doriel hisses. "And you have no idea what harm this will cause. For fucks sake."

"Aug-Augustine?"

"Joanna." He swipes his blunt thumbs through the muck on my cheeks. His next words come out in rapid French, blurring into one. I am not even sure he realises he isn't speaking English. A hand moves to my nape, into the spot that burns from his bite, fingers digging into the muscles until it eases the rising tension. His thumb massages the base of my scalp until my lips part and my head feels heavy. "There you are. Take a deep breath."

"Disgusting."

"Seeing as I am no longer needed, I shall take my leave. I have already missed a call from Emmi this morning." Nash grips the corded leather leash from his dog, Buster, who leads him around us. "See you on Tuesday."

There is something about being reminded of the time when you have lost complete sense of it, that feels like a bucket of cold water being dumped over your head. The gasp that leaves my mouth is overdramatic. How much time had I lost? What time was it? I clamour up to my feet, awkward and aware of the men staring at me. The blanket sticks to my skin uncomfortably and my balance is all over the place. It almost feels like I've drunk a whole bottle of wine myself.

Or lost a lot of blood.

JOANNA

When I was nineteen, and desperate to keep my bed in the student flatshare I was in, I donated plasma regularly. It was easy cash for when I needed to buy textbooks or coffee. But often, I would leave too soon and still feel a bit unsteady on my feet. The clinics always made me uncomfortable. The nurses were always a little too eager to take a stab at the donors.

This feels about three times worse. As I grip Augustine's arm, my stomach threatens to fall right out of my body.

"Joanna?" He sounds concerned, curious, confused, and a slew of other C words I am sure, but my mind is running a million miles a minute about how I was going to explain to Patrick I missed our morning call. Gary will have found the mess at the site office, my blood all over the floor.

I have to fix this, I can do that.

"Where's my stuff?" I demand, my words harsher and more bitten off than necessary.

"Your clothes are ruined. Hawthorn cut them off."

"I had Arlo take your purse to my house for safekeeping after he found it," Augustine explains softly.

"Mother-" I smear a hand over my face and cringe at the stickiness. *Take a deep breath, Joanna. You are late already, so rushing now won't do you any good.* I swallow the welling anxiety in my throat. I can't handle going from one extreme to another like this. "I am late for work."

Augustine and Deg'Doriel stare at me like I have just announced myself as the new queen of Scotland.

"Joanna, who cares?" Augustine looks genuinely confused, because obviously he is. Why would an ageless, nightmare man care what other people think of their work? "You were attacked, or have you forgotten? And we have to complete the bond."

He leads me to sit down on the chair, just like last night. I bit my lip at the creak of leather, the squeezing feeling around my hips. I don't want to sit down or talk about the bond. It is a clear source of tension between the two monsters left in the room and I'd rather not be around for their argument. Everything is upside down and twisted and I need to straighten it out and make a to-do list so I can see all the problems being shoved into my face all at once.

Then I can think about this bond or die situation.

"Who hasn't been mugged?" I ask.

"Joanna," Augustine growls.

"And I can't miss work. Ya know," a breathy laugh breaks my speech, "if this bond thing is serious, what better way to get to know me. I am bailing a second time because of work. I do that."

"I-"

"This is why you have to speak with the humans before you get your dream dick wet. She is clearly broken." Deg'Doriel cuts in, bending around Augustine's desk, a tail snapping against the wood, and tosses a plastic bag at me. My cheeks burn with embarrassment. He doesn't have to be so right this early in the morning. "This is what I had. My flesh suit is a bit bigger than yours."

"Than- your what?"

Before Augustine can protest, his friend bursts into purple flames and reveals a shorter, portly priest. A wretched burning smell permeates the room and I am gagging again. The man at Augustine's desk smirks at me, a dimple appearing on his round cheek.

"The books, Deg'Doriel," he groans, leaving my side to open a high-up vent on the back wall.

JOANNA

I take my opening and shoot up, rushing out of the door of the office. I clutch the blanket and trash bag to my chest. The library is quiet except for the sound of feet slapping against the hardwood with each step I take. An emptiness settles in me at the thought of how my world has changed, how things I thought were true aren't, fiction and nonfiction blurring together as I dash around the stacks towards the toilets. I don't know what is real any more.

That's a lie.

Work is real, and it will be a big problem if I don't get my ass across the road. All the lads at the office and site must be calling my phone, trying to figure out what the fuck is going on. Patrick is going to flip his lid when he finds out the site was broken into. The mountain of work I will have to do to get everything sorted is giving me a headache already. Those few precious hours of recovery I have enjoyed will have to tide me over until this is all sorted.

Shoving against the heavy fire door until it is shut, I lock the bathroom the moment I can. My eyes close as I listen to the delicate sound of shoes pacing in front of the door. I pull away and for the first time in a while, I look at myself. Covered in itchy, drying blood and something slimy, my body is still mine. Brown hair, brown eyes, double chin. It is all the same old Joanna Cole. My breasts are still comically small compared to the rest of me. The stretch marks that decorate my stomach and sides are still purple, but they are matched with mottled, discoloured skin.

Tears prick at the corners of my eyes when I meet my gaze.

I was assaulted. In my place of work, no less. Nothing about it was by chance, I know that, but I can't believe anyone would do that to another person. I can feel the spit landing on my cheek and boots crashing into me. The words echo around my skull as I stare at my reflection. *'He will remind you again and again until you learn your lesson.'* I don't know who my attacker was referring to. I can't think of anyone I could have upset so much for them to do that to me.

In a panic, my fingers swipe through the symbol on my stomach, smearing the meaning into nothingness. I yank a paper towel from the dispenser and wet it under the sink. This stuff has to come off me. The cheap paper rips and tears with each swipe, but I scrub at my body until I can see my pale skin. The discoloured flesh of my torso reveals splotchy, yellowing bruises that wrap around my body. Tears lead tracks down my dirty cheeks as I keep bathing myself. I dunk my head under the sink. The angle hurts my neck, but I need to be clean now. The overwhelming urge to peel my skin from my body, goading me into making it work, is driving all logic from my body.

The water is cold, but I stay bent over until the water runs clear. When I stand back up, Augustine stares back at me. I shriek, wincing as my hip rams into the counter and trying to cover myself at the same time. He looks annoyed.

"Joanna." Definitely pissed.

"How did you get in here?" I demand, turning off the water and grabbing more paper towels.

He raises his hand, and a tendril of sand leaks from the tip of one of his fingers. It floats for a moment before taking shape and solidifying. Well goddamn.

"What on earth are you doing?" he asks.

"Getting ready for work."

"Absolutely not."

"Yes."

JOANNA

Augustine rushes me. Sands wrap around my wrists, locking them to my body, as he towers over me. His hazel eyes flicker gold behind his glasses and I swallow. I am not scared. The vivid memory of my most recent dream, of Augustine's true appearance, has broken me in some way. I want him like that. I have tasted the sweetest sins I could imagine, and I want more of it. I want to feel him surround me and break me with purpose and control and put me back together.

But I have a job. I have to go to it. I have to. Because as much as Augustine made me feel alive in my dream, my real world is crashing down around me. That is the world I am stuck in, the world that I know more than the new one being laid out before me, so I have to fix it, prop it up on stilts, and hope all these new revelations don't drown me.

"I am not letting you anywhere near that building," he seethes, fangs flashing and lips splitting wide. "You are coming home, and we are discussing this bond. I meant what I said to you. *You are mine, Joanna.*"

"You want to talk about this bond?" A swell of anger rises in me like I've never felt before, twisting inside me until a sneer that matches his intensity stretches across my lips. "My life-or-death situation?"

"There will be no death." The sands around my wrists writhe around more of my arms, creeping up to my neck. "You will not deny me."

"If you want me, you must deal with all of me, Augustine. And all of me has fucking bills to pay."

"Watch your mouth, *mon abeille*." He leans into my face, his lips nearly on mine. I swear I can smell sea salt and books on him. My eyes flutter closed as the sands complete a loop around my neck. The fine grains tickle the sensitive skin and

I bite my tongue to keep my whimper to myself. "I know all of your desires, everything you fear. There is not an emotion you experience that I cannot taste. Do not try to convince me for one moment that you are not moments from collapsing with exhaustion or panic."

Augustine backs me into the cold tiled wall and presses his whole body to mine. His fully clothed body to my damp, nude one. My thoughts of work stutter for a moment, heat pulling in my belly at the power he is holding over me. I swallow hard. *Focus, Joanna, you are angry with him, not aroused.*

Can I be both?

"You are going to call in sick to work, you are coming home with me where I can bathe and worship you, and then you may discuss your concerns about the bond with me in private."

"What if I don't want to?" I ask, feeling the urge to deny him, to make him force me to do what he wants.

"This is not a game," Augustine asserts. "I want you all to myself, *mon abeille*. We have spent long enough suffering in the dark, in dreams, from the bond."

It all crashes into place in my head in a moment of clarity. Like a rubber band has snapped across my wrist. Privacy. At home. Hidden away. He wants me and isn't afraid to show how he desires me in private, in my dreams. However he doesn't want to be seen with me. What's the point of making the bond, of living, if Augustine doesn't want to live with me?

They were right, they *are* right.

Prove it. A tiny voice in the back of my head whispers those words I told him in my dream.

"No," I say, even as I feel my lower lip tremble. "You want me, date me then."

"Do not be ridiculous. We are past courting."

JOANNA

"I am not- I deserve- I-" My breath sputters and chokes on a sob as a wave of hopelessness threatens to drown me as I remember the harsh words whispered to me in a dark office. "I belong."

"Who said you did not? Joanna, you are not thinking straight-"

"I belong," I whimper. "I don't want to die."

Suddenly, I am lifted off my feet. I am crumbling, drowning, awash in the anguish of defeat I felt last night. Augustine's long arms wrap around me and hold me close. In the back of my mind, I feel a sense of confusion and I don't think it's mine. It only makes me cry harder. Fully, completely overwhelmed by everything. *I don't want to die.* The words repeat over and over again in my head. I want to be alive. I want to live a life worth remembering, and I want to belong.

Fingers dig into my scalp, and a hand soothes my shuddering back as sobs rack through me. I can't stop the tears as they pour from my eyes once again.

"You are not going to die," he says. "I will not let that happen. You are my queen, *mon abeille*. Even if you grow to hate me, I will do everything in my power to make your dreams real. I will not let anything happen to you. I cannot experience that terror again, of not being able to feel you."

Augustine presses kisses into my hair and forehead. There is a rattling, the spines at his back moving as he shifts to set me on the counter. I hadn't even felt the change in his size. My broken mind accepts the monster as much as the man. They are both him. They will both be mine if I complete the bond.

"Please, come home with me."

"Okay," I whisper.

11

Augustine

0 days

Had I known that when Joanna is not drowning herself in work, she is an incorrigible busybody, I would have chained her to our bed instantly. Like a worker bee in a hive, she buzzes around, desperate to keep herself busy. I try to brush it aside, but I can tell it is something deeper. It is almost as if she believes movement is the key to her survival. That if my human rests she will suddenly expire, or perhaps she needs the constant distraction.

The taste of her emotions is so much stronger on my tongue now. Like the last eighteen months have been nothing but a scattering of crumbs for a starving man, and now a feast has been laid out before me. Our bond is so near completion my sands scrape across my flesh in desperation to complete it.

But *mon abeille* is not ready.

The woman is manic, filled with so much worry it makes even my head spin. The vagabonds and caffeine-addicted students who usually suffice as meals at the library are nothing compared to my human. I sit in the conservatory off my kitchen and watch a freshly showered Joanna tap away at her phone that she snuck out of her bag like her life depended on it, dressed once again in the raggedy clothes Deg'Doriel gave her.

The first requirement after our bond is complete is getting a new wardrobe sorted.

"You are supposed to be taking a sick day," I remind her, nudging the cup of tea I made for her closer to her hand. She should really drink it before it goes cold.

I bring my tea to my lips, the tangy notes of Earl Grey nothing compared to the taste of my human. She is right here. She is in my home. *Our home*, I correct myself even if Joanna tries to claim it is not. Something in my chest settles at this, like a piece of my eternal puzzle finally fits into place. I have never shared my home with another, but thoughts of her filling all my spaces warms me.

"Well, trying to lie my way around a police report and a legal team is pretty hard." Her adorable little nose scrunches up as she reads the words she has just typed out. She was not pleased to learn she was entering a world of secrets and that she would need to become adept at lying. "That Arlo guy did quite the cover-up."

I try to hide my disgust. Arlo's ability is unique, and foul. I do not want Joanna anywhere near him or the rest of the people I am forced to associate with. Her only requirement in this bond was to accept me, which she has done magnificently regarding my form but atrociously in regards to allowing me to treat her the way she deserves. She is precious, a queen among the plebeian monsters of this city. She does not need to bother herself with them. She is above them now.

And will be for the rest of eternity as soon as she allows me to complete the bond.

Joanna's mobile phone begins to blast some annoying tone, and her anxiety spikes. It tastes like corked wine, a stomach-turning sour flavour. Before I can snatch the device away, she is answering it.

"Hi Patrick." Her voice is squeaky, and I hate the sound instantly. "No, no- I know. Yes, I will be- Yes, I saw that email- I- Noted. Patrick-"

Every time she starts to speak, her voice cuts. She is not allowed to get a word in edgewise in whatever conversation she is having while she is supposed to be resting after being brutally attacked. Whomever this Patrick is, he has just gained himself a very dangerous enemy. Nobody will ever be so offensively rude to Joanna again. I will not have it.

I hold out my hand as the voice on the phone becomes so loud I can hear Patrick's clipped tone. She looks at me with almost fear in her eyes, and guilt as she places the device in my palm. *There is my good pet.* This shall be a good teaching moment for *mon abeille*.

"-Jesus fucking Christ, Jo-"

"I have it on good authority that is not how that happened."

"Who the fuck is this?"

"This is Dr. Croft," I reply, slipping into a role I have not played in a long while. "I have advised my patient to rest and avoid stress while she is recovering from *her assault*. And I will advise you, free of charge, sir, unless you are ringing to enquire about her well-being and wish her well, do not call Joanna for the next ten days. She will be unavailable."

"I- Dr. Croft, you can't just-"

"I most certainly can. I am sure a call to her union representative would be beneficial in clearing up this *harassment* if you feel the need to call again."

There is silence on the other end of the line. A sense of satisfaction brings a smirk to my face as I take a sip of my tea.

"Good day," I say, ending the call when it sounds like he is about to speak again.

Joanna is red in the face with anger for some reason, and I can only feel more smug about the outcome of this. Surely if she is angry with me, she will not be thinking about anything else. A perfect solution to a quite annoying problem. I slip her phone into the pocket of my casual trousers and take another sip of my tea. Her cute, delicious mouth falls open.

And suddenly, her indignation brings me a spike of arousal right through my centre. I recross my legs to adjust the swell of my cock discreetly. I have been ignoring the need that dwells just under the surface. Our bond is burning inside Joanna, but it is a raging, chaotic hive of bees inside me. Every grain of sand, every atom of my being vibrates with a primal need. They want her, need her, and I am only just controlling it.

Mon abeille is fragile right now. She does not need a beast; she needs a gentleman. I suppose that does not mean we cannot play.

"Augustine. Give me my phone." Her tone is measured, an adorable firmness that makes me smile. I want to hear her beg.

"And if I refuse?" I ask. "What will you do then, *mon abeille*?"

"I'll go home."

"You will?"

"I can't stay here. All of my stuff is at my flat."

To a mortal man, that would probably sound logical enough. But I am not mortal. I have more money than I could ever possibly spend lying around in accounts across the globe. It would be nothing for me to replace any material thing Joanna owned.

"I will buy you new things."

Her soft cheeks puff out as she blows air into them. She wants to argue but is holding herself back from me. Already I can see her deflating. Well, that just will not do.

"Strip," I command.

"What? No."

"This is not a request, Joanna. You know what to say if you do not feel comfortable."

I take a sip of my tea and study my mate. Her fingers slowly trace the handle of her teacup. The blunt, bitten nails curling around the decorative design of the porcelain taunt me. She has not picked it up yet, but I am trying not to be offended. There is still time to learn her preferences. We have eternity.

Once my cup is empty, I set the saucer down on the table and relax deeper into my chair. Beneath the hem of my trousers, my sands begin to wind their way to Joanna. The black tendrils creep across the floor until they reach the thick sweatpants she wears. Her eyes meet mine just as two of them grip her ankles, spreading her legs apart.

"Augustine." She says my name like a warning. Her cheeks are red with a tinge of embarrassment, and I can taste her arousal in the air again.

"Joanna." I simply state. "You agreed to be mine in this realm, or have you forgotten."

"No," she says. "But this isn't what I agreed to."

"Is it not? You are my queen, but you are also my pet. And

good little pets do as they are told." The sands slip up her legs until they meet the warmth of her inner thighs, not touching just yet.

"Augustine," she breathes. "I can't."

"Can't or won't? Because I would joyously undress you if you allowed me."

"I won't. I know the moment I am naked in front of you, three things will happen."

"Tell me, *mon abeille*."

She swallows hard, fingers fidgeting with the ties of her sweatshirt while she stares holes into her teacup. I bring one hand to the table, teasing the wood with a clawed finger. My sands wrap tightly around her thick thighs, and I let them tease her core, applying hints of pressure over the cotton material. Apprehension and arousal battle for dominance in her taste.

"I will be freezing."

"Fixable."

"I will feel self-conscious."

"A preposterous feeling to have when it comes to us."

"I will want to complete the bond."

My sands tighten around my mate and my claw scars the wood. Joanna's gaze flicks from her cup to my hand.

"Do you not want to complete the bond?"

"Not until we talk," she explains. "I need to think, to process what the fuck is going on with my life."

"Language, Joanna." I hum.

My skin itches with the need to disagree. There should not be a need to process anything, for it is all very clear to me. She is mine, and she will always be mine. I will do anything to keep her. At this moment, that means pulling back the beast and showing her the gentleman I have spent centuries creating.

"Come, I will show you some of your new home, and we can have our discussion in a more comfortable space." I stand and hold out my hand for her.

To my delight, she grabs her tea and my hand. The warmth of her skin against mine, of my sands coiling around her fingers, brings me a small amount of ease. I take her on a short tour of the ground floor, showing her the drawing room and some of my less rare prints and paintings, before taking her to the first floor. There is a smoking room I rarely use any more. It is mostly for when Deg'Doriel and Kragnash visit since I no longer host parties like I used to. But more importantly, this floor holds my decorative library.

As I open the door for Joanna, she gasps. Her gaze darts towards the large fireplace, to floor-to-ceiling bookcases that cover three of the walls, to the statues, to the settee and chairs placed around the room. This library is set up for entertaining, with a heavy curtain separating it from the smoking room. The books in this room are valuable, but nothing priceless or not worth the risk of cigar smoke.

Joanna gently sets her now empty teacup on a side table and wanders up to the statue of a Rubenesque woman holding a pitcher. I watch her for a moment before lighting a fire. The room warms slowly as I let her explore the small details of the space that I am sure we will be spending many countless hours in. I can already picture her draped in a silk robe lounging on the settee while we read together. It is cosy, and wholesomely warm with just an underlying hint of more.

Desire quickly melts the innocent image into one, her spread out in front of the fire, my sands teasing her body while I enjoy an evening drink. Joanna is whimpering and writhing as I tease her, feeding off her need until I am satisfied enough to allow her release. The toe of my shoe presses into the ornate rug in front of the fire. I will need to procure some kind of pad to place under this rug.

"Joanna," we turn to meet each other's gaze. "How are you feeling, physically?"

"I'm-" She cuts her speech off and tucks a strand of damp hair behind her ear as her cheeks colour. Her embarrassment perfumes the air, but so does her sweetness. "Better after the shower, still a bit sore, but shit, I feel like I'm gonna crawl out of my skin if you don't fuck me."

I do not understand why the foul words that come out of her mouth irritate me so, but they do. She is decadent, and those words are below her. I take a deep breath and crook a finger at her to come to me. Joanna comes on command.

"Now, I have spent over a year in your dreams. I know all that you desire, *mon abeille*." I start, "But I would like to discuss them and the bond. Would you like to sit down?"

"No," her voice squeaks and she clears her throat. "I, um, have tried to have relationships like that before, and they haven't gone well. We don't need to do that stuff."

She folds her arms across her chest and the sour taste has me pursing my lips. I am not jealous of Joanna's past relationships, but something inside me threatens to snap at the idea of someone treating her poorly for simply having desires she wishes to explore.

"Why didn't they go well?"

"The few exes I dated didn't like that I wanted to be forced. They wanted someone more giving. It made them uncomfortable." She refuses to look me in the eye now, shame overwhelming my senses as she takes a deep breath. "It's fine, I know it's a 'niche' interest."

Joanna makes quotes with her fingers around the word niche, but it feels deeper than what she tells me.

"Nothing is 'niche' to me." I take her hands and lead her to one of the chairs in front of the fire. It takes me tugging on her hips to get her to sit down on my lap, but when she finally does sit perpendicular to me, her body leans away from mine. "Is this uncomfortable?"

"Are you comfortable?"

"I would be if you relaxed. Trust me when I place you somewhere."

That colour rises to her cheeks again as she eases into her position on my lap. I place one hand in the middle of her back to support her and let the other rest on the chair. Joanna's heart thumps beneath my touch, strong and steady. I do not stop the tiny tendrils of sand that slip from my fingers.

"I meant what I said, Joanna. I want to worship you, treat you like the worthy queen you are, but I also have those darker desires that humans shy away from. I want to possess all of you, and I will, by any means necessary."

"Possessions are replaceable," she says, head turned towards the fire.

"But once we complete the bond, there is no breaking it. Your soul will be mine for the rest of existence. You may decide you do not want to play our game, or maybe you will grow to hate me, but I will always crave you, *mon abeille*."

"Augustine, I can't- we barely know each other, and- and- and…"

"We have eternity to know one another, and to grow together. I have spent months waiting for you, anticipating your visits to the library. I am not going to change my mind."

Joanna nods along, her fingers twisting around the strings of her sweatshirt again. Honeyed arousal floats off of her the longer she ponders my commitment. The tendrils of my sands support her back, allowing her shoulder to relax the longer we sit. Her weight on my legs only threatens my control. More of my sands thrash against my skin just to hold her, to taste her, but I remain a gentleman for now.

"I want a date, a real one, before we complete the bond."

"If that is your stipulation, then courting you shall be my pleasure." I take one of her hands and kiss her knuckle. Finally, she looks at me again, and I see the heat in her gaze. My sand slips from the hand holding hers and surrounds her fingers. "Are you agreeable to discussing the relationship you dream about?"

"Yes," she says, her tone hushed suddenly.

"Can you confirm your hard limits with me?" I watch Joanna's throat move as she swallows, while visions of where my teeth will sink into her pretty skin make my sands grip her harder.

"No degradation, no mess like food, no feet stuff."

"Thank you for telling me, *mon abeille*." I kiss her knuckles again just to watch her blush. Her thighs shift across my lap and I smirk against her skin. "I know you have a verbal safeword, but I would like you to think of a hand signal as well."

"Two snaps," she says quickly, doing the action. Her fingers loudly click, something easy enough to hear. "I, um, have fantasised about this a lot and thought knowing more would be good."

"You are a very good girl, aren't you?" My words cause her

arousal to spike and sweeten the air between us. Joanna leans further into my touch now, moments away from curling up in my lap like a tired kitten. "I know it can be common in these types of relationships to have rules, but I only wish for two things, *mon abeille*."

"Okay."

"As mine, you will do as I request, and we will be honest with each other." I look into her eyes, watching her brow soften at my words.

The sands supporting her back travel up and slip gently around her neck to form a collar, more of a delicate black necklace, but a symbol all the same. It will do for now until we complete the bond. Then she will carry my mark forever. Her breath shudders and her eyes close. I wait, inhaling her scent, her desire, and her arousal until I can no longer stand it.

"Until you are ready to complete the bond, I will not gratify you sexually." Her eyes snap open and she looks ready to argue with me. My sands around her throat tighten noticeably enough for her to hold her tongue. "If I get another taste of you, I will finish our bond. And you requested a date."

"I've had plenty of sex without a date," she says. "And won't it kill me?"

"Next Thursday I have a reservation at a club for dinner. Will you join me?" I change the subject. I neither wish to hear about Joanna's previous sexual partners or her death if the bond remains uncompleted. Already I am addicted to her taste. To keep feeding it without completion of the bond would just put her at risk of me overfeeding.

"Yes, but I'm still nervous about the bond, Augustine." Her hand rubs her cheek and she sighs. "I want to trust you."

"Let me prove it to you then, *mon abeille.*"

12

Augustine

7 days

Even in her dreams, Joanna anxiously paces up and down the beach until I can get to her. She calls to me every night. I never see her sneak into the library, but I sense it. The moment her honey arousal enters my domain, my mouth waters. I stand at my desk studiously and wait to be called forth. Wait for *mon abeille* to shed the shackles her conscious mind holds on her and to let herself be free.

Only then will her worries cease, only then will she stop pacing and look out at the water. She sits in the sand in her loose linen clothes, often giving me a matching set and staring at nothing. It takes everything in me not to feed off her when she calms herself. I know these moments are precious, I don't wish to sully them with my more beastly behaviours. Not until the bond can be completed. Her aura hums with a golden sweetness that calls to me, begging for my sands.

She is delicious. The honey taste of her lust swells like

the waves on the beach. I know the bond is burning inside her. The flush on her cheeks is vibrant and her arousal drips from her every pore. My sands pulse under my skin like a heartbeat every time we are close like this, where I can feel our connection burning between us simply by touching her hand.

The bond is why she is venturing here at all. I know she has mostly remained at home. My messages are read almost instantly, and Joanna responds in a series of short answers one right after the other, like she is scared she will not be able to get her full thoughts through before I respond. She claims I text like I am writing a formal letter, but she messages me like a serial killer.

```
Mon Abeille: Do you have to eat real food?
Mon Abeille: Or is it a choice?
Mon Abeille: Do I still get to eat food? I won't
give up coffee.
Augustine: Joanna, while food is not a requirement
for me to sustain my eternal life, it is enjoyable
when done well. I enjoy human cuisine. I would never
dream of cutting you off from your precious drink.
A.R.
```

It has been the only way we have communicated in the mortal realm. When she comes to me in the evenings, it is like that first night all over again. I catch a small taste of her on my tongue but nothing more before she drifts off to her favoured chair.

In her dreams, *mon abeille* is living, wild and free. She speaks to me without restraint here. Her words flow in a beautiful mess of storytelling. Joanna reveals herself to me in laughter and sorrow. How her mothers died when she was young and why she dreams of this beach. How she does not feel like she is living trapped in a cycle of fear and change. There is a depth to her existence she has yet to tap, hindered by the exhaustion of life and society. She tells me more about her job, why she feels guilty, and why she will not leave. She tells me about her waking dreams or what she can decipher from them. Her wants are muddled with menial things like funds and time.

I promise to make them real if she will only let me, but she just shakes her head at me every time, demanding I kiss her, chase her, own her until she forgets this is all a dream. Each time I reinitiate the bond, a precaution as we wait for our date. Every night I have watched my queen, *mon abeille*, blossom in the safety of her dreams and I want to bring that life into the mortal realm if she will only let me.

In the mornings, when her flavour is still fresh in my mind, the memory of her on my tongue drives me to my office. I can still smell how her arousal has leaked onto the leather chair when I sit down on it. The memories of that night are coated in blood and feastings, but this chair will forever be a shrine to my first waking taste of Joanna. I can envision her thighs pressed against the arms, her leg draped over one of them as I feast on her cunt. Her fingernails digging into the leather just at the top of the chair. It is imprinted with her mark. Jealousy and reverence go hand in hand when I look at that chair. I want to carry her mark on me. It makes my cock ache all the more to think of the little scratches her nails could make.

I've been discreet thus far with that most pressing aspect of the bond. I am giving her time, which was not what I originally planned. If we were not meeting in her dreams every night, I believe she would be genuinely suffering. However near we may be there, it is not enough to calm the storm raging beneath my skin. So for the past five days, I have been taking certain matters into my own hand, stroking my cock to thoughts of plump, supple flesh wrapped around my waist and my sand pinning her down while I ruin her in a library constructed just for us. The floodgates have blown wide open, and these small acts are what are keeping me from losing my sanity.

A week ago, I was so close, our bond practically overflowing with completeness. Now, I fear it will never be completed. My wills are at odds. The rules of gentlemanliness that I endeavour to follow are saying I should be respectful of her wishes, provide security and do everything in my power to shower her with delicate, chaste affection. While my sands, the primordial part of me that seeps and drips and craves like a starved beast, gnaws at my insides for completion. Of feeling our bond, our souls sewn together in divine and primal perfection.

Joanna keeps refusing to accept my courting gifts, which does not help matters. After attending her home on Wednesday evening, I made a note of her address, which seemed most sensible at the time. On Thursday morning, I arranged for breakfast to be delivered to her flat. The delivery driver called me after she 'fobbed me off and wouldn't buzz me in'. Which is fair, I suppose I should have messaged her about the delivery, but now I do not know if she is eating well enough.

At least Friday's flowers arrived without issue. A selection of wild roses, red carnations, and honeysuckle to convey my feelings from our imposed distance. Except then she texted me a series of messages thanking me, telling me how beautiful they were, but that she had to bin them because of a pollen allergy. I nearly threw the book I was rereading at the time.

I was so close to doing the right thing and then failing once again.

Saturday was easy. Joanna called me to ask if I had plans, which I did, but they would be irrelevant if she needed something. She enquired about going to the park *to chat and have coffee*.

Perfection.

Truly, a lovely idea for a date if she would have allowed me to call it that. There were very strict rules around what she thought of as a date, and apparently a stroll in the park is not it. It was a perfectly fine courting excursion the last time I felt so inclined. I am not sure what exactly my Joanna qualifies as a minimum to make a date, but this side of her, assertive and assured, makes my sands and I want to wrap around her and never let go. This little peek at the Joanna in her dreams out in the mortal realm is delicious.

I arrived ten minutes early out of a sense of urgency I still cannot place, if only to prove to her that I am a suitable mate in all forms.

But gods, the outfit she wore.

Leggings are one of the most genius inventions of humanity. The stretchy fabric moulds my mate's body beautifully, elegantly, with the grace she deserves. When she met me at the gated entrance, I was shameless, as anyone with taste would be.

"You tease me with these trousers. I would devour you right here in front of everyone, *mon abeille*."

Joanna turned such a lovely shade of blush, her arousal, syrupy sweet, seeping from her pores. It took everything in me to remain chaste after that. I could gaze at her for the rest of my days and never tire, but there was something truly sinful about the way the material of her leggings clung to her bottom. Walking around with my cock at half-mast is not exactly an enjoyable experience.

As we approached the café, however, she refused to let me purchase her drink.

"I found ten dollars in the pocket of these leggings this morning. I can buy our drinks. Save the big money for Thursday."

I do not think she understands the depth of my coffers, but there was something like pride in her soft aura as she grabbed both of our cups from the barista and handed over her money. I want to nurture that feeling in her, that she should be proud of everything she does, by existing.

Now here I am, Tuesday evening, sulking in my wooden chair with my cracked ceramic mug of tea from an industrial-sized bag of some store brand variety mix. It has been one disastrous attempt at courtship after another. Even when I think I am making ground, Joanna pulls the rug out from underneath me. Oh, but does she have another thing coming. On Thursday, on our official date, I am going ravish and spoil and show her exactly what it will mean to be mine for eternity. How to be treated like the queen she shall become.

"Auggie. Augustine."

A large, earth-toned hand waves in front of my face. Nora looks confusedly at me and then at my notebook, which is unopened on my lap.

"Just because you're getting pussy, doesn't mean you can't take notes," Ramón hisses, just as annoying and fearless as ever, like our disagreement last week never happened.

"Ramón, shut the fuck up," Nora scowls at him, but there is little heat in her voice.

"I mean no disrespect," Arlo's soft Appalachian accent is almost shocking amongst our group. "But will she be joinin' us on a count of her becomin' immortal?"

He is looking healthier; his pallid skin almost has a flush to it now and he is not as fidgety as he once was. It seems that little meal he had last week did him some good. At least someone benefited from that insanity.

I purse my lips. To be perfectly honest, I had not thought about it because my main focus is keeping my queen all to myself.

"Not if she doesn't get the cravings." Kragnash spreads his legs before resting one ankle on his knee. Buster lays next to him, leash off and relaxed. The bags under his eyes tell me he has not restored his powers yet. His age is showing just enough to make you believe he really is centuries old. Maybe Ramón's one-armed friend could be handled more efficiently than I had initially planned.

"She will not," I assert, before quickly changing the subject. "Where is the sea witch? She is never late."

"I haven't seen Orthia since she stormed out last week," Nora says.

"Do you think *Her Love* has taken over her again? I haven't heard of anyone going missing in a while." Ramón scratches a claw over his chest. "But then again, I'm not sure we really would. I'll ask my guy."

I try not to think about who or what guy Ramón means. It is not uncommon for the monster community of Gwenmore to have more unscrupulous connections, but Ramón has made running the underworld his life's mission. The sewer rat views himself as some sort of don, but that always comes with baggage the group has to deal with. There is no denying that his connection to the human underworld is the best, which has come in handy many times.

"It's not that," Nora says. "I can't feel their energy. Normally there is a rippling in the woods between the veils when they are feeding."

"Where is Deg? This meeting needs to get rolling, I have a press breakfast in the morning." Kragnash grunts, displeased as usual when things do not work to his time frame.

Again, as if speaking his name has summoned him, Deg'Doriel marches into the parish centre basement. A burst of flame and his human form turns to ash as his demon form expands. His lavender skin looks more grey than normal, and I find myself concerned for his well-being. However, his first words to me erase any concern I have for him.

"You haven't completed the fucking bond yet. Thank fucking Lucifer."

He sounds almost relieved, and I hate him for it. It exposes knowledge about me to others that they did not need to know and even though the demon is my friend, he would happily see me unhappy and mateless than with Joanna. I grit my teeth together to control the response that tickles my tongue and begs for my retort.

"Wait, wait, wait," Ramón leans forward on his stool. "Bond? B-O-N-D? Like mates and shit? Are you saying we get to have those with humans now?"

"Absolutely not." Deg'Doriel's voice shakes the ceiling tiles and flames flicker around his crown of horns.

"But then why does the tight-ass rule follower get one?" Nora asks.

"He shouldn't get one at all." Deg frowns at me. "There is a delicate balance that must be protected here. Mating with humans permanently is dangerous. We haven't spent over three centuries building this world for us to coexist with them only for it to be ruined by a fucking one-night stand."

"Wet dream." Ramón snickers.

My human facade disintegrates as my sands explode from my body. Arlo and several of the other lesser monsters scatter to the corner and Deg'Doriel sneers at me with a viciousness I have never had directed at me. He does not understand. He has never known these feelings; the loveless beast claims he is incapable. The hellspawn knows nothing of what the mate bond is like on the mind and body. How it feels to have something slowly torn away, like a rack dragging over your skin until there is nothing left. He gobbles up souls so greedily for a being who has never had one. His aura is dark and sharp, an empty husk of foul emotions that taste of burn and blood.

"Alright, put your dicks away, lads." Nora's tone is ethereal, the fae queen's eyes glowing bright white as she oozes the power she wields to soothe and pacify and lure her victims to their doom. "Let's get this meeting over with. Not everyone here wants to listen to your bickering."

I take a deep breath, my sands refusing to retreat, the spines having ripped through yet another one of my jackets. My tailor will be getting quite the bonus from me this month. I pull back enough to sit in my chair, but my claws and eyes refuse to shift. I can see the auras of emotions around the monsters in the room more clearly than when I mask my abilities to appear human.

"Joanna will not be mortal for much longer," I say with complete certainty. "So there will be no issue. Now who would like to speak first?"

"Finally," Kragnash growls and begins the meeting proper.

The rest of the meeting goes on with as much ease as possible. There is tension among the lesser monsters, the weres in particular, seem a little more cagey, but that will most certainly be because of the full moon this weekend. Arlo recounts his side of the events of Tuesday night. But since he has yet to actually kill a human, I do not mark his number of days as changing. Of course, Kragnash is back to seven, just like I am. The battered security guard Arlo found in a closet of that basement had to be sacrificed for the blood ritual to work on Joanna.

Once everyone shares what they wished for the evening, Deg'Doriel ends the meeting with a reminder that our existence in harmony with the humans is like balanced scales, that if it swings in either direction, it could topple all the work we have done to build our community. The lessers leave. Arlo also tries to slink out of the room, but Deg grabs him by the scruff of his oversized jacket and drags him back to the inner circle.

"I really don't think I need to be here. The good shelter near the mortuary will fill up if I don't get there soon," he claims, his fingers digging into his dirt-stained jeans.

"You've proved yourself useful, O'Shea." Deg'Doriel drops him into a chair. "So you are staying. Make sure everyone else gets your phone number before you leave."

Arlo pulls a flip phone from his pocket and begins to pass it around.

"Kragnash," I say, before Deg'Doriel can begin his lecture on balance anew. "You still need to restore your power, correct?"

"Yes, sir." He grunts, "Emmi has been running me like a dog for the past week, so I haven't had a moment of peace."

"Well, I have the information of a man who needs to be

removed. I meant to do it Saturday, but something came up."

"Since when have you ever shirked a duty like that?" Nora snorts, a ghastly noise.

"Exactly," Deg growls. "Since everyone clearly needs another reminder of why soulmates and bonds and all the lovey bullshit with humans is a dangerous risk, let's start with Augustine Ravenscroft's Horrible Mate history, shall we?"

"That was told to you in confidence, Deg'Doriel."

"Yes, but last one ended with the human committing suicide because they couldn't handle their world becoming so scary. Nightmares that are actually real. The scales tipped."

"Jamie was an accident."

Saying his name out loud brings a chill to my skin. I have not spoken his name in decades. My accident, my innocent lover from an era of secrecy and closed doors even between humans. Much like Joanna, I had never planned to form a bond with him. The opium and refined wine that blurred his senses had also affected me that night. I would have loved him, could have grown fond of him over the years we would spend together. But when he saw me outside of his dreams, he could not handle it. The young man overdosed before I could save him.

In the end, when the urges of the bond faded, I was left feeling oddly relieved. There had been disgust flavouring his emotions during our last meeting. It taints my memories of him, only leaving a bad taste in my mouth. Jamie's death was never my intention, but I do not think I would have ever actually completed the bond.

"Joanna reacted impressively well to seeing us," Kragnash says. "But that could be shock."

"She is different," I argue. "For starters, she has told me she would complete the bond with me. She has fully consented."

"That doesn't matter if she is more trouble than she's worth."

"Deg'Doriel," I scowl, the skin of my cheeks stretching as my sharpened teeth are revealed.

"Question," Ramón says, ignoring the struggle between us. "What exactly does a soulmate feel like?"

Ambrosia, nectar of the gods, fulfilling.

"Pure light," Nora sighs, and I swear I can almost taste a wistfulness in her emotions.

"Victory," Kragnash says with such certainty. I do not know much about orcish cultures, but I do know they form bloodmates, which can cause war or peace between clans.

"Hogwash." Deg'Doriel finally states.

"Well then," Ramón grins, "I have one. She is a human as well. So mark that in your little notes on me, Auggie. She is my princess."

I cannot stop the sounds that bubble up out of me like a fountain. My chuckle turns into a raucous laughter that shakes the room. Deg'Doriel's anger, in combination with Ramón's absolute certainty, is just too much for me to contain myself. This has turned into one of the greatest group meetings we have had in years. An honest to god tear comes to my eye as I look at the horror on Deg'Doriel's face.

"Look, let's put it to a vote," Kragnash has to shout over my laughter. "I move to drop the rule regarding bonding, mating, or engaging humans in long-term relationships."

"I second," I say, with a nod at Kragnash.

"All in favour, say aye."

Everyone but Deg'Doriel and Arlo vote in favour.

"I-I-I- don't feel comfortable votin'. I ain't here for politics." The ghoul shakes his head, eyes flicking to the door, to his phone, to his lap again.

I have to bite my knuckle to stop from cackling again like a madman.

"That is four to one then, Deg'Doriel. So unless you have some *substantial reason* you'd like to share as to why we shouldn't, the motion passes."

Kragnash stares down the demon, his mouth set in a firm line. I can see Deg's mind working, desperately trying to come up with a logical reason why we should not. The excuse must be on the tip of his tongue. His emotions are a riot of spicy burnt flavours that makes my stomach shrivel up. Whatever he wants to say, he keeps to himself.

"This does not mean you can broadcast this information to every beast or creature in Gwenmore. I refuse to be responsible for humans dying because some fucking troll or lich decided to fuck them."

Something in Deg'Doriel's emotions shifts. The spiciness turns sour and curdles on my tongue. He is lying. For whatever reason, he is lying to us about why he does not want us to mingle with the mortals. I check my watch. It is later than I would like it to be. I know Joanna will have already arrived at the library. My human is waiting for me.

I am at odds with what to do. I will not press Deg'Doriel in front of the others. Whatever secret he is hiding, I will find out, but I cannot leave my mate. I watch as the others leave, Kragnash and Ramón chatting jovially about the one-armed man, while Nora slips Arlo some money. I make a mental note to look into what services the library has to offer to make sure Arlo doesn't become a danger. He is useful, but beyond that he deserves better. We have all been in his position at some point during our existence.

Deg'Doriel's sigh sounds more like a growl as he walks over to the small refreshment table. I watch him pour the burnt coffee into a mug and top it up with a flask from his jacket pocket. He sits back down in his chair and unclips his white collar.

"Do you want to tell me the truth?" I ask.

"No," he grunts, rubbing his hand across his face. "Just know that when the time comes, we are going to have to make some tough choices."

I hum softly for a moment, contemplating what he could mean by this. Life is nothing but choices, and I have spent a good long time taking the safer and more boring of them. Perhaps a few hard decisions would liven up all of our existences some.

"Whatever the future holds for us, Deg'Doriel, know I will be at your side. You are my friend. My bond with Joanna will not change that. I think you would like her quite a bit."

"You barely know her."

"Yet, I know with all my being, that she is meant to be mine and will add a new sense of purpose to my life that I was missing."

My friend sighs, taking a long drink from his coffee. "You are disgustingly in love, and I hate it."

"Do you? Or do you simply hate that it is not you?"

I stand up, placing my empty mug on the table. My sands pulse with need and hunger for *mon abeille*, but I am not sure I can leave my friend just yet. The worry he is feeling sets my teeth on edge. We have been friends for centuries, since the fall of the Medici Bank, and yet I have never seen him like this before.

"On Friday, let's have supper," I say. "I will pay."

He snorts, "If you can't pull yourself from your human, bring her too. Since she will become a permanent fixture."

"No." It's dual reasoning. I do not want my Joanna to leave my bed after Thursday, but I also do not wish Deg'Doriel to believe that mating with humans means they will become everyone's whole existence.

We will always be the monsters that lurk in the night, first and foremost.

13

Joanna

I am going stir-crazy. Or maybe just regular crazy.

I can remember exactly when I last had time off work. It was when I spent the week at the seaside. That was three years ago. Since then, I have spent every day, including weekends and holidays, trying to stay on top of work. I haven't taken a sick day or a day of leave for anything. My life has revolved around my job because I am not sure who I would be without it.

Now, I am not sure who I am.

After spending Wednesday afternoon curled up on Augustine's lap, allowing him to direct me, to move me, I know I'm not scared of being his. Even when we both remained clothed, he proved he would possess me just like he said, just like I wanted. He doesn't scare me. Seeing the monster that lurks under beds and hides in the dark corners of my dreams made me alive. Finding out there are other beings existing on Earth is radical and freeing more than terrifying. It opens up a whole new world of chances that I can take. And having Augustine as my hot professor just makes it better.

I spent Thursday thinking and writing and processing some more. I had made the decision that living is certainly what I want. After everything that happened that night, I know it wasn't some freak incident. Someone is sending me a message, but I have no idea why. Early in the mornings, when I return from my late-night rendezvous at the library, I feel like someone is watching me. There's a tension in my neck I have never felt before and it makes me move faster until my feet are pounding up the stairs to my door and I'm sweating.

Nothing about my past, my moms, or my previous foster parents explains why any of it happened to me. I have done nothing but work and go to the library for months. Whoever sent the message made sure I got it loud and clear, except I'm not going to respond.

Something in me has sparked to life.

The Joanna Cole, who was a doormat, milquetoast with a glass of water and a Tuesday lunch of salad, is done for. No amount of placating or being easy to be around had saved me from that beating. The old Joanna Cole can't rule my life any more. She can't be in the driver's seat any more. Being safe has done nothing but work me to the bone and make me feel like shit. It's a lie I told myself over and over again. Augustine asked for honesty, so I am going to give it to him, and to myself.

She needed to die, and I guess a near-death experience is all it took to bring me back to life.

Augustine makes me feel alive too. He has brought out a side of me in my dreams that I have kept hidden for years, from everyone, simply by listening. The side of me that is loud and laughs and takes up space is alive in my dreams. It is time for me to be that person in real life. No more trying to hide. No more biting my tongue. No more allowing others to make me feel uncomfortable. If I want to feel alive, to enjoy being who I am for real, I need to be honest with myself.

I belong.

I would like to say I have spent every day since becoming the new and improved Joanna. That in this crazy week, I have become the new and adventurous person I am in my dreams. But in reality, after catching up on all my laundry, I was too tired to do much of anything else that all those influencers and self-help coaches talk about on social media. The advantageous list I had made is stuck to my fridge with none of the more impressive things marked off.

I didn't go out, I didn't start a new hobby to better myself. I didn't really do much but lay on my bed and text Augustine. He sends me a message every lunchtime, asking if I have eaten, rested, and hydrated. He reminds me that I am worthy of rest, and that my value is for me to decide, not the amount of work I produce.

He is constantly on my mind. If his odd attempts at gifts weren't enough, the bond certainly keeps me constantly reminded of him. The pull of the bond is ever present in me, like a string tied around my heart, pulling me to him. I feel connected to him even when we are apart. It's physical, bone-deep and aching, but it reminds me that that part of the night was very real—the part I want to live in.

That first evening I was alone, when my hand wasn't enough to keep the heat off my flesh or my pulse from racing, I went to the library. I don't know how I knew it, but I could tell that Augustine knew when I had arrived. This new Joanna I want to be still couldn't approach him. So like the coward I was, I slunk to my chair and waited for Kant to lull me to sleep. Or for whatever freaky magic Augustine had to put me to sleep for a few hours of rest.

On Tuesday, I had a bit of panic. What am I going to do for the rest of forever? I have never thought about immortality and what that would mean for me. Augustine had been in a weird mood because of a discussion he had with Deg'Doriel, who I learned is an honest to god demon and his closest friend, so I didn't voice my concerns about immortal work.

The more I learn about Augustine though, the brighter and more hopeful it all seems because he believes in us, in me. There is something in his voice when he tries to convince me once again that I can quit my silly job that makes me want to believe him too. Eternity, however long that is, won't be scary because he will always be there for me. I hang onto those words desperately, that he won't leave me or simply disappear one day.

People always leave you, whether they want to or not. I know my moms' accident was exactly that, but I also know if my friends really wanted me around, they'd answer my text messages about meeting up. I spent my early twenties pushing people away and claiming I didn't need them. Unlearning that instinctual gut reaction is hard, but now I will have eternity to work on myself, which is almost as overwhelming as getting attached to someone. What if this is the best I can be?

By Thursday morning though, I am buzzing, completely and utterly excited for Augustine to take me on this date. In the early hours of the morning, before I could sneak out of the library, he caught me to tell me the dress code of the club we were going to tonight. I didn't latch on to all the details, too distracted by the feeling of his hand in mine, the way his thumb rubbed circles across my skin. My skin was on fire, screaming at me to let him touch more of me there and then.

I take extra care to get ready. I wash and style my hair. I put on makeup, which I haven't had the energy for in ages. I guess those short little naps in the library are paying off in more ways than one. My outfit is daring, at least for me. It is something I bought during a flash sale two years ago when a friend announced she was getting married. I didn't get an invitation like I thought I would, so I've never worn the dress.

Now, standing in my bathroom on my tiptoes to inspect myself, I am feeling a bit uncertain. I know it fits the dress code, but I am nervous about wearing it out.

The strapless dress is so structured. Even if I had boobs, I am not sure I would need to wear a bra. Its fitted short skirt stretches around my shapewear to give my more streamlined silhouette a hint of tummy rather than the whole show. The sleeves aren't attached but act more like opera gloves without hands. A flat, floppy bow accents my waist, yet it doesn't really add much, not like it did in the picture online. My stud earrings don't add anything to this, and I wish I had kept more of my mom's costume jewellery, except it is what it is at this point.

I am slipping on my tallest, sturdiest pair of black heels when my buzzer goes off. *He's here.* I swallow the anxiety and nerves. This is an opportunity to be me. There is no reason to be anything but honest.

"I'll be down in just a second," I tell him on the intercom.

I rush to my bathroom and check my reflection again before grabbing my bag and dashing out. With each step I take towards the door, my hands shake with excitement. The smile on my face is so big my cheeks ache. *This is going to be amazing.* I can see his outline through the glass of the fire door and I take a deep breath as I pull it open.

"Wow." Augustine's eyes flash a familiar golden hue before they turn hazel again and his olive cheeks darken a shade. "Apologies, you look truly stunning, *mon abeille*."

My cheeks flame under his adoration. The only word I can think to describe how he looks at me. I look at his outfit to break our eye contact; the fine suit is a lush navy colour. His tie is intricately knotted, and his matching waistcoat creates an ocean of blue that reminds me of the seaside. There is a shining gold bee pinned to his lapel.

"You look very handsome," I say, even if the word feels a bit awkward in my mouth. Handsome doesn't begin to describe what a beautiful vision he is. His golden hair is shining in the setting sun and his glasses somehow soften the sharp angle of his face in such a way that makes me want to take them off to kiss every inch of his features to see if they will cut my lips.

"I have something for you that you cannot refuse this time." He smiles, a sense of satisfaction just flickering across the back of my mind that I know is the bond now. "May I?"

My fingers itch to touch him, to feel his skin on mine. "Yes."

He produces a jewellery box from his jacket and carefully opens it to reveal a gorgeous set of earrings. Golden with pearls and what I can only assume are diamonds. Definitely not glass costume jewellery. A refusal is on the tip of my tongue because there is no way I can be trusted with something so priceless looking, but he is already reaching for me as I lean in.

His delicate fingers remove my studs and place each piece of art into my ear. They should be heavy, but it feels like they weigh almost nothing. His fingers ghost over the shell of my ear and I feel the heat of his body through the fake satin of my dress. He doesn't touch my skin any more than that.

I make a small noise when he steps away. He stares at me with such intensity, a hunger swelling in his gaze that makes the heat on my skin rush between my legs. Augustine holds out his arm for me to take and walks me to a long, black Cadillac from a different age. The type of car you are meant to be seen in, to show off wealth. The windows are tinted, the chrome shines, the tires are white-walled. He opens the back door for me to slide in and only then does it occur to me that there is a driver.

"The vehicle is mine, and the driver is Marcus. He owed me a favour and I wanted to ensure we could have as much fun as you'd like tonight." He explains as he buckles my seat belt over my lap before I get the chance.

"You know what I want," I tell him, heat creeping up my chest. I want to complete the bond. I want to belong. I want to be owned.

He gives a nod to Marcus, who promptly raises a privacy screen and begins to drive. My fingers tap against the cheap pleather of my clutch and the excitement I was feeling twists back into anxiety. This feels like too much. It is much more than I'm worth. It feels like more than just a date.

A date is a dinner where you order a whole bottle of wine and not just a glass. It's drinks at an upscale cocktail bar. I feel like I am on my way to a completely different universe. Will I ever feel like I belong in this part of his life, or will I always be lower? The bond thrums between us so easily. He makes it easy, so why am I making it difficult?

Augustine's hand is so close to my thigh but not touching me. My dress has ridden up so high, the shapewear I have on peaks out.

"Why are you nervous?"

"I feel out of my depths." I explain, "Like I am swimming too far out into uncertain waters."

"I suppose, in a way, you are. This is a whole new world that I have thrown you into." His knuckle slips up my thigh to trace the seam of shapewear. A thrill runs down my spine as he meets my gaze. "But I am here to be your guide, to sweeten you up with honeyed words and decadence like the queen of my eternity deserves."

"Augustine." His name comes off my lips like a prayer. His eyes turn the deepest, glittering shades of black and gold that melt my insides. The clawed hand that grips my chin is so gentle, the sharp talon of his thumb catching on my bottom lip.

"I promised myself I would be a gentleman tonight, but you tempt me worse than any siren, *mon abeille*."

His lips are like a drug. The moment they touch mine, I crave another hit. His fingers dig deliciously into my chin as he holds me in place. Just as I begin to reach out, to feel his beauty under my fingertips, sand wraps around my wrists and keeps them pinned to my bag.

A whimper rattles in my throat, but sharp teeth nip at my bottom lip. I open them eagerly, letting Augustine control the kiss, greedy to taste him for real and not just in my dreams. He angles my head to the side and strokes his tongue against mine. If I can't touch him with my hands, I will with my lips.

I suck on his tongue, just like I would his cock if he ever let me.

He groans so deep in his chest it almost sounds like a growl. It's animalistic and makes my heart stutter. My panties flood with my arousal and I squeeze my thighs tighter together. He knows this move all too well from me.

"Whatever happens tonight, I want the bond. I want you, Augustine," I say, panting against his lips.

"Joanna," he draws out my name like he wants to keep it on his tongue. "You are a temptation I cannot deny."

Augustine's other hand drags my knees as far apart as my dress will allow. I feel his sharp inhale against my cheek and that only makes me want to sink deeper into the kiss, into the syrupy sweetness his attention brings out of me.

His sharp fingers are careful as they slip up the inside of my thigh. My breath hitches with every little pointed tap of them. Augustine's sand squeezes my wrists before pinning them to my sides. His knee knocks against mine as he moves in his seat. This new angle pushes the bulge of his crotch right against my knee, and I could nearly cry. He is right there, hard and hot, but I can't touch him.

I want him. I have for months, even before the dream when he first bonded with me two weeks ago. This hunger and desperation are different, wholly insane. I can't believe I agreed to eternity with someone I barely know, but right now it feels like this could be the greatest choice I have ever made in my whole life. My skin is alive to each touch, each rush of air as he breathes me in. I am *alive,* and this is where I belong. With him, under him, between his thighs, wherever Augustine needs me to be, that is where I will go so long as he keeps making me feel this way.

Two fingers slide over the centre seam of my shapewear. The dampness, the teasing sensation of his touch driving my hips up.

"Centuries of evolution, yet women still feel the need to wear such restrictive undergarments." He sighs when he breaks the kiss. *"Mon abeille,* I will not ruin these like I did the last, but know I never want you to feel like you must wear these. Your softness, the plushness of your body, is perfection. The Romans would have tripped over themselves to paint and sculpt your perfect form."

I don't know what to say to that. My mouth dries up and tears come to my eyes. This compliment feels different because Augustine would know. He would know exactly what artists of antiquity would like. His Adonis form is the envy of every Greek sculpture I have ever seen in pictures, and he is calling me perfect.

"Are you sure we have to go out?" I ask when he begins to kiss my neck, inching closer and closer to the source of all this.

He chuckles against my skin and I can feel the way his lips have stretched. The largeness of his mouth against my skin feels surreal. His moustache tickles my exposed shoulder and brings out a sweet vulnerability. An urge to bare my throat and submit to his every whim has my muscles relaxing. My neck falls to the side to allow him more space to kiss me, to tease my mark.

His fingers press against my core, right next to my clit. I moan and tug at my restraints. This is too good. It's so much more than the dreams, than the memories of it while I touch myself in bed. I need him.

"Augustine," I whimper.

"So sweet for me," he murmurs. "Should I make you cum before the fun even begins? Would that make everything better, *mon abeille?*"

"Yes, yes, please."

His fingers wrap around my nape and pull me into another

kiss. My heart pounds in my chest and my thoughts slow to nothing. This slowness, this sweetness, is comfortingly familiar and yet halting. To be awake and feel this pressure drip from the base of my skull like honey is exhilarating. I don't want it to end, a craving I have never experienced before overtaking all my actions. I lick the seam of Augustine's lips, his mouth parting just enough for me. My tongue teases the sharpness of his teeth—a dangerous thrill skittering across my body at how they might feel against my skin.

His fingers are methodical and consistent against my core, pushing against me until my folds make space, until he can stroke my clit through my shapewear. Stomach muscles tightening and pussy clenching at nothing, I move randomly. I chase my need while Augustine pushes my knees further apart.

A rush of excitement heats my skin when his hips move against me. When the outline of his cock presses harder against my body. Augustine is as desperate for this as I am. That alone has me teetering on the edge. He is as hot and needy as I am. My boogeyman is just better at controlling it. It takes all of my concentration, but I rub my knees up and down his length.

Augustine moans into our kiss before breaking it. His forehead rests on mine as I keep moving. I can't see him clearly, not when we are this close, but I feel his lips move against mine. French slips from his lips as his touch becomes more demanding. My jaw is slack, my lips slick with our combined spit, and I feel utterly beautiful.

"Augustine," I whimper. "Own me. Own me. *Own me.*"

Words that I have never spoken aloud pour from my mouth. Words that I have moaned and screamed in my dreams are mumbled and whispered against my lover's lips like a secret now. I need to be his.

"*Mon abeille*, you know that I do. Everything that you are belongs to me. Your excitement, your worry, your pleasure. It is all mine. And the sweetness of your climax will be mine when I am ready for it. For now, we wait."

A knock against the privacy screen makes me jump. Augustine's hand slips from between my thighs. He brushes a loose strand of hair from my heated face with a soft smile, like he wasn't about to make me have the most explosive orgasm of my life.

The chasteness in his kiss against my cheek makes me blink. He smooths the skirt of my dress down and unbuckles my seat belt. My mouth snaps shut when he opens the car door and I see the bulge of his cock, the only thing that reminds me I am not at the tail end of a fever dream.

As he stands, he buttons his suit jacket up and extends a hand to me. For a moment, I want to demand he get back in the car and take care of what he started, but I don't. I am the one who asked for this date. Demanded it before I would finish the bond.

It is now or never to be the real me.

14

Joanna

The club, as Augustine calls it, is absolutely fucking insane. In gilded letters, *The Gin Palace* glows in the almost red light of the setting sun. There is a black carpet up into the building and velvet ropes with two men at the door wearing black suits who look like they will snap me in half for looking at them. Augustine's hand rests on my lower back as we glide up to the building. At least it feels like I am gliding or floating. It's all very surreal, and I swear I see a group of people with cameras lingering just down the pavement. I suck in my gut on instinct and straighten my shoulders.

I am not an eloquent, society type, except right now I pretend long enough for Augustine. He nods to one of the bouncers and we are ushered into the dark entrance of the building. My nails dig into my clutch as I lean a bit closer to him.

"I feel like a little heads up would have been nice."

"I gave you the dress code. You could have asked for the location," he whispers into my ear.

I huff at his stupid rightness. There is that urge in the back of my mind to be petulant, something I have never really been before. Maybe it's the crawling feeling of denial that is making me feel that way. Most of my sexual encounters before him were lacklustre at best, yet Augustine has proven to be more than capable of making me cum. The fact that he has chosen not to has flicked a switch in my head.

He smiles with a cold politeness at the host in her fancy dress. Her costume is reminiscent of something from an old stage show. Waistcoat and tails, wide fishnet stockings and short heels. She leads us up through the lobby and into a private box. It's only when the heavy curtain is closed do I let my jaw drop.

"Holy shit," I murmur, ignoring Augustine's slight frown at my foul language.

This is a full-blown theatre. Around us are more boxes where fancily dressed patrons chatter and below us are tables and chairs beginning to fill with people dressed in their best going-out clothes. Our table is covered with pristine white linens and a large candelabra in the centre, already lit. There are more forks and knives than I thought could possibly be necessary already laid out and shining in the warm glow. Definitely more than a simple date.

"I have said it already, but it seems you keep forgetting. You are a queen, and I will spend the rest of eternity treating you as such."

Augustine's half smile as he looks at me makes my knees weak. He pulls out my chair and dutifully waits for me. There is a moment, when I look at it that I think it won't be sturdy enough to hold me. It's a nagging feeling in my chest that always rises when I am somewhere new. If the chair breaks, it will be a sign from God and the universe that I don't belong here or with Augustine.

But as I sit down, I just feel supported. With ease, he slides me closer to the table and sits down opposite me. I can just see over the edge of our box and around the other boxes. They are doing much the same as me. A server comes and goes, Augustine ordering a bottle of something expensive that will make my eyes water. Like so many others, I am too enraptured in looking and seeing everything to even think about what I am planning to order.

"Oh my god," I whisper. "Oh my god, that's- and that's-"

I can't get the celebrities' names past my lips. When I whip my head back at Augustine, he is smiling at me with indulgence that makes me feel like a pet. I swallow with an ease that suddenly doesn't feel right. My fingers skim across the base of my throat, a haunting feeling of missing sands where my skin touches warm flesh.

"This show is internationally renowned," he explains. "But I have known the owner since it began in 1873."

There is a moment when he looks down at the stage. Again there is that flicker of a feeling at the back of my head, but I don't know what it means. Before I can speak, the server returns with a bottle of wine. They make a show of presenting it to Augustine and quickly uncorking it. I don't think I have ever drank wine from a corked bottle. He tastes the small amount of red wine poured into his glass before allowing the server to pour my own. I can't take my eyes off of him.

Once we are alone again, Augustine raises his glass and I do the same.

"To you, *mon abeille*, my eternal queen."

A blush erupts across my cheek and chest until I feel more

like a tomato than a person. Augustine's glass ghosts against the rim of mine before he takes a delicate sip. I try to do the same but end up taking more of a swig that coats my whole mouth. The flavours burst across my tongue. It is thick and rich as I swallow.

"You seemed…" I skim my vocabulary for the right word, "wistful when you looked at the stage."

"Ah, well, I used-"

"Monsieur Ravenscroft!" A heavily accented voice erupts from a short woman just as she bursts through the curtain. She seems almost larger than life as she moves to our table. Heavy makeup and a revealing dress show off her lithe form. Her smile is wide and wicked when her gaze moves from Augustine to me. "Oh, my friend, they did not tell me you had a mademoiselle as your guest. My darling-"

The sweet name makes my gut seize, muscles locking as if waiting for someone to hit me. One time, it was one time, and a simple word has been ruined for me. As I inhale, phantom pain in my sides has my teeth on edge. Augustine is quick and polite to cut her off from continuing.

"Nicolette, please refrain from calling my Joanna that endearment. It leaves a bad taste in our mouth."

"Of course, of course, you know I never wish to upset a guest. *Cherie*, I beg your forgiveness." The woman grabs my arm and I feel myself moving closer to her, a saltwater taffy scent in the air that makes me blink. "A friend of Augustine's is a friend of mine."

Her pupils turn to slits and I can't stop myself from nodding.

"Nicolette, she is not on the menu." Augustine scowls and sand tickles my fingers. "She is my mate."

There is a gasp, overdramatic and high-pitched. "After

JOANNA

Jamie, I was certain you would never. Lady of the Ravens, Monsieur Ravenscroft, in love and mated at last. My goddess. *Cherie*, what spell have you cast on him to make such a thing true?"

A polite, albeit awkward, smile stretches across my cheeks at that question and the drama of the situation. *After Jamie.* Jealous adjacent rises in me, simply for not having found Augustine sooner in history. As though I had a choice in the matter. Whomever Jamie was, they clearly meant something to Augustine, but they aren't here now. Why? It's a question to save for later because Nicolette is staring at me like she wants the details of whatever spell she thinks I am capable of.

I can't exactly tell this woman the story, even if she would think it was normal. I start to say something, but then another theatre staff member rushes in. They whisper something in Nicolette's ear and she rushes off with more apologies. I delicately try to sniff my nose to get rid of the taffy smell.

"You were saying?" I ask, my smile softening when I look at Augustine.

"In the twenties, I used to dance here. Lady of The Ravens was my stage name." His eyes go a bit soft, and he glances at the stage. Again, I want to know so much more about this other side of Augustine. What other lives has he lived?

"I haven't asked, but what is your preference? He or they or?"

I leave the other options in the air. It never occurred to me that Augustine might use all sorts of pronouns. He is some ancient being, after all.

"He or they is fine. When I created this form, became more than the sands, that is, it was easiest to be a man. Choosing a name took much longer, but Augustus was popular, and I enjoyed it well enough, so Augustine was born."

"You created your body?" I lean forward in my chair, fingers twirling around the sand. I can only dream of creating my perfect body. "I wouldn't even know where to begin."

"It was not overly hard. I had centuries upon centuries of living amongst humans." Augustine blushes, and for the first time I realise he might not have had this type of conversation before. Or maybe it's the way my fingers are stroking the sands like they are something more firm.

I take a sip of my wine and smile. There is so much for me to learn about who I'm binding myself to for eternity. Lifetimes of stories and adventures he can share with me. So much knowledge and wisdom that I thought had just been scholarly but is, in fact, honest-to-goodness first-hand experience.

I can't wait to spend my eternal life learning it all.

Augustine orders us a tasting menu of five courses, each with their own wine pairings and instructions. It's rich and lavish, and my stomach is bloated and a little achy by the time we are done. With every little bite I take, he smiles. I don't hold back the little moans as one thing melts in my mouth while the flavours of something else burst on my tongue. I have never had such decadence in all my life. I'm sure we will eat like this again, but I'm not sure I'll ever get this sort of experience again.

For his part, he eats with absolute grace. I am transfixed, watching the silverware slide between his lips and watching his expression for flavour balance.

"It was passable, not the chef's best." He says just as our small dessert plates are taken away.

My eyes nearly fall out of my head at the comment. Passable? This has been the finest meal in all the world. I don't have time to tell him exactly how I feel about it because an orchestra begins warming up, and I am swept into the world below.

Overhead, Nicolette's voice booms through the speakers, making my full stomach flutter. She announces the show will begin shortly and that it is the last call for drinks before intermission. On cue, two men walk into our box. They clear everything from the table and carry it to a far corner. One of the men looks at me directly and I hastily rise. I watch them a little stupidly, buzzed on wine and cosy warm with food. Augustine rises with grace and a new plush chair is brought forward.

Just one chair.

I stand for a moment, thinking they will bring in a second, except they don't. The men leave and Augustine takes his seat in the new chair. My mouth opens to ask him what's going on, but his hand rises, and two fingers beckon me to him.

Heat blooms in my belly and cheeks at what just those two fingers can do to me. God, that night feels like a million years ago already, and it's only been a week. I follow my instinct and take his hand, letting him direct me how he likes.

In all the times I have seen him sit down, Augustine has always crossed his legs, at least at the ankle, usually with one long, lean leg tossed over the other in a careless manner that makes me jealous. Now his legs are spread apart and he leads me between them. I look down at him, the low light gleaming off his glasses and golden hair.

"Mon abeille," he murmurs so tenderly.

His thumb brushes over my fingers once or twice before a claw drags across my skin. A shudder racks down my spine and my eyes close. There is a flickering at the back of my head, and I can feel his emotions through the bond. Augustine's desire hungers so much that my own is barely a craving in comparison. My breath catches in my throat when he yanks me down into his lap.

"Augustine." My fingers dig into his lapel and my eye catches the bee pin. How it shines, the intricate details of the wings mesmerising. I wonder why he chose to wear it tonight.

"Shh," he hushes me. "The show is starting."

On stage, the heavy curtains begin to open and the orchestra plays a sultry melody. Augustine's hands touch me everywhere except my skin. One grips my thigh in earnest to keep me anchored to his lap, the black talon-tipped finger splayed across my hips. The other runs up and down my spine, from the curve of my ass to the top of the zipper on my dress. My knees press together, and I do my best to focus, but the goosebumps on my flesh and thrumming heat between my legs and on my neck make it so very difficult.

Beautiful people in beautiful makeup and gowns sing songs that make my head float. They dance seductively across the stage in patterns that make my eyes feel heavy. Augustine slides my wine glass into my hand, refilled with wine from the bottle he ordered for us. The flavour tastes newer, headier on my tongue now. A small droplet leaks from the corner of my mouth. Just when I feel the embarrassment tighten in my chest, fingers grip my chin and draw me in.

He licks the wine from my mouth before his tongue plunges past my lips, and all I taste is honey. Lusty, heady honey that sends me reeling into sweet oblivion. I am lost to everything but the feeling of Augustine. He breaks the kiss softly, teasing the corner of my mouth with another before gripping both my hips. In one sure motion, I am straddling his thigh and my back rests against his chest. He hooks his chin over my shoulder, the wide split of his mouth and moustache tickling the heated skin of my neck right over where my mark will go. *Permanent, forever, eternity.*

"Watch the show, mon abeille, do not take your eyes off it until intermission." Augustine's husky voice washes over me.

I nod, muscles in my thighs relaxing and the hem of my dress rising obscenely. There is no fear that we will be seen. Like everyone else in the theatre tonight, we are entranced by the performance on stage. For a few moments, his hands remain on my hips. Those strong fingers dig into my soft flesh and I sigh. Throughout the meal, I've felt the heat of the bond. It's simmering under the surface, but now it's threatening to boil over. I do my best to focus, for the performers on stage are magnificent. They deserve my attention.

But just as my guard relaxes, the hands so innocently resting at my sides begin to move. It starts with his thumbs massaging soothing circles into my low back. They dig into knots I didn't even know I had. I bite my lip to keep the moan I want to release in. I melt further into my boogeyman until I am laying on him more than anything.

"I can do that," Augustine whispers, just as a dancer in very high heels does a fancy kick.

I am so lost in thinking about just how flexible he can be, that when I am lifted ever so slightly, a squeal comes out of me. My hand slaps over my mouth and heat rushes to my cheeks. Augustine arranges me over his lap so his two thighs are now between mine, keeping me spread so far open that if anyone looks into our box, they will know what's happening.

My breath stalls in my throat. I could be seen, we could be seen, and it makes my belly swoop with desire at the very thought. Augustine doesn't care if we are seen together; I am worth the risk to him. My clit throbs and my head swells at all the thoughts floating around it.

His hands go back to my hip, holding me steadily to his warm body. For as tall as he is, I am still much wider. My body practically swallows him up in the chair, but I can't find that I care. If he didn't want me this way, he would have placed me somewhere different.

I could be on my knees between his spread thighs, with his collar of sand decorating my neck and his clawed hand massaging my scalp while his cock stretches my throat. I could be worshipping my monster. The thought makes my pussy throb. I want to do that, to show Augustine how well I can serve him if he were to ask.

A hand slides across the expanse of my stomach until it just rests under one of my breasts.

"Mon abeille, you are not thinking of the show, are you?"

He kisses my throat, right on the epicentre of all the heat, and I turn to putty. Something inside me feels on fire and alive, and I squirm in Augustine's hold. With every beat of my heart, I swear it is saying more, more.

"Will you give me your honey?" His teeth, razor-sharp now, drag across the column of my throat to my ear. "In front of this audience, will you let me serve you, my queen?"

My skin erupts in goosebumps. I should say no, absolutely not when we are in public. I am tipsy, to say the least, and have already indulged so much tonight. This sort of dalliance will get us put on a list if we are caught.

Fuck it. I am going to indulge, be a gluttonous creature that I have always tried not to be.

"Own me," I say.

I have pleaded, and moaned, and whispered those words so many times in my dreams. But never have I said them with such command. Augustine hums against my skin, and his hand leaves my hip. I feel the creep grain by grain across my exposed shoulder until it delicately circles my neck like a fine gold chain would. I whimper and my eyes close, ready for the teasing and pleasure.

"Keep enjoying the show, mon abeille. It's very good." He sounds smug, like he has read me like one of his books. He knows how my mind swims and sweetens for him, how hard it is for me to focus on anything but the pleasure.

My eyes snap to the stage just as a single claw trails a path from my knee to my dress, pulling the material up to my hips. My beige shapewear shines a little under the light reflecting from the stage.

"I love your form, Joanna, how the universe has filled and stretched your skin to perfection. I don't want you to wear these for me or because you feel you must."

His finger moves to my inner thigh and the sharp talon snags on the seam.

"But if you, and only you, want to wear them. I will accept that." He continues. For some reason, that makes my heart flutter. A soft, gooeyness sticks in my throat. "It does just mean I will have to tease you through these, and you will not get to feel my fingers in your perfect cunt."

My heart stops, my thighs try to squeeze together. Below us, the orchestra crashes and pulses as the music begins to build again.

"Ruin them," I whisper, my hands searching for something to grab onto, for him.

Just as my fingers wrap around the wrist on my sternum,

sands envelop them, locking me to Augustine. Sands grip my ankles and keep them secure on the floor. The single claw between my thighs slices each centre stitch, one by one. Each snag a point of relief from the tight confines of my shapewear.

"The taste of your arousal is going to drive me mad, mon abeille. Do you have any idea what you do to me?" he asks, his speech slowing, punctuated with deep inhales. "How my control just vanished the moment I stepped onto that beach with you?"

I shake my head, and make a little noise of denial as I feel the cool air hit my damp, swollen flesh. My pussy clenches around nothing when even the subtle pressure from Augustine's finger disappears.

"It was like that first taste of cool water after wandering the desert for days. But I did not have an inkling that I was doing without. For eighteen months, I have had little drops and dribbles of your sweet nectar."

He cups all of me at once, the heel of his palm pressing into my mound and his sharp talons digging into the delicate flesh of my ass. A rumbling sound vibrates against my back and sends a delicious chill down my spine.

"This delicious honey is all mine now, Joanna. You make it only for me, from now on. It is my reward for serving you for the rest of eternity. Nourish me with your lust, your arousal, your darkest desires."

A single, blunt finger slips into my pussy and I nearly come off his lap. Augustine's grip on me tightens, the sands restraining me harder.

I am panting, biting my lips so hard it hurts even my teeth. As much as I want to shout with joyous relief, I can't. I can't interrupt the show. Trying desperately to focus as I was instructed to do. His finger strokes me slowly, with luxurious ease. An obscene, wet sound that I pray isn't as loud as it seems, makes the heat rise in my cheeks and more slick drip from my slit. I have never been so wet, my body so willing to give and relax.

He slides a second finger into me embarrassingly easy, my pussy clamping down on the digits the moment he is knuckles deep in me. For a moment, Augustine holds them there. His palm rubs circles into my clit, while the two talon-tipped fingers outside of me tap along to the song being sung.

As the music builds, the singer's voice grows stronger and louder to match the orchestra, so do his strokes. He pulls them out in time with music, making sure to drag the pads up with each stroke. It's a teasing amount of pressure to mix with the almost unbearable press of his palm. Just as I think I am going to cum, when the coil in my belly tightens and is ready to snap, he removes his fingers.

The song ends.

I am gasping for air, for more pleasure, for him. I am so close to finishing. The orgasm from the car that was ripped away from me is screaming inside me and weeping for release. My skin is on fire, boiling sugar surging through my veins with each pump of my heart.

On stage, the curtain closes and lights slowly rise. Intermission.

"No," I whimper.

"Would you like to get an ice cream?" Augustine asks coolly. The sands slither away from my overheated skin and a tear comes to my eyes.

He holds me tighter as he sits up slightly, encouraging me to stand. I turn to face him when I am again on my feet and can look down at him. There is a tickle at the back of my head and my mark aches with the second denial of the night. Slowly, he brings his two fingers to his lips and sucks my arousal off of them. My breath stutters and heat pools in my belly all over again.

The urge to stomp my foot like a child overwhelms me. Augustine stands before me, and my heeled foot collides with the carpet for this injustice. The plush carpet of the box silences the sound, but the huff that puffs out my cheeks shows my displeasure. He told me he wouldn't make me cum until he could complete the bond. He didn't say he would torture me.

I hate it.

I love it all the more.

He smirks down at me, placing my hand on his forearm and guiding me out of his box.

All the childish petulance leaves me when I'm passed the security of the curtain. My thighs rub ever so slightly together where my shapewear has been sliced. Slick arousal cools against them. I swear I can smell myself on Augustine's breath as he leans down to my ear.

"Stay close to me. My respect for the others is minimal, and I do not want them to get ideas."

He says 'others' with a level of haughty disdain that makes me scoff. It sounds like plain rudeness to me. There are other monsters here, blending in with the humans and enjoying an evening of fine food and theatre. He doesn't need to sound like a dick about the whole thing.

"If we're going to spend eternity together, you're going to have to be less *holier than thou* about shit," I say, trying to be a bit more relaxed with my word choice than I normally would be when we are something so fancy.

Just because he holds himself to a standard, doesn't mean we all meet it. Augustine holds himself like he is a god among men. He clearly doesn't believe that others, monster or human, are of a standard he appreciates. I certainly don't meet the standards he clearly has, but here I am at his side. It seems like we both have something to work on as we move through eternity together.

"I simply know what I am worth, mon abeille, and I know what you are worth as well, especially to me. Let the commoners worship you from afar and know they will never be able to attain a queen like mine."

This classist bullshit shouldn't make me blush, but it does. As we round the corner in an indulgent and plush art deco-designed bar, my cheeks burn brightly and my pussy is way too interested in being worshipped. I try to remind myself that as amazing as my dreams are now, real-world antics are a much different story. This world has rules, laws that we have to follow. My free hand brushes over the warm spot on my neck in a nervous tick I've developed.

As we approach the bar, I see the heads turn. Augustine walks with ease and grace while I stumble along next to him trying to make sure my skirt doesn't ride up and that I am keeping my gut sucked in. Not that there is much more I can do with my Span, even being unable to hide my food baby. A few people nod at Augustine, but most just avert their eyes once I catch them staring.

One person does approach us. He is about my height, broad and barrel-chested. His charcoal suit is finely fitted, and he appears to be in his late fifties. In the back of my head, I feel a hint of disgust, but I push it aside. My brain is too busy making me feel like a sausage stuffed in this dress with how the man's eyes keep darting from me back to Augustine.

"Mr. Ravenscroft." The man's voice is rumbling, if not a bit grating. "You haven't felt the need to grace us with your presence in a long while."

"I have been very busy, as of late, and before that, I saw little point in conversing with you." He responds, voice as dry as his sands.

"Augustine."

I can't keep the chastisement out of my tone, even as my lips perk up. It is rude, but it is also funny. To feel so aghast over his statement makes me want to laugh even more. Never would I ever have spoken like that to anyone, friend or strangers. I am polite and kind to a fault, which I suppose is how I got into the situation I have with my job. But it still pays my bills and puts food in my mouth.

The other man cracks a smile just as Augustine sighs heavily.

"Robert Vanderburg." He extends his hand, and I shake it just like my mimi always taught me, a firm grip and eye contact. "I haven't seen you before. Who is your family?"

It strikes me, then, just exactly how high society this evening is. Family? He means to ask if I am from a founding family or another one of those fancy east coast names. Ones that are placed on statues or holding seats of government.

My moms were both from different parts of the country. They moved here for college and always said the rest was history. Their parents didn't care so much for their "lifestyle," so I don't know them. I have no idea what kind of family I could present to him that wouldn't sound as poor as I am.

So I'm honest.

"Joanna Cole, my moms weren't from Gwenmore."

"Ah," I see the subtle way his face ticks at the knowledge I have two moms, though he quickly presses on. "New blood is always good if it means Mr. Ravenscroft is out again."

"Yes, well, we are going to make an order with the bar and return to our box." Augustine makes a move towards the bar, but Robert stops him.

"I'll join you. Give us a moment to chat about the upcoming election this fall."

"You know I will not discuss politics, Vanderburg."

Ah, so he is that kind of rich.

"I am looking forward to the election," I say, nervously filling the awkward silence that stretches as Augustine places an order for some kind of cocktail made with tea and affogato for me. "I met the mayor recently, he was lovely."

"Hawthorn is not so lovely, darling."

My fingers tighten around Augustine's forearm. The hairs at the back of my neck rise and I desperately want to rub away the goosebumps that rise up on my skin under the sleeves of my dress. It doesn't sound the same, but I am suddenly exposed and vulnerable. My stomach tightens like it knows it will be taking a hit.

"Leave, now, Vanderburg." Augustine's glare is ice cold. He angles his body in front of mine. "I will not in this life or the next ever support your bid for mayor. You are a vile bastard who would see our city coffers drained for your personal pleasures."

Robert's face turns violently red, his jowls shaking as he grits his teeth to avoid saying anything in return. Augustine stares him down until he walks away, joining back into a crowd of people.

"I'm sorry," I whisper. "I'm sorry I-"

"Mon abeille," Augustine's soft fingers grip my hand, gently kissing my knuckles before placing it against his chest. "Are you alright? It felt like you were about to have a fit."

"He called me darling." I swallow hard, trying to push the lump down in my throat. "It's silly, but I was just... back in that room."

"There is nothing trivial about trauma recovery or what you are feeling, Joanna. It was barely a week ago. You almost died."

Our drinks arrive, and Augustine passes me a martini glass with a small golden spoon nestled in a dainty scoop of ice cream swimming in rich, aromatic espresso. His whiskey glass is smoking, or steaming, but the ice in it is cut into a perfect sphere.

"What a vibe killer," I mutter, holding my glass at the steam to keep the ice cream cold. "Sorry."

"Would you like to return to our box or go home?" he asks.

There is no evidence that if I chose to leave, to be driven south of the river and away from all the people that Augustine is so used to being surrounded by, he would be upset. He would graciously take me away, kiss me goodnight, and call me when he got home to arrange another date. I have no doubt of that. Even if the bond is affecting him the way it is me, he will put it aside to make sure I feel comfortable, safe. He is a gentleman, first and foremost, and my boogeyman second.

I take a deep breath, letting the murmurings of the crowd and the cold drink in my hand recentre me. It takes a few moments, but he waits for me and I smile when I see the look of adoration in his eyes.

"I want to finish what we started."

JOANNA

A blush tinges my cheeks even though I already knew I was going to complete the bond tonight. I want Augustine, I did before the bond, and I hope I will forever.

15

Joanna

In true gentlemanly fashion, Augustine keeps his hands to himself for the rest of the show. He insisted I remain seated on his lap, but his touch was nothing but soothing. The second half of the show is a bit confusing because I couldn't tell you a single thing that happened in the first half. It is beautiful and heart-breaking all the same, and I want to beg Augustine to take me again.

Marcus is waiting for us at the front of the building, exactly where he dropped us off. The privacy screen is already up when I'm ushered inside, and I'm not sure if it's for his benefit or ours. Augustine buckles me in, and the fluttering feels set off in my chest. Unlike the first journey, there is no teasing. I lay my head on Augustine's shoulder and hold his hand in my lap. His thumb traces little patterns around my palm.

Joyous and peaceful calm washes over me. There is nothing about this moment that feels wrong or strained. The silence is blissful. The smell of tea and musky cologne sets something in my soul at ease. There is a rightness to being at Augustine's side that I have never felt about anyone or anything before.

JOANNA

Maybe it is the bond, or trauma, or extreme loneliness, but I think I might be in love. A few months of a crush and two weeks of knowing him, I feel like my life has turned upside down for the better. Every little defence I had about keeping people away so I didn't get attached just blew up with Augustine. I want nothing more than to be attached to him.

That is the most terrifying thing about all of this.

The knowledge that what howls in the night and lurks under beds is new and scary, but it makes no real difference to me. I have Augustine. He believes he is one of the scariest things in the world, but in my world? He is a dream come true and only keeps proving it to me.

The drive is short. His townhouse is on a side street in the historic district. Marcus pulls up to the curb and idles for us. My lover opens the door and holds out a hand for me. He tells Marcus to return the car to the garage and that's the end of it. A quick business goodbye and then it is just us standing on the pavement in front of the stairs to his front door.

"Joanna," he hums my name like it's a beautiful melody, a hand cupping my cheek as he looks into my eyes.

"So, are you going to invite me in for a nightcap?" I tease.

"I would much prefer breakfast."

His smile is downright sinful. Augustine grips the back of my neck and drags me in for a kiss so luxurious it rivals the entire evening. He pulls my body flush to his. A hand settles on my hip, holding me in place for his pleasure. Sands tickle the base of my neck as it drips across my throat, smoothing over my bare, heated skin.

He breaks the kiss with a smile reminiscent of that first night, when I was trying to sneak out of the library after that dream. It spreads a bit too far across his cheeks, and the lights from street lamps make his face look sharper. My hand cups his cheek, thumb tracing over the seam that hides his sharp teeth.

"Put me to bed then," I whisper.

Most of Augustine's house is exactly like the library. It is stacked upon shelves upon piles of books ranging from titles I have seen made into movies to books older than this country. He pulls me up the stairs in a rush, narrowly avoiding the art decorating every wall. Another time, when I am not recovering from a life-saving ritual or near delirious with lust, I will enjoy the decor, but now all my focus is on him.

With need and arousal pulsing to life between us, the heat of the bond washes over my skin like hot sand. It's comforting and turns me softer, if that is even possible. The need to bury myself in this feeling is almost overwhelming. To hide away from all the real parts of life and just live in this dream. The fact that Augustine would give that to me is a threat to my sanity.

As I think this, Augustine slams me into the wall. Frames and sculptures clatter around me, but my focus is on him, his body shifting, sands dripping from his hands and around his neck. His eyes are dark as night, the iris glowing a hypnotising golden shade that I once thought was just a trick of the light.

He grips both sides of my face with his blackened, clawed hands. "Mon abeille, I cannot control myself around you. Every grain of sand in my body is begging to touch you, swallow down your emotions as they happen."

My breath catches as I feel them. His sands crawl up my legs with a slow gluttony, luxuriating in all my curves, sneaking underneath my shapewear.

"Allow me, Joanna, grant me the greatest pleasure of my

existence to have you. Tell me, now."

"Augustine," I gasp softly. My heart threatens to explode out of my chest and tears threaten to spill down my face. "I want you, *all* of you."

He lets go of me only long enough to open the door next to us. Then his mouth is on mine. His teeth scrape across my bottom lip and I moan. The sharpness of it sends a shiver down my spine that pools right between my legs.

"The sweetest ambrosia," he mumbles against my lips, guiding us into his bedroom.

Augustine shucks off his jacket as I pull him into a deeper kiss, teasing my tongue across his lips and teeth until he lets me in. I stroke my tongue against his. A groan vibrates from his chest, and the soft, warm sands that I thought surround me turn molten.

"No games," he says. "When I own you here, worship you, I do not want there to be any doubt. Every word is true. As soft and vicious as they may be, they are real. You will never doubt me."

He rips his waistcoat and shirt off, exposing his smooth, golden skin to me for the first time. It's the first time I have seen so much of Augustine. Dreams are so wildly different. They cast a haze over everything I do and see. Now he is all I see. In the glow of the city lights seeping through the bedroom window, I see the boogeyman. His chest heaves and thin black veins pulse through his skin. They decorate him like a work of art. My fingers reach out and trace one from his solid abdomen up to where his heart should be. The hardened spines at his back shine and shudder as if they are his heart, alive and pulsing with life.

"I don't know what I did to deserve you," I whisper.

"Nothing," he drags my hand to his face. "You do not have to do anything to have my love, mon abeille. It will be yours for eternity."

He kisses my wrists and leads a trail of them up my arm over my sleeve until his lips hover over the bonding mark he leaves me in my dreams. Every night for the past week, I have felt his teeth sink into my flesh with his honey ichor dripping from my lips like a drug. It's a pleasure and pain that are fighting to see who will drown the other first as I'm dragged to oblivion. I will never be the same if even a drop of those feelings hits me tonight.

I will never be the same either way, but Augustine makes me feel alive when I have felt nothing for so long. A selfish part of me wants to keep feeling that way. A little voice in my head shouting that I don't deserve happiness or love. A deeper voice echoes in my thoughts, *'sticking your nose where it doesn't belong, darlin'*. I inhale sharply, trying to blink the voice from my head.

"Are you sure?" I ask, belly quaking as fear twists up in my gut. "Augustine, you don't have-"

"I know what you are going to say, and I hate interrupting you, *mon abeille*, but..." His lips brush against my ear as he pushes me back towards his bed. "I have lived thousands of years and have never been more certain. I know what you are worth, my Joanna. Let me show you."

The spines at his back catch in the light again and I am desperate to touch them, to feel them soften to my touch or resist me. Augustine pulls the zipper of my dress down slowly, avoiding the snag where my waist flairs. It falls to the floor easily, my sleeves coming next, and then he steps back. Slips of sand remain on my shoulders, and my neck. They trickle down my sternum until they reach my nipples. They pebble at the sensation, my chest heaving as I wait for more.

He is appraising me like he does his books, taking in every part of my naked torso with keen, hungry eyes to evaluate my worth. I swallow as heat pools in my lower tummy. This should make me feel sick. If anyone in the past had looked at me this close, it would have, but when my body reacts like this for him it feels so right. Augustine inhales sharply as a smug grin stretches his mouth again. He strokes clawed fingers over his moustache and then his dark gaze flicks to my shapewear.

"Hold still," he whispers, his features softening for a moment.

Once again, the sands sneaking up my legs suddenly shoot up my hips before arching down like a scythe. They cut through my already ruined Span and now I am completely and utterly bare to the monster, my boogeyman. Augustine's gaze turns hard again, assessing and critical. I want him to own me as he does in my dreams. To be his pet and the object of his desires, so my only worry is pleasing him.

I am holding my breath, fighting my urges to cover up and suck it in. I don't need to, I have never needed to, but old habits are hard to kick. Everything about Augustine's reaction to seeing me like this tells me he wants me. He crosses his arms, taking a moment to make a turning motion with his fingers. I do as he says, twisting on the balls of my feet and squeezing my hand into fists.

He groans, a noise so pleasing and hungry that my pussy clenches. I am the one he loses control over. There is a rush of power at the thought that makes my head buzz and my stomach flutter. It's a glorious sweetness I want to savour.

"Shall I tell you my evaluation while I devour you?" he asks, already moving. "Or should I make you sit on my cock while I list off every fine detail about you?"

"Fuck me," I murmur, my lips parting just enough for the words to drip from my tongue.

Augustine's smirk deepens as he takes another deep breath. He pulls my hands to his mouth and kisses the knuckles again. A fresh blush rises to my cheeks, and I bite my lip. It feels ridiculous to be blushing like a schoolgirl at that action, but I can't stop myself. This is the most surreal experience of my life. A merging of my darkest desires that I keep locked away and the romance I have deprived myself of in real life because I was convinced it wasn't real.

"Lie back on the bed for me, mon abeille, so I may tell you exactly what you are worth."

I do as he says, propping myself up on my elbows to watch him. Augustine removes the last of his clothes, and I think I could be receiving this information much more effectively on my knees while worshipping him and showing him what a good pet I can be. His cock is hard and I can already see the quills surrounding it. Golden precum leaks from the slit and I want to lick clean.

He kneels at the bottom of the bed and grabs my ankle. In one swift motion, he has me completely flat, my arms raised above my head with my foot pressed to his chest. His sands circle my wrists and hold me down. The kiss he places on my ankle is tender.

"Let's start here, I would pay the Fates a thousand souls in annual tithes for encouraging you to enter my domain and for our paths to cross that night. How I would kiss the ground you walked on if you so desired it, my queen."

He kisses a path up to my thighs, sharp teeth scraping over

the top and making me shudder with excitement. *Devour me, take me, own me, bond me.*

"Your thighs," he groans, placing open-mouth kisses over the stretch marks he can see. "How the Valkyries would honour me if they were to crush me. How the Norse kings would exalt what a glorious death it would be to die between them."

Augustine kisses the crease of my hip and stomach, moving up across the wide plain to my other hip. My breath stutters in my chest as I watch him move. His spines sway and his golden hair glows in the low light. When his eyes catch my gaze again, they shine like the sun, bright and warm.

"How the great sculptors of old would have worshipped you, mon abeille, how Michelangelo would have carved the most jaw-dropping statues of you. How he would have transformed marble to match your softness. How the Medicis would have commissioned hundreds of works in your honour."

His moustache tickles my stomach as he moves higher. His tongue teases one nipple while his sands pinch the other. Augustine's hands dig into my hips as he raises me to him. My pussy rubs against his cock, quills teasing my folds and clit. Slick drips out of me at the friction and I moan.

"*Mon abeille*, the price of you does not exist. Kings would go to war, goddesses would steal you away, and still, they would have to worship your beauty and pray to one day be worth a moment of your time."

Augustine rises to my face, kissing my nose and cheek before resting his forehead against mine. He takes a shuddering breath and I think this is it. He is finally going to fuck me. My body is wound tight with anticipation and my hips rock against his, reminding him how much I want it. How I need him to fuck me.

"Yet all those things are nothing compared to your soul, mon abeille. How it tastes, how it holds your emotions with such divinity. Your body, for all its perfection, is a vessel for what is most true. The goodness inside you that tastes of the heavens and joy that makes me want to do horrible, devilish things to you until you can think of nothing but me."

Tears prick in my eyes. This honesty is more than I expected. Augustine isn't lying to me and I am not sure I can face this truth. My lips tremble against his as I reach to kiss him.

"When I look at you, I feel alive," I tell him, a brutal honesty in my voice I almost don't recognise. "I have wanted you for months, thinking it was just a dream, and in two weeks you have made almost everything come true. Please, Augustine-"

I can't get the rest of the words out. My body is burning with need and words are getting lost in the thickness of my emotions. He can spend the rest of eternity unravelling them, plucking them from my mouth, but right now, I need more than words.

Augustine lifts my hips off the bed and thrusts into me in one full stroke. His cock is thick and the quills that run the length of it spark every nerve in my pussy. The air punches from my lungs, and I'm drowning in the overwhelming sensation of fullness. He presses his whole body into me. Sand drips from him, caressing my body where his hands aren't.

He slips from English to French nonsensically, his lips bumping against mine in a taunting motion. Claws dig into my ass as he moves, grinding my clit against his pelvis rather than pulling out of me, like he can't bear the thought of leaving me for even a second. It feels so good, but I know he can do more. I know exactly what he can do with the right encouragement.

"Augustine," I moan, trying my hardest to be sultry, to be in charge for even a moment. "Is this how you worship your queen?"

I have never been anything, but mostly I have never been a dominant, an alpha, A-Type, or a go-getter person. But when Augustine whimpers, with his eyes squeezed shut and his hips still grinding into mine, I feel some part of me open up. Like I am the queen he sees me as.

"Prove to me." I swallow a moan as his sands twist around my nipples. "Prove you know what I am worth, that you are worthy of me."

"*Mon abeille*," he draws out the words, lifting his upper body up enough to look into my eyes. I stare into his golden eyes, let the heat in his gaze turn me syrupy sweet and melt deeper into his bed. "I will spend eternity showing you I am worthy of you."

He shifts his weight and moves my thighs higher up, pulling one up to his shoulder in a stretch that burns my muscles, but drives his cock deliciously deeper inside me. Augustine looks from my eyes to where our bodies are joined. He pulls his cock out slowly, and for the first time ever, I hear him curse.

"Fuck."

The word is harsh and hushed, filled with lust so real I can almost taste it. It loosens the muscles in my neck and heat spreads through my body. It's a victorious compliment to hear him say such a word. My head swims with the sound of it on his tongue and in my ear.

The spines around his cock pulse against my fold like they are desperate to be back inside me. My pussy clenches around just the tip of his cock and he growls. My boogeyman loses his gentlemanliness; the little bit of control he kept to tease me slips from him. Augustine slams his hips forward so hard I move up the bed. His skin slaps against my wet flesh with a deep, primal rhythm. My body sings as each of the spines press against my pussy.

Every thought in my head is begging for more, to cum, to feel full of him, to taste him. My jaw turns slack, I can't close it. Every sound of our flesh meeting is followed by a moan from my mouth. Each sound gets higher and higher the closer I get.

Augustine's hand wraps around my nape. His fingers dig into my hair and my eyes struggle to stay open. I am drowning in the sounds of our bodies, my thoughts slow and wispy like spun sugar, but I want to see him. I want him to know that I am thinking of only him as he is now. Tears return to my eyes and I feel them slip down my cheek into my hairline.

"Own me," I whimper. "Yours, Augustine!"

I cry out when he pulls out of me, a hollow feeling taking over me. He wraps my thighs around his waist completely and sands cover my ankles. My head spins when Augustine lifts me up, the blood rushing through me straight to my throbbing clit.

"I want to feel you everywhere when you cum on my cock, *mon abeille*." He licks the tears from my cheek and it only makes me cry more. His tongue scrapes across my skin like it truly wants to devour me.

Sand encompasses us. I am surrounded by black sand and a soft glow from Augustine. His eyes flash as he looks at me again. He bites his tongue, and I see his ichor. The golden honey fluid drips from his sharp teeth and his bottom lip.

I open my mouth in want, waiting for him to give me this. Every fibre of my being wants to lean in, to lick and kiss and suck at his tongue until I can't think straight.

A devilish smirk I have only seen in my dreams marks his cheek. His cock teases my slit, the tip rubbing against my clit as the quills taunt my soaked flesh. Augustine grips my neck harder, pulls me closer to his lips, and spits into my mouth. The ichor barely hits my tongue, but my body is already shaking. He has never done this before. I am vibrating out of my skin and floating out of myself. Honey, warm and golden and laced with Augustine's perfection, slides down my throat.

"You are mine," he growls with finality, like he is making a promise before God to be pious for the rest of his days. Augustine's other hand cups my ass and lifts just enough to position me above his cock. "Who do I belong to, Joanna?"

"Please," I pant, anticipation tensing my muscles, my pussy dripping obscenely down his cock. I can't see it, my tummy is in the way, but I know it's covered in me.

"Who, *mon abeille*?" Sands tweak my nipples and wrap tighter around my body, holding me in their embrace. "Who?"

"Me," I whimper. "Me, mine!"

My voice is punched out of me as I am dropped onto his cock. Augustine's spines expand inside of me as he rocks me against him, lifting me just enough to rub against that delicious spot inside me. He thrusts his tongue into my mouth and I suck on instinct. The sweetness on it makes my head reel. He groans against my lips with each stroke.

My lower belly tightens, the coil of my arousal tightening to the point of snapping. Tears cool against my heated cheeks, sweat forming in my hairline, but I never want it to stop. I have never felt anything like this. Augustine's hand in my hair moves me, bending me to his will as he deepens the kiss.

I am surrounded, ready to surrender to everything and anything he has to give me. My hands grip at Augustine and his sands. The grains trail across my body and raise me up higher. My thoughts are of nothing but my boogeyman, of this monster who has turned my life upside down and inside out. He has brought me back to life.

He breaks the kiss, only to kiss me again. His sharp teeth cut across my lips and I taste the copper tang of my blood as it mixes with his honey ichor. We moan in unison, lost in the taste of each other.

"*Mon abeille*, I am going to cum. I need you with me." Already I'm nodding, words lost. I am so close. My head is empty except for him.

He kisses my jaw, down my neck, right to the bond mark. The pace of his thrusts picks up, the deep strokes coming in quick succession as he chases our release. I am impossibly full of him, and he hasn't even cum yet. Tendrils of his sand slink around my ass, around our joined body, until they are coated in my leaking arousal. They wrap around my clit and I scream. Whatever Augustine is doing, it feels like he is sucking on my clit. Everything goes white and gold as I cum. My pussy clenches and gushes around Augustine.

"Yes," he praises me, teeth grazing my skin. "Give me everything, Joanna. Let go of everything and be mine."

His teeth sink into my soft flesh with ease. I scream as pain and pleasure rip through my body. Everything is alight and frozen. Time stops as all the pressure drips from the base of my skull and I feel the bond. Every emotion rushing through Augustine is rushing through me. My syrupy thoughts mix with the drunken high of my mate. *My mate.* The word rings out in my head as my eyes close. I can't help it. I am awash in ecstasy and dreams.

I wake up to the scent of lavender and hands smoothing over my back. I don't think I could be more relaxed. A soft and slow smile spreads across my lips as the aches in my body come to the surface. My neck hurts, of course, but my pussy throbs with a delicious pain that is only a reminder of how well fucked I was.

"*Mon abeille*," Augustine chuckles, and I feel his mirth. It's an odd sensation, like tickling behind my ear.

"My mate," I mumble into the plush pillow, the words coating my tongue like caramel. "Did I pass out?"

"Yes, I briefly panicked. But it was only for a few moments." His teeth nip at my ass and I squeal. "Stay still so I can finish."

Augustine leans across the bed, and then I feel slightly warmed lotion spread across my thigh all the way down to my ankle. It smells more like honey than lavender now and my body warms to that.

"What do we do now?" I ask when he finishes.

"Whatever you would like, Joanna." He wraps me up in his arms, my face pressed into his neck. "My preference is a cuddle and tea as a post-love-making ritual, though that will require leaving the bed."

I giggle. The boogeyman likes a cuddle. I run my fingers over his sides, feeling the shorter spines give way to my gentle stroking. Augustine groans and rolls his hips against the thigh I have pressed between his legs. I kiss his neck and pull back enough to stop teasing him without letting him go. I don't want to ever stop touching him. His warmth radiates through my hand like the sun touching my skin after a cold, rainy day.

I look into his eyes and feel it again, the tickle behind my ear, and I know what it is. What that feeling is, but I can't bring myself to say it just yet. *Soon*, I promise myself.

"I like this too," I whisper. "But what about tomorrow or Monday? I have work, a life that I can't abandon."

"I am not asking you to do that, *mon abeille*. We have eternity to do as we please. It is your choice how you spend it." He kisses my forehead, breathing me in so gently. "Just let me be a part of it."

16

Augustine

14 days

I will not say that I am restless. It is ridiculous to feel this jittery after Joanna's extended stay with me. Friday morning breakfast had blurred into a weekend of carnal desires the likes of which I have not known since the days of old. Deg'Doriel nearly threw me out of his office when he saw the look on my face when I dropped by on Sunday for our lunch. Even in her dreams, she called to me, begged for me as if I was not the reason she was asleep.

Joanna is insatiable.

If anything, I should be collapsed onto a settee in complete and utter bliss. I have found Elysium, Valhalla, Heaven on this godforsaken wasteland, and its true name is Joanna. I never want to be away from her. *Mon abeille's* softness must always surround me. I cannot handle this separation. Even the thought that I am missing her smiles, her laughter, and her worry has me ready to throw my notebook across the room. I make a note in the margins of my book to give Joanna the number for the moving company I prefer. Her scent is already fading from my sheets, from my house, and I cannot have that.

It has been two days, one night without her, and I feel like I am losing my control even worse than before. She expressed concerns that we were doing this all backwards. Bound to me for all eternity, yet she still wishes to go about courting. *I don't want to feel like I'm missing out on any part of our love story.* At the time, it seemed odd to explain that she was not prepared to leave her old life. Her words vibrate through my sands now as I think about what else she misses.

I am supposed to be listening to this vampire sob about killing a human like it matters. They are clearly too young, maybe in their early twenties, but fate has been cruel to them. Deg'Doriel reminds them that mistakes happen, but that if they do not harden the fuck up he will make sure there are not any others. Our group is about second chances, after all, not third, fourth, or fifth ones. Controlling oneself and one's baser instincts is all a part of the struggle, along with planning and scheduling when you intend to take a human or fifteen completely.

My baser instincts are screeching at me to go to my mate, to abandon the plan and just run to her. I take a deep breath to steady my emotions. There is hunger wafting off nearly everyone here except Arlo. I suppose his snack two weeks ago has kept him sated for now. Another note in the margins for this meeting. That ghoul needs to find permanent residency in the city. Deg'Doriel has expressed an acceptance of his usefulness, so it is best to get him settled somewhere low-risk where we can manage him.

Orthia still has not returned since she stormed out. There have not been any reports of out-of-season storms or ships washing up to shore, but who is to say she has not begun causing problems down the coast again. The ship she uses as a facade is still moored at the northmost point of the Docklands, the crowds of tourists growing more prominent the closer to summer we get. As much as Her Love has been feeding on the sacrifices we allow her every year, they will also be feeding off her energy in some way. I am sure of it.

And she, they, were livid when they were last seen here.

"If you're around the docks or beaches and you see anything more unusual than normal, give me or Ramón a shout." Deg'Doriel yawns and flashes his sharp canines at the room. "Otherwise, get the fuck out of here."

Like last week, only a few trusted members of our group stay behind. The lessers are as quick to leave as they are to arrive. None of them are keen to linger and hear chats about diplomacy or risk being removed from the group. Everyone except Arlo, who stares at his shoes, turns to me once the room is clear.

"Like a bunch of nattering old bitches," Deg'Doriel grumbles, his tail flicking in agitation. "Nicolette spilled all the saucy details."

"Auggie," Ramón starts, and my disdainful look at him does nothing to dissuade him from continuing. "You fucking player."

"Maybe I should start going to the library to meet humans," Nora smirks at me.

"Do not." I frown. That is the last thing I need. These idiots in my domain, in my library, making an absolute mockery of everything it stands for just to meet a human. Absolutely not. "Besides, my mate will be here shortly to meet you all officially."

This was not my idea. While enjoying a selection of fruits and cheeses on Saturday afternoon, Joanna asked about my friends. I was quick to point out that the creatures here are my colleagues, aside from Deg'Doriel and Kragnash, but she insisted on calling them friends. And of course, since they are my friends she must meet them.

Joanna wants to be involved in all aspects of my life. She wants to continue courting despite the bond. My mate tugs at a romantic side of myself I have not truly explored before. I had played the flirt for a time, when Jamie was in my life. He enjoyed the coy gestures and the hazy opium dens as much as any well-off merchant's son would during that time. He was easy prey, and I underestimated my hunger and the drugs flowing through him. But like the smog that covered London then, my thoughts were clouded by his ruby-red aura.

But even the short stint in his dreams and the much shorter time we were half bonded, I never felt the drag to him the way I do my Joanna. She wants me, wholly as I am, and that touches something inside me I have never considered before because I do not have one. My heart.

There is an interesting reaction among the group. Arlo's pallid cheeks flush red, Ramón and Nora both grip each other's hands like schoolgirls, and Deg'Doriel looks downright furious.

"Augustine, you know-"

My phone vibrates in my pocket, and I pick it out of my jacket. Only one person would be calling at this hour. Joanna's name flashes on the screen and I answer.

"*Mon abeille*, are you here?"

"I'm so sorry. I'm sorry. I can't. Work has been more full-on than I expected it to be. I'm sorry. Lance told me yesterday things had been fine while I was away, but every time I look up from my computer, there are like ten new problems." She rambles on, something about hiring processes and budgets not adding up, but it does not really matter.

Joanna is still at work at ten o'clock on a Tuesday night. That is abhorrent. The sands under my skin ripples and my eyes change in a blink. Protective, instinctual urges rise up in me. Providing for her, taking care of her, making sure she is safe is all I can think of doing, but how do I keep her safe from herself?

I stand up from my chair and leave the parish centre basement recreation room to stand in the darkened hallway. My clawed fingers scratch against my phone.

"Joanna," I say her name with authority, ownership. "Are you alone?"

"Yes, well, I mean the building has a security guard, Pauly," I hear the pause in her speech like she is waiting for me to speak over her, but when I do not, she keeps explaining Pauly to me. "But he did his rounds like an hour ago so he won't be back until like three."

"And you have this Pauly's work rounds memorised because?"

"Oh- well, I have been known to burn the midnight oil, and he likes the same trash soap operas I do," she confesses this grave sin of wage theft to me in such a weak tone, I should not be surprised with what follows next. "I'm sorry."

"Have you eaten today? Drunk water, anything more than that sugary coffee you like?" I ask.

"I had some snacks at lunch, and I reheated the leftovers

from Sunday."

My pause in the conversation is heavy, and I am sure if she could see the look I am making she would blush and apologise again.

"And I will take a five-minute break to fill up my water glass and rest my eyes."

I want to argue that she should leave work tonight, and for good, but Joanna is an adult. When I said we had eternity to figure it out, I meant it. If she wants to work, I will encourage her to do just that. But I cannot watch her dig herself into a hole like this.

"I will be finished here in about fifteen minutes, and then it is just a short walk to your office. Shall I pick you up and take you home?"

There is a heavy sigh on her end of the receiver. I do not need to be a monster to feel insecurity and sadness in just that. I should not have asked. I should have told her.

"I- oh, um, I-" she sighs again. "I can't. I'm going to finalise some forms here, and there is a massive pile of laundry I have to start."

"Do you want to have breakfast with me?" I ask. "I would like to see my mate even if she insists on working herself to death."

"Yes, absolutely," she responds instantly. There is a rustling, followed by a low tone in my phone. "I have sent you a place I have always wanted to try. It's near the library. Seven sound good?"

"Perfect, mon abeille, thank you."

We hang up after a short goodbye, and I am left riddled with concern but not sure how to address this. I thought finding Joanna out so late on that very first night was a fluke. Then again, the night of her attack, I assumed it was the bond that had drawn her out so late. Now I am not so sure. These are not the habits of someone who knows how to take care of themself. Her work is not an obsession, or at least a healthy one. It seems to have rewired the parts of Joanna that know how to relax and breathe and enjoy life. What would have become of my mate if we had never crossed paths?

I wonder what else can change about my human in just a few days.

21 days

I am not restless this week.

After a weekend of pulling Joanna away from her laptop and her incessantly ringing phone, I have come to realise that her work is not something she does to sustain her lifestyle. It is something she does compulsively as if she will cease to exist if she took even a moment's break. While it makes every moment I am able to have her full attention all the more precious, every moment her focus is elsewhere, I am scheming up new reasons and ways to make her realise her work is not her life. That she now, in fact, has many lives she will get to live, so she should start a new one as soon as feasibly possible.

At our Wednesday morning breakfast, I tasted her guilt mixing with my tea.

"I'm sorry," she yawns. "I feel like I am trying to live two different lives at once here."

"You know I want you at home Joanna, but I also understand modern courting involves dates and time. Are you sleeping alright?"

"No." Her admission makes the guilt in her taste rise. *"I've been getting these annoying spam calls at all hours of the night. I'm*

getting nothing done at work because all I hear in my head is my phone ringing."

She has endeavoured since then to come see me before she rushes to her flat to prepare for the next workday. Every night, she has worked late, well past midnight, only to stumble into the library shortly after she sends me a text message. I do not know what she could possibly be doing at her office that keeps her this late. She does not dodge the question. Her answer has just always been the same. Emails, presentations, budgets, suppliers.

So I make a cup of chamomile tea with a dribble of honey and sit her in my office. She has taken to asking me about different time periods in my life, which eases my worries. I find myself sharing details about my life I have not with anyone before. I remember little anecdotes that I had otherwise forgotten. The joy that pours from her as she laughs at my reactions or encourages my stories warms me. Little forgotten parts of myself come to the surface of my existence, and Joanna is the cause of that.

"If you wrote a book, I would be the first to buy it." She's told me this multiple times, but I scoff.

"I am not a writer of books but a keeper of them." I remind her.

"Were you at The Library of Alexandria?" She asks after taking a sip of her tea. The bags under her eyes are heavy tonight, dark circles adding a hollow look to soft features.

"If I had been there, mon abeille, it most certainly would not have been lost." I say, a smirk on my face as my own cup of tea hovers just over my lips. "I do have a few scrolls from their collection in my private archives, though."

"Show me."

The Parish Centre for Our Lady of Mercy was, in essence, rebuilt in 1976 after a troll brawl collapsed a portion of the tunnel that connected to the building. Deg'Doriel had been furious at the time, as before that, it was one of the oldest buildings in the city. We had to blame the whole incident on a sinkhole and rally the parishioners for funds to rebuild it. Now, as I look at the outdated layout and overly scrubbed linoleum floors, I think perhaps it is time for another brawl to destroy the building.

I do not wish for the group to cease meeting, just that I am tired of staring at these same wood-panelled walls outside Deg'Doriel's office, where pictures of all his past skin suits are lined up in chronological order like a shrine to every man of god he has ever corrupted. There are a few hours yet until we have to move down into the basement recreation room for our group meeting, but I want to have a discussion with our leader, and with my friend.

The shrill voice of Margie Lawson rises as she cackles at something Deg'Doriel has said. Whatever it is I am sure it is not a joke and that he was serious. The door handle clicks suddenly and the laughter echoes around the building and threatens my ears' safety. I blink as if that will stop the terrible sound, but soon enough Margie is speaking to me.

"Mr. Ravenscroft, I hope you haven't been waiting long! Fr. Doug and I had to go over last month's minutes before the meeting next week," she says.

Had to go over or had to quiz him on them to make sure he was listening?

"I have no other engagements, so it was no bother to me, Ms. Lawson. Have a good evening." I end the conversation before she can go into a discussion about her birds.

Usually, I would not mind a discussion about animals. Still, Margie enjoys teaching her parrots different bible verses and I have never heard of a more annoying and boring hobby in my long life.

Deg stands in the door, looking almost ashen, while he waits for her to be all the way down the hall. Gods forbid the woman turn around and try to continue a conversation with us.

"I swear, there are times I believe that woman is an agent of Lucifer sent to spy on me," he sighs, closing the door behind me as I enter. Quickly, he sheds his human skin and unclips his white collar. His tail does not flick or move before he collapses in his chair. "Did you know that we have been experiencing a three percent year-on-year growth in Sunday collections despite the national average being a seven percent loss?"

"And I am sure it is all thanks to your rousing sermons," I smirk, but my friend throws his head back and sighs again. "Would you like to discuss what ails you? You are practically grey."

"No," he grunts. "I have been overextending my abilities recently. Do I actually look grey?"

His head swivels back up quickly, and his clawed hands are digging around for his phone. For a moment, I watch Deg'Doriel assess his hellish appearance on his phone and then he puts it away. The demon has always been a bit vain. Like myself, he likes to put forward a very specific appearance. When we first met at a dinner hosted by the great Cosimo de Medici, he was wearing the suit of a cardinal from Florence, and I was simply a patron of the arts. Deg'Doriel still dawns that suit when he needs to appear a bit more regal.

"No," I concede. "Now, shall we talk about why you lied two weeks ago? Or shall I, your oldest friend, remain in the dark?"

His eyes flick to mine and his horns catch in the fluorescent lights in the ceiling, shining a bit more brilliantly. His scent is subtle and he is actively trying to keep it that way. Whatever secrets he is keeping are either of a divine nature or something so earth-shattering it would rip the fabric of space and time if he told me. While he may claim that the others gossip and natter, he thrives off secrets. Where I search for the truth and knowledge in others, Deg'Doriel lives for lies and admissions of guilt. The only thing steadier in his life than our weekly Tuesday meetings, are his Wednesday confession hearings. I have seen more than my fair share of souls lost to that ornate box of his.

The fact that he is keeping one himself simply makes me hunger all the more. I raise an eyebrow at him as I wait for his response.

"It is a secret that I can't share and may never share if the time does not come. Just keep your little human to yourself."

"Slightly difficult, seeing as Nicolette has been introduced to her and the siren was enamoured, to say the least."

"You are the reason I drink," he groans, dragging his mitt-sized hands over his face. "Speaking of, do you want anything, or did you bring it with you?"

"I abhor thermoses, Deg, you know this. Fresh is the best way to consume any tea, even the cheap nonsense your parishioners drink."

"Fine, fine, fine." He pulls a flask from his jacket and takes a long swig. "So now that you don't fucking reek of sex, tell me about your human."

We have made no plans for Joanna to meet the trusted few of the group this week, and I have already decided that when she answers my call after this meeting, I will be going to her office and dragging her home by her hair if I must. She surely cannot keep this pace up.

She has spent more time with this human called Lance in the past week than she has with me. He seems to act like her shadow. A scuttling, annoying shadow that asks too many questions. It seems he has an ever-increasing interest in making sure the job at the armoury goes well, and that he will do whatever he possibly can to make my Joanna's life easier. Liaising with contractors, filing work orders, and all sorts of other things that I had no desire to understand until a month ago. If he wanted to make her life easier, he could simply cease to exist for all I cared.

Even now, when I am taking notes, the very thought of him agitates my sands beneath my skin.

It is most certainly not because she speaks so highly of him, fawning over his work and dedication like he is some paragon of capitalistic society.

"I don't know what I would do without him, I swear," Joanna says to me, her breath huffing out of her as she rushes to some other site visit. She has not returned to the one across from the library and I am grateful for that small victory. "I'd completely forgotten I'd booked this meeting two weeks ago. Normally everything is on my calendar, but I must have scrolled over it. But I guess ten minutes late is better than totally missing it."

She should not have to rush anywhere. From what I understand, Joanna's job is administrative, a people manager. Why on earth would she be attending a meeting about a budget review with clients? Even more, two weeks ago, she was not even at work. Meaning the cretin booked the meeting for her without her knowledge.

"Ravenscroft," Nora says, snapping her fingers around my head. "You alright?"

I stare at her over my lenses. "Why would I be anything but apathetic to be sitting in this basement every week?"

"You've driven a hole straight through your paper." She points down at my lap.

Of course, she is correct. The nib of my pen has soaked the paper in ink and ripped a hole through several pages in my book. I grit my teeth and swallow that annoyance. It is my own fault, feeling anything regarding stupid human matters. My fingers trace over my moustache, and I close the book.

"I will be taking my leave. Goodnight."

A few of them call out goodbyes, but my thoughts are miles away already. Once outside the church's low stone walls, I ring Joanna.

"What's up?" She answers almost instantly, an urgency in her voice that does not make sense to me. It's nine o'clock at night. What could she possibly be doing that is so pressing?

"*Mon abeille*, are you still at work?"

"No, no, no, I'm at mine. I'm sorry I can't see you tonight. Just- just getting this presentation finalised, and I am on a roll... I think, I hope. Who's to really say, this could all be crap. Lance promised me he had time first thing tomorrow morning to look at it, so I want it finished tonight. I know he's super busy. I already feel bad taking up his time with my stupid questions. I should be able to do this on my own by now."

I take a deep breath. She is talking a mile a minute into the receiver and I blank everything that comes after *his* name.

"Very well, Joanna." I keep my tone even, but it drops easily as worry rises in me. "Please make sure you get some sleep this evening. Will you meet me for breakfast in the morning?"

"Our spot?" I can hear the smile in her voice. We have gone to the small French inspired cafe twice, but already it warms me to hear her call it our spot.

Small victories, I remind myself, as if I am not some ancient creature of darkness who could crush my human into submission with a flick of my wrist. Joanna is my mate, and I am doing everything I can to respect her wishes. I am honouring my queen.

"I look forward to seeing you. Sweet dreams, *mon abeille*."

"Night, Augustine."

She hangs up and I start walking down the main road towards the library. The wind picks up and is surprisingly warm. New season blossoms have come into full bloom and are already starting to fall. Their delicate petals decorate Gwenmore's historic district's dark pavements and well-maintained cobbled street. The light pollution hides the stars, but the moon shines overhead, full and heavy. A beautiful night for a stroll. If only I had Joanna to share it with.

Up until a few weeks ago, I would have laughed right in any creature's face for even speaking such drivel as 'you will have feelings towards a human', but I most certainly have deep feelings for my human. Cliches from all eras of time come to mind when I think of the depths of feelings I have for her. The ironclad grip I have maintained over my control for years vanishes when I see or think of her.

But to have such strong feelings towards any other human should be absolutely absurd. And to have found my arch nemesis in a disgusting human of all beings.

Lance.

17

Augustine

28 days

The sun is high in the sky when I exit the library at lunchtime. Humans are bustling about and monsters that easily weave into society move about them. There is a short lull in tourist activity, not much by any means, but with the two city universities closed for the summer and local schools still in session, it means that there is less of a crush through the pavements as I make my way down the main road and through the side streets of Gwenmore. This is the opposite direction from my home. Where I live closer to the Harbour Crest neighbourhood, Joanna's office is nearer the west side in a slightly more business and affordable part of the historic district.

In fact, the office that Joanna works in is not even a part of one of the buildings originally planned for the city. The office has the street facade of an old factory, but that is it. The bricks are suspended by wires attached to the building's modern frame. They have not even left the old windows in, all that remains is their hollow sills. Inside, there is a reception and wide lobby with a cafe tucked into the corner. Large, albeit fake, plants are dotted around the space as if to make up for the lack of natural light in the building.

The woman behind the wide counter types away furiously as I approach her, and I wait a moment for her to notice me before I finally clear my throat. Her aura swirls around her in soft, green wisps as she looks at me. Between the ventilation and the number of people around the lobby, it is challenging to pick out which emotions in the air are specifically hers, but I catch a scent of intrigue as she looks me up and down.

"Appointment?"

"No, Ravenscroft for Ms. Cole at Concord Construction."

She holds up a finger to me as she dials up the office I wish to attend. My gaze drifts around the lobby again as I try to decide what sandwich I am going to recommend Joanna try at the Italian deli I plan to take her to. *Mon abeille* is not a fussy eater, but I want to make sure her first taste of what I consider a Gwenmore institution is superb.

"She's in a meeting, but they said to send you up."

I nod and sign where directed before heading towards the elevators. I haven't been inside this building before, but a stylized directory tells me the office I want is on the fourth floor. A large group of businesspeople exits before I can enter the first available carriage and I catch a whiff of a werewolf I have not met. Before I can make eye contact, though, he is gone and I am slowly travelling upward towards my mate.

A giddiness takes over me as the digital display ticks up. I have never been one to smile, or show outward emotion beyond disdain, but the simple thought of Joanna has my flattened teeth showing in the mirrored walls surrounding me. I inspect my appearance quickly; my tie is straight, my hair is styled correctly, no very obvious wrinkles in my jacket or trousers. It is odd for me to preen in this day and age. Another time that was all there was to do. It was all the people cared about, really, preening and subjugating, that is.

Yet another side of me that Joanna has dusted off and brought to the surface. While my appearance has always been well-kept, now I make an effort to appeal to someone other than the monster I see in the mirror.

The lift arrives and opens up into a wide hallway filled with doors. As the directory stated, the office I am looking for is clearly labelled room 416. The sight I walk in upon however, is not that of a bustling office.

It is dead silent.

The stale, recycled air reeks of anxiety and stress, as if everyone in the room is waiting for a guilty verdict from some unseen judge. Nobody looks away from the door in the corner or their screen. If they are not hyper-focused, they are waiting on something or someone. A woman nearest me rushes up before I can even take a step further into the room. Her navy aura is barely visible and her own guilt wafts up to my nose like the smell of fungus on a hot day.

"You must be Augustine," she whispers. "I'm Andrea. I've worked with Joanna for two years now."

"It is nice to meet you," I say with sincerity, warmth blossoming in my chest at the thought of Joanna telling her co-workers about me. "I'm taking her for lunch."

"Good, somebody needs to-"

Before she can finish that thought, a deep shout reverberates through the closed door that everyone is now staring at.

Andrea's fungal guilt smell intensifies, and when she looks at me again, it is tinged with fear.

"Patrick's not normally like this, I don't think."

It takes every grain of sand in my being to hold myself back. He is yelling. At my mate. There is a human who has the audacity to believe that he can speak to my queen with anything but reverence. How dare he? The words I am going to have with this man. The people I am going to speak to so that his life becomes so immeasurably difficult that he will have to go back to whatever Spanish hellhole he crawled out of. As my rage threatens to expose the more beastly side of myself, a tremor of fear arises in the back of my mind.

He is scaring my queen.

The door bursts open and Joanna rushes out, head bowed and running straight towards a different, secluded part of the office. She does not look up from her shoes, but she flinches when the door slams shut again. The visceral scent of her defeat and misery trails behind her until it is abruptly cut off. I take a step forward, absolutely ready to drag my mate from this laminate-floored prison.

This is supposed to be a nice surprise for my overworked mate. I never meant to come upon a scene such as this. I am out of my depths of human emotions, but I need to comfort her, to offer Joanna protection against every dark part of her world, and prove to her again that she is safe with me. The paltry woman standing next to me places a hand on my arm and stops me from following. She rushes after Joanna, and I'm right behind her before another hand grabs me and a familiar voice stops me again.

The rude man from the library quickly removes his hold on me when I glare at him. A deep red surrounds him and the smell of his contempt is so subtle, it blends effortlessly in the concerning emotions of this office. While his appearance meant nothing to me weeks ago, now I look at the middle-aged man in the harsh fluorescents of the office space anew. He is average looking, gangly in a way that most people would find attractive. His hair is overly styled, but the grey around his temples and streaking his hair shows his age.

"Let the girls deal with it," he says. "Lance Jameson."

Lance. His name sticks in my head like a fly to paper, buzzing until it will drive me to madness. This is the man my Joanna is so desperate for approval from, who she showers in praise for the smallest things as if he is not your average male. I pull the sneer from my face. Civility and poise are the best course of action here. His name is already on a short list to be taken care of in some fashion.

"Yes, you viewed the Milson Bushwhipper book a few weeks ago."

"Yeah, yeah, real interesting book. Didn't know there was so much folklore around the city, but you know what they say," he smiles, and I raise an eyebrow at him.

"No, I do not know what they say," I state.

A new tension rises in the air and I breathe in the scent of his nervousness. I hold back my own smirk. This is a good feeling for him. He should be nervous around me. He clears his throat as his eyes size me up, lingering on my lapel pin. It is the one I wore the night Joanna and I completed the bond—a nod to her honey sweetness and her as my queen, *mon abeille*.

"That's a nice pin. Do you mind me asking where you got it?"

"It is a family heirloom," I lie. While the pin is certainly old enough to be considered an heirloom, I have been its sole owner since sometime during the Napoleonic wars, worn as more a fashion statement rather than a show of military prowess. It holds meaning now because I have my own honeybee, but previously it was just one of a collection. If Joanna had told me she hated it, I would have tossed it aside and found something she loved.

"You here to see Patrick?" he asks, changing the subject abruptly when I do not further explain my adornment to him.

"Not this time," I sneer, thinking I should see this man at some point soon to have a discussion of sorts. "I am here for Ms. Cole."

"Oh, you have a meeting with Jo? Is she working on a project with the Library? I am sure Patrick would be more than happy to discuss-"

"No." I cut him off quickly. "This is not a business call but a social one. I have come to take my partner for lunch."

"Partner?"

On the rare occasion that waking humans lose a grip on their emotions, their auras pulse as their feelings and consciousness try to balance out. Lance's red aura pulses a spark of vibrance before the air scents with his surprise, a spicy savouriness that reminds me of creole food I sampled during a short stint in New Orleans at the turn of the twentieth century. I let my smirk spread ever so slightly across my lips, the barest hint of my lips turning up.

Maybe I should be perturbed that my Joanna has not told him that she has a mate, a partner for all eternity, the way she has Andrea, but instead I am pleased she does not share personal details about her life with this man. She may view him in a way that I find vexing beyond comprehension, but he is nothing more than a work colleague. He is not worthy of her conversation outside the context of work. Lance is not worthy of her conversation, period.

"Yes, and I do believe that is the correct term for our relationship." The words do not taste correct on my tongue, but I know humans would not understand the depths of my bond with Joanna.

Another tense moment passes before Andrea and Joanna walk in our direction. Audible only to me and my mate, the guilty woman reassures her that budgeting errors happen. That whatever is going on, the company will survive it. My sands pull tight in my chest at the sight of the tear stains on her cheek, the way her eyes and nose are redder than they should be. Her golden aura is dull compared to how it was last night when she arrived at the library. I never want to see her lose the vibrance of her soul, the brilliance shining in her that only I can see being sucked from her by this place, these people.

"Augustine," Joanna tries to smile, but her lips tremble. Her attempts to cover the bitter taste of her have me pulling a clean handkerchief from my inner jacket pocket to hand to her. She does not need to hide her emotions from me; I will handle all of them and be what she needs me to be as she experiences them. Today, I will be her shoulder to cry on.

"Mon abeille, are you ready for our lunch?" I phrase it as if I am not surprising her at work. I want to make it clear to both Lance and Andrea, who linger at a desk near the entrance, that my mate has a new priority, and it is not this job. I feel her hesitation in the back of my mind and see her deliberating to decide if she can leave for her allotted lunch break.

"Yeah," she sniffles, her fingers gripping the piece of fabric I just handed her. "Let me grab my purse."

"Am I being unreasonable? Is this what humans are actually like now?" I stare at the group after explaining the scene I walked in on this afternoon.

"She was cryin'?" Arlo fidgets with his shirt sleeve and looks just over my shoulder at me. An improvement I should make a note of.

"Practically inconsolable," I groan, slouching into my chair. Slouching! Me. Truly that shows the state I am after spending most of the afternoon reassuring my mate that she did not deserve that sort of treatment. "I thought it would be a nice surprise, except when I was buzzed into her office, some Andrea woman rushed me."

"Rushed you?" Deg'Doriel sounds more bored than I have ever heard him when it comes to another suffering.

"Rushed me," I repeat. "The whole place reeked of stress and burnt coffee. Truly hellish, you would have loved it, Deg. I imagine more than one person there would have traded their soul for a moment of peace. All that was missing was the screams of the damned. God, the lighting and decor made my skin crawl. There was plastic everywhere and cheap laminate flooring-"

"Augustine, focus. This is about your human, not your delicate sensibilities." Nora snorts and throws a huge, muscular arm around me. "Tell Auntie Nora her name again? Abby?"

"My mate," I lift her appendage off of my person with my sands, "was crying because her boss returned from Spain yesterday and has been causing havoc. Something about incorrect accounts."

"Ya need me to rough him up?" Ramón asks. "I can break some kneecaps or chomp his fingers?"

"No, no, when I get my hands on that scoundrel, he will

feel terror like he has never known, before I suck his soul clear from his body." I take my glasses off and rub my eyes. That decision came only after Patrick made Joanna's guilt skyrocket after she called in to take the rest of the afternoon off sick. "Lance, however, you may eat."

"Lance? What kinda fucking name is that?" Deg'Doriel sneers. "Does he have a brother called Spear?"

"He is her co-worker. She practically worships the ground he walks on."

"So you're jealous?"

"I most certainly am not. That human is gangly, and he is far too nosey. You cannot trust a man who willingly searches out the works of Milson Bushwhipper, that idiotic druid, really should have known when to leave better off alone."

"Is she alright now?" Arlo asks, turning the subject away from that horrid druid. I am going to remove that book from the collection of viewable antiques.

"Yes," I lie. "She is at home now. I was able to convince her to at least take some time for her mental health after that whole debacle."

Honestly, I do not know if Joanna is alright. All I could tell of her emotions before leaving was a deep sense of guilt. I could not drag much else out of her, spending the afternoon with her head on my lap as I read aloud some nonsensical poetry about transcendentalism. She swirled her fingers around the sand that slipped through gaps in my shirt, but that was it. She did not wish to speak of the finer details.

It sickens me to think that she is not well. That she is putting herself through this horrendous job simply because that is what humans do. I know my telling her to quit would not solve anything. It would just cause her more stress. I have seen her desire for success. She craves the feeling of accomplishment that has been bred into humans since the industrial revolution. Like worker bees, they have made work their whole lives.

But *mon abeille* is not a worker or a drone or anything so plebeian. My Joanna is a queen, a goddess among mortals. They should be stabbing their own eyes out for fear that even looking at her beauty would bring shame upon them. I have told her I will provide whatever she needs, whether physical, emotional, or financial. I just do not know how to make her see that she does not need to be causing herself harm in this way.

18

Augustine

28 days

I decide not to work at the library this evening. After wrapping up the meeting, I find myself practically sprinting to get home. My mate needs me. We are too far apart for me to feel her through our bond, but even as I left this evening, her anxiety was creeping in again. I move through the dimly lit street with ease until I get to the library.

It is hard to believe this building is considered historic. I remember drawing up the plans for it in London with Deg'Doriel. It was the only way he was ever going to get me on that laughable ship of his to come to the new world, to settle in the new world for good. He had some sort of master plan and he sought me out personally to be a serious contender to add weight to the investment.

I stare at the golden placard and recall the sense of peace it gave me in those early decades. There is still peace here now, but it is dull. I need excitement and life. I suppose that is why the fates brought me Joanna. My life has been a whirlwind since she arrived.

Behind me, there is a loud clatter, louder in the dark, near-empty street than it would have been during the day. I look over my shoulder at the scaffolding-covered armoury. No light is coming from the building, nor does it appear the security alarms have been tripped. There is the sound of boots hitting the ground in the alley between the buildings, it echoes off the stone walls like they want to be caught.

It really should not concern me for a moment what anyone, human or monster, is doing back there, but I know this is Joanna's big project. Her proof to Patrick that she is capable and competent. If my check-in on the exterior of the site means she has one less thing to stress about, then I shall do it for my mate.

I cross the street quickly, blending into the shadows created by the scaffolding and hoarding. Three men huddle next to the labourer's side entrance that I have seen trucks back into during the day. I am close enough to smell their apprehension in the air and my sands begin to thrum under my skin. Being surrounded by Joanna's emotions normally invigorates me, satiates the hungry beast inside of me. Still, after this afternoon, all I feel is a greater ache to alleviate her feeling, to feed and make others feel the way she does. I want to be a nightmare once again if only to make my mate feel anything else.

"He wants it to say this?" There is doubt in this man's emotions, giving him a starchy taste I don't care for. "Kinda weird, right?"

"Look, I don't fuckin' know. All I know is that a cheeky extra two grand bonus is gonna look nice in my wallet." This one tastes a bit desperate.

"Hurry this up, before we get caught." The fear wafting off this man tastes savoury on my tongue and I decide a late-night snack might just be what I need to calm down before seeing my human. What better way to solve a problem for Joanna than to simply remove the root cause?

There is a rattling of cannisters, quickly followed by paint fumes. I watch for a moment; graffiti has never been my interest, but I will not stop art in action. I move closer to the hoarding, my sands slipping from my limps and my form slowly shifting until I am taller, my arm too long, my mouth too wide, my eyes too dark. My sands grate against my body in anticipation of such a bountiful meal.

"She seemed nice enough the one time we met. A bit flat looking, but she's not a bitch." The doubtful one arches his arm in a wide sideways arc.

"Yeah, but we don't know what Cole's like. Man's forking over six big ones to send this message." The desperate one shakes his canister and covers his mouth. He will not have a mouth for long. I plan to tear his lips and tongue from his body before I end him. How dare he even speak Joanna's surname?

"Yeah, because the two guys before disappeared." So the fearful man has an ounce of sense about him. That is right, little human. Be afraid, believe the rumours of a disappearance, for you will be joining them soon.

"Those two fucks got fired, c'mon I wanna get home. I'm fucking exhausted."

Sands rip through my jacket, silenced over the canister rattling and the noxious paint spray. My spines crackle at my back, flexing and reaching for the fear I taste in the air. I move away from the shadows and finally understand what's being created on the hoarding around the office.

"Bitches get stitches," I read aloud, my jaw cracking around the words and echoing in the service alley. "How eloquent."

Fear spikes, a rush of it as their heart rates increase and they whip around to look at me. I cannot help but grin. My spines rattle and flex across my back as I move further into the light. The fear morphs into terror, such delicious terror. It covers the smell of paint and construction with its meaty, savoury delight.

"Who the fuck are you?" The desperate one demands, a canister raised like it can be used as a weapon.

Out of the corner of my eye, I see the fearful one edging away.

"Oh, no, wretch, you are not going to want to miss this." My sands lash out, wrapping around his torso and coiling around his neck. "Now explain to me what you are doing."

"Look, man, we just needed the cash." The doubtful man drops his canister, and they all jump.

The leader of the trio sprays me with paint, but it is too late for him. His fear, along with one already in my clutches, has enticed my sands too much. They lash out like vipers, keen to sink their fangs into the prey before them. I watch as they both writhe and jerk under the intrusion. My sands pierce into their ears and noses until their eyes are covered in black. Their screams are silenced as their brains scramble. Blood soaks into my sand, and I can feel their souls being absorbed into the mix. My sands drain and soak up their essence with ease until their bodies go limp.

In a dream, I can control this better. It's painless. My sands can sink into my prey while they sleep. I enter their dreams to bring their worst nightmares to the front of their subconscious mind. Dreams are short bursts, REM as it has come to be known. It adds a balance to how much I can feed, usually. I feel the shift in their neurons as the brain tries to move on to the next memory to categorise. I move on when they are ready to move on.

When they are awake, though, the fear is right there on the surface, begging to be consumed.

The doubtful one is all that remains. His stench has morphed into one of terror, reaching into delirium and urine. He trembles against the paint-stained hoarding.

"I'm sorry, I'm sorry, it was just supposed to be easy cash. A-a-a sign-on bonus, he called it." He keeps apologising as I creep closer. Depositing his useless accomplices on the ground next to him. He shrieks as my sands slither across his body. "I'm sorry, please, man. I don't even know the bitch."

My clawed fist pierces his chest before I can stop myself. I cannot even bring myself to be angry. The slippery grip on my control vanishes once he utters that vile word. I drag in a ragged breath as I watch shiny fluids coat his front and his mouth slackens as he chokes on his own blood. It is not enough. It. Is. Not. Enough.

My spines sink back into my body only to be pushed into every crevice of this filth's corpse. He bursts like an overripe grape. Viscera drenches me and the surrounding area. My sands flow back into my being, shucking off the useless waste before retreating into my human form. I take a deep breath and remove my lenses. My clothes are ruined, but I tuck the frames into my breast pocket, anyway. I do not need them for poor eyesight; they simply mask the way my eyes shift upon occasion.

I shake my hands free of as much muck as possible and gingerly pluck my phone from my inner jacket pocket.

"Mr. Ravenscroft?" Arlo's voice is quiet, and I can just hear Ramón behind him.

"I'm having dinner by the armoury. Join me?" I take a deep breath again, more winded than I expected to be. "Bring the sewer rat with you."

"Yes, sir. We'll be right there."

My hair has fallen loose from the weight of some hunk of flesh. This is typical. I swipe it away and stare at the graffiti. *Bitches get stitches.* Someone is targeting Joanna. That assault four weeks ago was not being in the wrong place at the wrong time or interrupting a robbery. Someone is out to get my queen, and I will find out who.

It takes nearly two hours for the three of us to clean up. Arlo easily disposes of the bodies, and Ramón knows how to remove the blood from the surrounding area. Neither of them commented on the graffiti that I attempted to cover up. The paint refused to stick after the solvents were applied to clear up the mess. We departed quickly after that, them through the tunnels and me creeping along the shadows until I was able to make it home. It was late enough that the neighbourhood was asleep.

I suspected Joanna would be asleep, but as I ascend the stairs to our bedroom, light seeps from under the bathroom door. I can barely feel her through the bond. My mate is closing in on herself, believing whatever that idiotic, soon-to-be-dead man has said to her. The blood that coats my clothing has gone stiff, and I am in desperate need of a shower, but I am frozen with indecision. It's not whether or not Joanna would find my hygiene distressing, but whether or not I should intrude on this moment. We spent the afternoon and early evening together. Does she need more time to herself?

"Augustine?" Her voice carries through the door, and I open it without a second thought, eager to answer the call of my queen.

My sands tremble at the sight of her, the scent of the bath swallowing up her own. I stand in the doorway, limbs stiff and sands slipping from my being. They crawl to the visage of my mate. I had once thought to remove the claw-footed tub because I find using the shower simpler. I do not wish to laze about in steaming water, but seeing Joanna's back as she rests against the edge, her hair pulled up to expose her neck and the bond mark on her skin, makes me wish we had done this every night.

The tiling in this room is a dark Victorian green metro-style, the fixtures golden brass, and the tub is stark white meant to draw the eye away from the walk-in shower. But my eyes only see her and the golden aura that flows from her body in lush curving arches. The scent of lavender and honey overwhelms the senses as much as my decor choice, and I cannot stop staring at my queen. I feel transported to a time when I barely knew how to control this form. My sands riot inside me until I am a husk, watching them slither over the edge of the tub to caress warm skin. I crave every moment of peace and joy I can give her. I want to feast upon her only to fill her again so viciously with every hope and desire she has ever had that we are lost to a never-ending cycle of each other.

Finally, she turns to me. The sad expression that dulls her face twists into shock and concern and I remember that I am covered in blood that is obviously not my own.

"I had to help Kragnash with something." The lie slips from my lips just like my sands and something inside of me sinks. "What are you doing awake, *mon abeille?*"

"Couldn't sleep without you," she hums, her eyes tracing me as I strip down. I will dispose of the clothes in the morning. "Feeling you near me reminds me I'm not alone."

The shower is too loud in the space of the bathroom, and the water is cold when I step under the spray, but I rush to scrub every trace of those foul things off of me. Cleansed so I may be deserving of the hunger I see growing in Joanna's aura as she watches me. My body is created the way I desire it, the fibres connecting as I see fit, but knowing she craves all my forms makes my thoughts turn to darker delights. My hands glide through the soap on my skin, the steam from the shower creeping up the glass panes to obscure her view of me. She makes a petulant little noise when I stroke my cock.

"Do you wish for a show, *mon abeille?*"

"If the Lady of The Ravens feels so inclined." Amusement drips from her tone like lemonade, sweetened by the hunger in her gaze. She is forgetting her worries about work, she is letting go and letting herself be who she wishes to be. The slight inkling of concern is still there, pressing into the back of my skull, but I will do anything to erase it.

"They do," I grin, but I do not stop stroking my cock. My talons toy with the quills on the underside. This was never the type of show I participated in all my years of dancing, but performing for her makes my sands come alight, buzzing under my skin with ecstasy.

"Augustine," Joanna whimpers my name, and her hunger seeps into me, filling and fuelling me.

I stare at her through the fog, a blurry blush of a being lined in gold and stained with tendrils of black wrapped around her throat and the peaks of her breasts. She leans out of the tub to get a closer look, to let my sands play with her, to reach for me. I do not wish to look away from her, but my eyes flick to the drain beneath me. The water has run clear and a cursory brush of my other hand through my hair remains clean. I turn off the shower and the only sounds now are *mon abeille's* heavy pants mixing with mine.

"Another time, I shall give a proper show," I say, moving towards her, a talon-tipped finger moving her chin up before she can lick at my cock. "This performance is just for you, *mon abeille*."

She swallows and the sands around her throat move delicately with the motion. I pull her back with them until she rests against the high back of the bath. Her hands move to touch me and I allow it this time. Her fist grips my cock and my quills thicken with my arousal, trying to fill out the space of her hand. I step into the bath slowly, letting out my beast; lips stretching, spines rattling, and body growing. Water sloshes out of the way, but it does not matter.

My sands move Joanna's hands away from me and pin them to the edges of the tub, her chest exposed to the humid air while my knees bracket her legs and keep them clamped shut. I feel her thigh tense under the water, the subtle squirm I have seen her do before.

"Let me perform for you, and this time you may decide if I am deserving of your favour, my queen."

Joanna is bright red in her blush which is not from the heat of the water. The strong scent of the bath oils is overwhelmed by her honeyed arousal and I let my sands go a little farther, trail up to her supple mouth to tease her lips. That is all I will allow for now, even as her tongue lathes against trembling sands.

Even without music, my body rolls to a rhythm as old as time. Rushes of memories in palaces, in temples, in hidden drawing rooms come to me as I display my dripping wet body for my mate, letting my arousal bleed from my every pore. I play with myself, teasing pleasure from my nipples until they ache as I watch my mate get lost in my being.

"Tell me your thoughts, *mon abeille*. Do you think you could command me?" I taunt her as my hard cock bobs just above the surface of the water. My quills leak precum and each time the head dips beneath the surface, it sends a shiver through my body.

"You are so beautiful," she moans. Her eyes follow the trail of black veins under my skin to my cock. "I feel so hot."

"Should we stop?" I stop moving, letting my hands fall to her warm skin. She does not feel feverish, but I do not wish to risk her feeling unwell from being in the bath too long.

"No," she pleads. "No, god, if you stop I might explode. I want the show I was promised."

A proud and victorious smile spreads across my lips to reveal my sharp teeth. "As you wish, my queen."

Joanna's breath stutters as I lean over her body and thrust into the water between us. I am careful not to touch her, but my talons dig into the lip of the bath. My breath teases her lips, and her mouth falls open in want. Her thighs tense between my knees as she squirms.

"Is there something you desire?" I moan into her ear.

"You."

"You already have me, *mon abeille*." My teeth graze the shell of her ear this time and my cock aches with each roll of my hips into the water. More of it splashes over the edge and more of Joanna is exposed to the air. My gaze drops to her heaving chest, the dusty colour of her nipples teasing me by simply existing. I recall her words to me the night we finished the bond. "Is this how a queen demands worship?"

"*Oh.*"

She shudders at my retreat, but there is a new fire in her. A burning sweetness that coats my tongue and has my jaw slackening. My hands traverse the muscles and dips of my body as I watch her subtle transformation, the wildness almost changing her hazel eyes.

"Tease your nipples again," she commands, her firm voice washing over me with a sense of delirium I have not felt before. Joanna moans when I do as she says, but I let my sands mimic me. They reach for her nipples and pinch the sensitive flesh in a way that I know makes her weak. She does not close her eyes. They stay locked with mine as if seeing who will win in this duel of pleasure. Her hips try to roll up between my legs, but my hold remains firm around her. I wonder if my wondrous mate could cum just like this?

"Do I please you?" I moan, the hard beads of my nipples ache and my quills are pulsating around my cock.

"Yes, fuck, Augustine." Her mouth stays open, her tongue wetting her lips again and sweat beads along her hairline. "Touch your cock, please."

I do not stop what I am doing.

"It is not a command if you are begging me, mon abeille."

"You-" Her voice drops into a whimper as the sands around her nipples tighten and pluck at her delicate flesh. "Fuck, stroke your cock. Now."

My hand grips my cock and pulls my quills forward in firm

tugs. Sweet, heated pleasure drips down my spine from the base of my skull as Joanna's emotions merge with my own desires. My sands do not stop teasing her breasts, but she is too focused on my cock to complain. She tries to lean forward again, but my sands keep her collared.

I am going to cum, my body folding over hers to grip the edge of the bath once again. Water splashes, and my balls draw in closer to my body the harder I stare at her mouth. Her flat teeth dig into her bottom lip and I taste that zesty tang of her amusement.

"*Mon abeille*," I moan, gripping hard at the base of my cock, trying to gather an ounce of control. "Have I earned your favour?"

"Not yet," she breathes, her eyes meeting mine quickly. "Do you promise to make me cum?"

There is a hitch in her breath when she asks me. The sands around her nipples flick the sore, beaded flesh to the same furious rhythm I stroke my cock to.

"I will do more, so much more." My thoughts scramble as my slick hand moves over my flesh. "Every day, any time you will allow it, I am going to devour your perfect cunt until all you feel is bliss."

"English, Augustine," she commands.

Had I spoken in another language? It does not matter. I repeat the words, adding further promises until I am on the verge of breaking the bathtub under my grip.

"In my mouth," she murmurs softly, in that reverent, wanting tone of hers that has all of me shuddering and ready to destroy the world for her pleasure. My sands slip just enough, and my body climbs higher up until my cock nearly touches her lips. I know if I were to, I would cum before I garner her permission. "Well done. You have my favour."

My body seizes, and every part of me threatens to collapse as I watch the ropes of my cum coat Joanna's tongue and mouth, how her throat contracts as she swallows, her pupils still dilated and her hunger scenting the air. Before she can say another word, I gather her in my arms and move us to the bedroom.

"Augustine," her squeal of delight is like a chorus of angels.

"I do believe I have a promise to keep, *mon abeille*."

19

Joanna

I keep getting flashes of Augustine covered in so much blood it should have been impossible. He reassured me again before I fell asleep it was nothing, something Kragnash needed his hand with after group. Still not something you just spring on a person when she is trying to take a depression bath if you ask me.

Even now, stirring creamer into my coffee, I can only picture the blood swirling down his shower drain. There was just so much of it. What the fuck was Kragnash doing? Was the mayor doing some kinda shady shit that should make me question my vote? Should I be concerned for Augustine's safety? No, Kragnash is his friend. I know that, and I want to believe that even if they aren't human, these new people are still good. I don't want these new people to be just as bad as those already in my life.

But what the shit was with the blood?

"Joanna!" Patrick barks my name from across the room, and I jump. "My office."

I swallow the sudden lump in my throat, putting my

teaspoon in the sink. I pick up my notebook and pen and the stack of files I might need from the desk maintenance dragged up yesterday morning. The moment Patrick returned from his midlife crisis adventure, he took over my office and now I sit in the far corner behind a pillar near the kitchenette. There's no window, and the light isn't great in this corner, but at least I'm not constantly being bothered, right? Nobody stops by my desk now to ask for a favour or if I want to go for a coffee downstairs. No more distractions, so I can be more streamlined.

Around the office, everyone has their heads down. There is some chatter, and the sales team is never truly quiet, but there is definitely a sense of dread going around this place. Everyone seems to believe they are moments away from getting fired. Except for Lance, he is cool as a cucumber; we all really need that right now. Andrea makes eye contact with me as I pass her desk, and there is nothing but sympathy written on her face. She told me yesterday she is looking for a new job and I wished her luck because what else am I supposed to do?

I don't know what I will do after this project in the next month for the rest of eternity, but I am not going to discourage others from chasing greener pastures. It's been two weeks of hell and upheaval that doesn't appear to have an end.

Inside my old office, Patrick has cleared away all my minimal personal touches. The plant that I was trying to keep alive by the window is no longer there and a box of files is sitting on the floor next to the desk that I am sure I will need to organise. He sits at what used to be my overflowing desk, and now there is only a laptop and an empty coffee mug.

"Shut the door," he says before I can even get a word in.

"Hey Patrick, what can I do for you?" I ask, doing as he requested.

I don't sit down immediately, half expecting him to tell me he wants another coffee, but when he looks at the rickety chair I have never trusted, I settle on the edge of it. The hard wooden arms dig into my wide hips and snag on my dress.

For a moment, he doesn't take his eyes off me. Patrick stares right through me, or too deeply at me, like he is judging my faded wrap dress and my soul at the same time.

"Where is the bid proposal for the Riverside Development?" he asks.

"I can check with the team, but I am not sure anything has been finalised yet. We only had the meeting Friday," I explain, and from what I understand, the meeting didn't go great.

"What do you mean it's not done?"

"Well, their board was trying to cut certain corners to get a cheaper price. We are reviewing with our suppliers-"

"I want this contract. What part of that didn't you understand, darling?" He leans forward in his chair. An icy shiver creeps across my skin, and my stomach muscles cramp. I don't know when he decided that's what he was going to call every woman in the office, but I wish to god he wouldn't. "It's not that fucking hard. I could have a deal done and dusted by now."

"I understand, Patrick-" I force the words out as my chest tightens.

"Jo, you've been here long enough," he starts and rocks churn in my belly. Oh god, he's gonna fire me. "You should know how to speak to clients."

"But I wasn't-"

"First the fuck up at the armoury site, then your ridiculous sick leave, the fucked accounts." He rubs a hand over his tanned cheeks and leans back in his chair. "It just feels like you aren't really here any more."

"No, I am," I insist, like this job hasn't aged me, or I haven't lost sleep because of it. Like it hasn't taken over my whole damn life. "I swear, Patrick."

"I know it isn't easy. Lance has-"

My phone blares the annoying ringtone I have set for Gary's site. Patrick makes a gesture for me to answer it.

"Hey, Gary, now really isn't a good time," I start, eyes darting between my paper-covered lap and my boss.

"It's worse here, Joanna. You're gonna need to come down to the site. I- uh, found something, and you need to see it."

My blood runs cold. Something in the air changes, or maybe it's just me heading further towards a panic attack, but I suddenly weigh two hundred extra pounds. I look over at Patrick again, and he just looks bored. I swallow, trying to get rid of the scratchy feeling in my throat.

"Alright, I will be there as quick as I can. Do you need me to call anyone or bring anything?"

"No, uh… just get here, and you can decide what you wanna do."

Gary hangs up without saying goodbye. He has never sounded so unsure of himself before. Gary is always sure and confident in his work despite how terse he can be, and crotchety. He can be trusted to get the job done right and without incident. The fact that this job keeps having issues is like a dark omen. This is my job, my contract. I have worked so hard on this project, and everything just keeps falling apart.

"I have to go to a site, Patrick. I'm sorry. Gary's having an issue." I start to stand up, my notebook closed. There really isn't a point in continuing this conversation. Patrick has said what he expects, and I will have to talk to the lead on the project about the bid and take over to make sure it gets done today. I'll text Augustine when I get done at the site and tell him I'll be spending the night at my flat instead of the library.

"Gary can fucking wait. That son of a bitch always has something to complain about."

"Patrick-"

"Joanna, I'm putting you on notice."

My ass falls back into the chair and pain radiates up my sides. For a moment, I don't think I understand him. What the fuck does he mean by 'putting me on notice'?

"You've always been an asset to the company, darling. You're like family." Alarm bells go off in my head, my ears are ringing, and the rocks that were rolling around in my stomach take a nosedive right into my shoes. "But you've been all over the place since you've been back. You've got a month to get your shit together, or we are going to have to have a harder discussion."

"Patrick, no, you can't. I-"

"Joanna," he sighs like this is causing him some great pain, but the life I've known is falling apart right before me. He's ripped the rug right out from under my feet.

"I can't lose this job. I have given you everything. I-"

"Ship up, or ship out." He turns to his laptop while I just sit there, stunned. "Doesn't Gary need you?"

I don't start crying until I am in the elevator. My cardigan is draped over my arm and my heavy purse pulls the neckline of my dress so far to the side my ugly, old bra strap shows. Hidden just under that was the scar left from the bite Augustine gave me. The flesh is completely healed now, much faster than what is probably normal, but it is raised and slightly discoloured.

The mirrored walls won't let me hide away from my emotions. I see every part of me, every exhausted and overworked roll and pudge that my wrap dress can't hide. The way my shoulders are hunched from staring at my computer for too long. The blotchy red quality of my skin only worsens as tears and snot drip from my face. My hands shake as I move to whip them away. I dig through my purse for a tissue and find a fabric handkerchief with Augustine's monogram embroidered on it. The gesture only brings more tears to my eyes.

As the doors of the elevator open on the ground floor, I run right into Lance.

"Woah there," he says, grabbing a hold of my shoulders. His voice quickly turns from jovial to something else. "Is everything okay? Did Patrick say something?"

Maybe it's because my ears are still ringing from the bombshell that was just dropped on me, but Lance doesn't sound worried. I can't figure out why, but I sense or feel or just plain know that he isn't one bit concerned. I don't make a habit of talking about my relationship or meetings with Patrick with anyone, and I won't start now.

"Just been a long day already," I sidestep my friend and make a move towards the front door.

"Ah, okay. He asked me about how you've been recently. I wanted to make sure he didn't do anything crazy."

That makes me pause. Why would Patrick ask Lance about me? Technically, my role doesn't really have anything to do with compliance. Lance submits applications and forms to me for a final review. Sometimes we have meetings together when talking to new hires so he can ask some technical questions, but that is about it. We are work friends mostly because I used to sit next to him when I first started at Concord Construction.

"Why?" I sniffle a little pathetically and wipe my nose. "Did you tell him something?"

"I just told him that since you were mugged, I've been a bit concerned about you."

The hairs on my arms rise as goosebumps run the length of them. I bristle under his gaze as he says the word mugged. A mugging is something everyone goes through. You can't throw a stone in Gwenmore without hitting someone who has been mugged or had their phone nicked by some kid on a bike. It just happens in cities.

I wasn't mugged.

I was fucking beaten to a pulp.

But that's not what I told the police. That's not what the incident report says. I've been telling everyone that some guy cornered me under the hoarding near the site, roughed me up, and stole my wallet. Nobody knows what really happened because I couldn't tell the truth. And I honestly didn't want to. Augustine served a better justice that night than the police would have.

"And with your new boyfriend, I think he's worried about your commitment."

"He doesn't need to be." I scowl. "I'll see you later. I've got shit to deal with at Gary's site again."

"You need a hand?"

"Nothing I can't manage." I force a smile and walk out of the building.

JOANNA

As I round the corner onto the main road, I almost head straight for the library. That's where my heart is calling me to. It's where I wish I was headed rather than to that site. I haven't had a reason to return to the office since the attack, and I have been grateful for that. With how I have been responding to the odd person calling me darling, I am not sure I will react well to being in that room again.

But like I told Lance, I can manage just fine. I can do my job, whatever the hell it may be today. I can do it. I belong at this company. Concord would have fallen apart after Patrick's divorce if I hadn't been there to hold it together. I'll prove to everyone just how focused and productive I can be.

I enter the building's main lobby, scan my key card to get through the turnstiles, and head straight for the elevator bank. The security nods his head to me, and already I feel a bit better. I keep up my internal pep talk until I land at the basement level.

Out in this hallway, I feel less secure in my skin. I remember it being barely lit, the feel of Augustine's hand on my back. I want to keep remembering that, but as I punch in the security code and enter the site office, every bit of moisture in my body dries up. My throat is dry and my skin itches. My stomach churns and I fight the urge to cover it with my arms. I grip the worn straps of my purse harder and walk through the clean room to where Gary sits at his makeshift desk, stepping around where I had taken that beating.

He looks up at me, but doesn't say anything until I sit down on the folding chair across from him.

"You alright?" He asks, pulling a face.

"Yeah." I try to wave him off, but my voice cracks. I am so far from alright. I want to run as far away from this room as possible. "So, what's up? Is everything alright here?"

"Not really," Gary grumbles. "We had a power outage last night around nine, the whole security system went down and it wasn't until the crew got in this morning that anyone noticed."

"Shit," I say, rubbing the bridge of my nose. My purse falls almost silently to the ground and I jump. "Sorry. Was anything stolen, do we know?"

"Not that we can tell. There wasn't even a screwdriver out of place. It's just that when we checked the log to see who last entered this office, it was your access code."

"Gary," I start immediately, a level of incredulity in my voice that would tip anyone off that I am moments from breakdown again. "I went home sick yesterday. I was most definitely not here."

"Now, Joanna," he leans across the desk and stares at me, "I know you work crazy stupid hours. Even if it was you, there's been no harm done. I just have to file-"

"I wasn't here," I insist. Tears spring to my eyes, I don't know how to get him to understand. The system is wrong. I was drowning in anxiety at nine last night. My access code to this specific site is known by three whole people. Four, I guess, if you consider that Augustine had to help me punch it in that first night, but he was at his meeting. There are a whole bunch of people who will vouch for him.

"The security guard was on rounds when it went down and since our system is separate from theirs, they had no way of knowing." Gary continues. "I just need to know how *you* want to handle this."

The room spins around me. Handle this? This is a major security breach that I don't know how to even remotely deal

JOANNA

with. My first thought is that I need to call legal and get them on my side. Or maybe get my access code changed at this site and every other one because who fucking knows who is trustworthy now.

I close my eyes and take a deep breath. There is no use panicking. There isn't. Nothing bad has happened. It is all totally fine. It definitely doesn't matter that if something had happened, I would probably be arrested. That would have been a felony offence, and then I couldn't vote or do anything, assuming I survive a prison sentence. God I don't think I could survive-

"Joanna, earth to Joanna?" Gary sounds more surly than he was a few seconds ago and I rush to apologies.

"If nothing is missing, and everything seems alright, then we don't need to do anything. This can all just be brushed under the rug. We can change my access code from here, right?"

"Sure, but I still have to report this. Clearly, your code has been leaked or whatever the computer people are calling it. Everyone on site will need to get a new code and that will mean a work ticket with the IT team at the main office because that's too big for me."

"Gary." I squeeze my eyes shut. "Please."

"Yo, boss man, you good with us covering up that graffiti?" One of the new workers stands in the doorway.

"What graffiti?" I ask. This area doesn't have a tagging issue, but hoarding normally does bring out the artist in people.

"Some schmuck wrote *bitches get stitches* near the service entrance. No fucking clue what kinda tag that is." He shrugs, his hands so casually shoved into his pockets. His hi-vis vest is stained with grime and he looks as relaxed as anyone could be, and I suppose rightly so. He's got a simple job today.

Everything about this interaction is casual, but I feel moments away from throwing up.

"You get a picture of it?"

"Yeah, should be on your email-"

"Sorry, I have to go." I rush. "Do whatever you need to, Gary, I trust your decision. You're the best site manager I have ever worked with. I'm sorry."

I grab my purse and run for the door. The guy is still blocking the exit, now just awkwardly staring at me until I shove past him. My chest is imploding, or exploding, I can't tell. It is hard to breathe, and my head is swimming. I stagger into the narrow hallway, my feet dragging across the floor until I get to the elevator. I smash the button for the lobby and collapse into the railing.

What in the actual fuck is happening to me? Is this a panic attack?

Thoughts keep rushing through my head as I get flashes of men in black masks. The feeling of spit on my cheek. The way my body just gave into the fist being shoved into it. There was nothing to protect me.

I scratch at my chest before my fingers dig into the mark on my neck, but it isn't helping. The nervous tick that has kept all emotions I have been keeping under a tight lid from boiling over isn't enough. My nails dig into the slightly raised flesh until the beds hurt.

It isn't enough. I am not enough. I am worthless.

I need to see Augustine.

20

Joanna

The brass placard shines in the afternoon sun as I wait for traffic to stop so I can cross the street. My fingers clench and unclench around my purse with every second that passes. There is so much noise surrounding me, it is all too much. I just need quiet for a few moments to breathe. The smooth purring timbre of Augustine's voice reminding me that I am enough will cancel out thoughts in my head. I keep telling myself that as I bolt across the street. My flats slap across the pavement as I yank open the heavy doors.

Book smell and recycled air assault my senses, and suddenly I am wondering if I've ever been here during the day. Is Augustine even going to be here? The new shiny extension bleeds into the majesty of the original library. The shelves turn from white to dark wood and the lights get softer. The art on the walls is much less stock imagery, bulletin notices, and more careful museum curation– objects that Augustine has collected through the years just like those in his house, our home.

The sun shines through the curtains, bright and warm. Dust

motes float across the room and guide me to his desk. He stands there resolutely, staring down at an old book with his pen in hand, notebook off to the side. Augustine looks up at me before I am even within speaking distance. Worry and confusion mar his brow when it clicks that he is seeing me in the middle of the afternoon. The mark on my neck pulses with my racing heart.

"Mon abeille?" he asks, voice a soothing balm for the ache in my chest.

"I- Something- It-" I sputter out a few nonsense words, and that's all it takes for him to pull me into his embrace.

Augustine wraps his arms around me and his sands slip across my skin. He takes me around his desk until we are almost separated from the rest of the library. My hands shake, refusing to let go of my purse. I can't stop shaking my head against his chest. The clip holding his tie to his shirt digs into my chin, but I push harder against it.

I am out of control. My breath comes in pants and short gasps. I don't know what to do any more. The clutter in my head buzzes and swarms like a hive of once orderly bees, only to be shaken and tormented by an angry bear.

"Joanna." His fingers grip the base of my neck and pull me back until I can look into his golden eyes. They flash behind his glasses and tears prick in my eyes. There are no words to explain what I need. I don't know what to do. "Are you hurt?"

I shake my head no, but then nod and say, "No, no, I was across the road and- and- and I just-" My words cut off again as I choke down a sob.

His fingers flex and I feel the sharp tips of his claws. Augustine's sands slide from his fingertips and around my neck. The weight settles me marginally. I swallow until my throat doesn't feel dry any more.

"Take a deep breath with me," he commands, instructing me and taking control of these instinctual acts. "One, two, three… One, two, three… there you are, mon abeille, again for me."

We breathe together for several more cycles. I follow Augustine's count until I don't feel faint any more. My thoughts scramble at the list of things I need to do yet and my gut twists with anxiety about being away from work. The terror I feel crawling across my skin like bugs has me shaking all over again. The sand around my neck tightens a fraction and my eyes flutter closed. I can't stop my body from heating, blood rushing to my cheeks and my panties growing damp under the pressure of my lover's touch.

Augustine inhales sharply through his nose, causing humiliation to burn through my panic. He presses me back into his desk. His pen clatters to the ground and echoes off the stacks. He nuzzles his cheek into my temple and purrs. The sweet siren song of my mate.

My knuckles brush against the buttons of his shirt as I breathe in his scent— spiced honey and warm tea.

"I am going to suggest something," he murmurs in my ear. "You may only say yes or no. Is this understood, *mon abeille*?"

I nod, but my eyes shoot open when a sharp talon tips my chin up so we can look at one another. Augustine squints at me. "Yes."

"That's my girl." The corner of his mouth tips up ever so slightly. "I am going to take you back to my office and we are going to calm you down. You are going to be reminded exactly how valuable you are. Then we are going to have a little discussion about your job."

"No," I say instantly, my gut twisting at even the mention of it. There is so much to tell him, yet anxiety is building in my throat. "No work."

"I have been patient enough, Joanna. I am not going to watch you attempt to work your newly immortal fingers to the bone. We will have this discussion. Your agreement is to whether you would like me to bring peace and pleasure beforehand."

It feels wrong to say yes. My head, even in complete disarray, has no issue continuing the tirade of put-downs to remind me that Augustine is too good for me. I am using him if I say yes to whatever pleasure he is offering me. My heart yearns for it, though. For my thoughts to be suspended in the devilishly sweet space. My body hungers for his touch all over me. I can't get enough of Augustine when we are together– mentally, emotionally, physically– he consumes me when we are near each other.

I have never known cravings like this for another person before.

"Yes," I say.

Augustine wraps himself tighter around me for a moment longer, applying pressure to my whole front, before he pulls away to grab my hand. He guides me to the back office just like he did that first night. There is no demanding bond pumping through my blood now, though. Every step I take towards this one is with the knowledge that I am going to let my boogeyman do whatever he wants. Whatever he believes that I need because I am his.

He flicks the switch just inside that turns on the low light fixtures and closes the door behind me, turning the lock with a sense of finality. I am trapped in this agreement now. There is no backing out. In this room, Augustine knows what is best for me and knows that I am his to worship and punish as he sees fit.

"*Mon abeille,*" he sighs. The words he has called me since that night sound heavy, like he is at war with his own desires and control. "What do you say if it becomes too much?"

"Iris."

"And if you can't speak?" He moves about the room, tossing a large cushion onto the ground in front of the chair I usually sit in.

I swallow at the thought. "Snap my fingers twice."

"Good girl," he hums.

I stand near the door as he prepares to bring my overwhelming nerves back to the surface. My fingers flex against my purse. I don't know what to do. Should I make tea? Sit down?

"Strip, Joanna," Augustine says, the command in his voice sending a shiver up my spine.

He stands in front of me again, looming over me like the scary monster he pretends to be, while I struggle to release the grip on my bag. His eyebrows raise over the thin golden frame of his glasses as I continue to stare at the intricate knot of his tie. He holds out his blackened, claw-tipped hand. There is a moment where I am not sure what it is for, but as I place my bag in his hand and watch how he dutifully hangs it from the coat rack, something settles in me ever so slightly.

I pull my dress over my head, and he takes that too, folding it neatly before placing it on top of his desk. With each strip of clothing I remove, Augustine takes great care to tuck them away. Even as he grimaces at the tummy control shorts I wear, he treats my clothes like they are made of the finest silks and not some cheap polyester. It isn't until he is kneeling before me I even remember that I am still wearing my flats.

Augustine gently lifts my right knee, kissing the top of my thigh before he removes my shoe. Butterflies explode in my stomach as I look down at him. His eyes glow softly, his claws digging soft little points into me. A warmth pools between my legs at the look in his eyes, the hunger that flashes as my mood settles into something sweet and carnal. He does the same for the left, tucking my shoes away at his desk, but he doesn't immediately get up. His lips trace the patterns of stretch marks that decorate my hips and tummy. I gasp at the feel of his sharp teeth.

"Augustine."

My hands latch onto his shoulders as he grips me tighter, kisses higher up my body until his tongue teases my nipple. Only when my hips rock against his hold does he stop. The way his cheeks darken ever so subtly tells me he forgot himself. He kisses my sternum once more and stands.

When he was on his knees, it was easy to forget I was the naked one, the vulnerable one. Standing face to face with him now, our power exchange is obvious, at the forefront of my mind because I am handing everything over to him. He may call me his queen, but I can't be that now. I don't want to be anything but used. For a purpose that is going to benefit someone who commands it of me with violent sweetness. I want Augustine to show me how worthy, and valuable, and lovely he finds me by making me into nothing more than a speck of dust on his shoes.

He brushes a strand of hair behind my ear and l can't stop the shiver that travels down my spine. Hints of my reflection appear in his glasses, in the blackness of his eyes, and I swallow. I am a mess, but there is only hunger in his eyes. Hunger for flesh, for emotions, for my very soul. I watch him move to the chair I usually sit in. He crooks his fingers at me, and I feel almost like I did that night at the theatre. Instinct drives me forward until I am standing between his spread thighs.

"I thought, perhaps, you would have learned by now, Joanna, that your place within the world is with me." Augustine grabs hold of me and spins, pulling me down into his lap so I am seated just like I was the night at *The Gin Palace*.

My head swims with the rush of movement, but he isn't done with me yet. Sands twist around my wrists and forearms, binding them together, before pulling me forward until my face and shoulders lay on the pillow between Augustine's legs. My legs are draped across his lap and my back bows with the soft touch of his hand. Sands trail down my spine until it coils around my throat.

I am exposed.

Blood rushes to my face, turning my cheeks pink. The whimper that comes out of me is almost as embarrassing as being balanced on Augustine's lap with my arms pinned beneath me and my pussy spread open, dripping and waiting for what's to come. He trails a talon across the back of my thigh. His other holds my hip firmly, a sureness, a secure grasp on the world to keep me from falling or floating. I know I won't fall. I know Augustine will move us if the position becomes too much of a stretch or if my back aches.

But all my focus is centred around the sharp claw dancing across my trembling body. I close my eyes. This is what I need; this time with Augustine will make everything sort itself out. He will straighten out all the chaos in my mind so we can make a list. If I can't control my mind, he can, and I don't have to worry about anything outside of the library right now. It's just us.

"*Mon abeille*, I can taste your honey a thousand times over and still it would make me hunger with desire. I need your taste on my tongue every morning from the moment you are awake to the moment you go to sleep, and still, I crave you. Seek you out in your dreams to feast on you."

A blunt finger traces the crease of my ass to my clit, gliding over my slit to smear the mess I am making across my skin. Another whimper escapes me as I try to push myself back into his touch. He tsks, wet finger tapping against my asshole with each sound.

"I have been so patient with you, Joanna, a doting mate who respects their partner's wishes, but I won't stand by and let you continue to do this," Augustine says.

His hand moves, the sharp tips of his fingers scrape across my ass. He inhales sharply as he squeezes and pulls at the heavy flesh. My muscles tighten and relax, my fingers gripping at the sands between them. My skin heats as he prepares me for what's to come.

We haven't done this in real life.

In my dreams, Augustine unleashes his true strength. He digs into my darkest desires and makes them a reality. He hunts me, chases me, takes me even when I say no. He punishes me at his whim and showers me with praise and acceptance. There is rarely a time when I don't feel the echoes of his hand imprinting itself on my skin. It grounds me and makes me want to fight against his hold when he easily thrusts into me.

After this afternoon, I will have a concrete memory of what punishment can be like when I am not taking care of myself like the queen Augustine believes I am. His handprint will stain my skin for hours, maybe even days, if I don't comply. The very thought that I could carry another mark has me squirming, provoking him before he has even begun.

"I am not sorry," I tell him. There are no lies when we are like this. Even when I am lying about not being exhausted or feeling spent from work, I will never lie when we are like this.

The first slap is gentle, if that is even possible. It makes my ass tingle and the flesh heat, but I don't react. I know what he is truly capable of.

"Your attitude will only make your punishment worse, Joanna. Is that what you want?"

"I-" I swallow the words that first come to mind, the ones that will provoke him. That isn't what I need or want truly. I want to feel. "I want to be worthy, Augustine."

"So you don't believe me when I say that you are?" he asks.

"No." A tear slips down my nose.

The truth makes my stomach hurt. I hate it, yet all the same, I say it. That's the root of all my problems. I don't believe that I am worthy of anything. People wouldn't leave me behind if they thought I was worthy. The more I fight to show people I am, the worse they have treated me. I am forgotten and pushed aside. A Tuesday lunch people won't remember because I am not worthy of a second thought.

It's why I am working myself to death. I don't tell myself that's the reason, but it is. Patrick showed interest in me, hired me for a job, and kept me. When he's gone off the rails, he has kept me close. And now he is threatening to get rid of me. Even my toxic boss doesn't think I am worthy.

"Joanna," Augustine snaps. The sands around my neck tighten and a shuddering gasp racks through me. "Are you with me, *mon abeille*?"

"Please," I beg. "Please, I am here."

Sand creeps up my jaw and brushes across my cheek as if it were his thumb. Augustine unleashes more sands. They wrap around my thighs, my waist, and my chest until I am bound tightly. The ropes of sand hold me in place and allow my body to fully relax. Both of his hands move to my ass.

"Tell me you are worthy, Joanna." He commands it with a harsh squeeze of my flesh.

I gulp and sniffle before I say it. "I am worthy."

The words are sour on my tongue and not at all like the sweet, honeyed words I am used to when we are together. Everything about Augustine is saccharine and divine and golden, but this phrase is tart and makes my chest ache. My mind can't drown that word in syrupy nothingness. It sits on top of me and keeps me from floating.

"I want you to repeat this affirmation every time I spank you. If I slap you three times in a row, you must say it three times before I continue. I want to hear every word, *mon abeille.*"

"Yes, Augustine," I say.

This time, when the palm of his hand lands on my ass, my whole body tries to jerk. The sting radiates through my core and up my spine. Augustine's hand holds firmly on the flesh while he waits for me to say the words.

"I am worthy."

The next slap lands on the other cheek, which hasn't been as warmed up. A wet gasp rushes through my lips. I say it again. The words are still sour in my mouth as I force them out. We continue like this for several more hits. The affirmation comes out of me increasingly sour, the words forced out of my trembling lips.

Claws dig into my flesh. Augustine drags his thumb over my

drenched core with a disappointed sigh that has my tummy fluttering. Tears leak from my eyes and stain the cushion beneath me.

"I can taste your disbelief, Joanna. I won't stop until you believe the words."

"I'm sorry," I murmur.

"You will be, *mon abeille*, my queen." He whispers the words against my low back, kissing me there before the sands around me tightens further.

He spanks me again. The force of his palm meeting my heated cheek echoes around the office as I choke on a sob. It hurts. The pain of it burns through me. I pull at my bonds, to try and escape.

"The affirmation," he hums, sinking his talons into my flesh until I am almost scared he has broken my skin.

"I am worthy," I choke on the sourness in my words.

The next two cracks against my skin make my back bow and my feet kick out. Augustine is quick to wrap them in his sands as well. I repeat the phrase twice between gasping sobs. With each strike, his hand becomes firmer and my bonds tighten. The words pour out of my mouth until I am hoarse and they taste of sweetness. They caress my lips each time I say them and each time I feel it.

I am worthy.

"There she is," Augustine hums softly, his touch turning just as soft.

He slowly massages my thighs and lower back, running his hands across my abused flesh while I sigh under the gentle pressure. My head swims as I lay against the damp cushion. This isn't the usual feeling. Syrup doesn't coat my thoughts, but the oblivion is sweet. My thoughts are quiet and a peace settles deep in my bones. When Augustine's thumb brushes over my slit, still dripping wet and fluttering, I almost cum. My body is oversensitive and suddenly screaming anew.

The pain that had been so consuming melts into a burning need. My eyes are slow to open, but when they do, I am met with a look of such adoration it hurts. Augustine looks at me as if I am the finest thing he has ever owned, that it is an honour to have me in his possession.

"Own me," I whisper.

"I do," he says, plunging a blunt finger into me.

He fucks me with his finger slowly, stroking and moulding my body until it is the perfect shape for him. The sands holding me vibrate with need. They massage my limbs and stroke at my skin so sweetly. I moan as they pull at my nipples, as they stroke my jaw, and caress my fingers. Augustine's thumb swirls around my clit as three fingers thrust into me. I moan with each retreat, my pussy squeezing him, trying to force him to stay inside me.

"Cum for me, *mon abeille*. Ruin your throne. Stain the leather so everyone who enters this room knows it belongs to you."

"Augustine, please, I-"

I cut myself off. I don't say the words on the tip of my tongue, but my body tells the story all the same. My legs shake and tremble as my pussy convulses and gushes. I feel it drip, hear the sloppy wet sound around his fingers as he keeps fucking me. My orgasm takes over my body and for a moment, I think I taste the ambrosia that Augustine always speaks about as everything goes black.

"Mon abeille, mon abeille, my beautiful Joanna, how I cherish you, how I worship you, how I love you."

JOANNA

The words are whispered against my temple, and warmth bursts inside me, soothing and lulling me into a realm of bliss. The taste of honey touches my tongue, and my eyes flutter open. Augustine sits on the floor with me cradled in his lap. Red stripes coat my body where his sands have grated against my skin. His hands are black, the dark veins pulsing just underneath the surface of his arms, the sands contained but present.

I nuzzle into his neck and kiss his skin. My body hums with cosy warmth and the thrumming ache of my punishment. I am pieced back together, in control of myself once again. It would be easy to stay like this forever, or for as long as Augustine will let me, but I need to come back to the present. There is so much to do and discuss.

"Augustine," I breathe out his name like a prayer.

"How are you feeling?" he asks, turning to kiss my cheek.

"Better, warm like the centre of a fresh croissant." I smile at the image that comes to mind.

He chuckles and shifts, causing his thigh to press hard into my bruised butt. I hiss at the pain, but Augustine hums another kiss into my temple. A steaming cup of tea is presented to me in a fine China cup, honey and floral. My fingers shake as I take it, but their grip is steady as I bring it to my lips. It soothes the ache in my throat.

Augustine brushes sweat-damp hair from my forehead while we sit in silence for a few more moments. I drink my tea and let the warm honey flavour soothe the ache deeper inside of me. The one that I always told myself wasn't there, or at least wasn't something to worry about. My life always had more pressing issues: college, bills, surviving. I'm terrified of people letting me go, so I either keep them at arm's length or hold on to them so tightly it breaks me when they leave.

But I need to leave. My job, at least. I need to end that relationship, but I am not sure how or when, but I can't stay. Not after what Patrick has said to me, not after everything that has happened. There are dots that aren't connecting, though. Something is happening at that job site, and I need to see the whole picture before I can go.

"It's crazy to think that if I don't quit my job, I will probably die," I say, staring at the overstuffed bookshelf against the wall of Augustine's office.

"You seem to be chasing away death left, right, and centre, *mon abeille*. First with me and now some desperate wretch at your office." His arms tightened around me as he sighed. "I have bad news and a confession to make before we start our discussion."

I wait for him to begin, unsure what Augustine could possibly have to confess to me.

"The reason I came home absolutely filthy yesterday was not because of Nash. I happened upon a group of scoundrels outside your job site at the armoury and had a rather aggressive discussion with them." He clears his throat and continues, "They were writing something vile on the hoarding around the side that I knew would upset you, so I intervened. What I was able to gather from before things got out of hand-"

"I know about the graffiti," I interrupt Augustine and his delicate explanation. He freezes underneath me, and I feel an inkling of some bad feeling just behind my ear again, but I press on even as my stomach twists. I will tell him everything that happened today, and I am going to make him tell me everything those people said. Although first, we need to go all the way back to the beginning. We need to step back and review every dot to make the connection we need to finish this picture.

"What do you know about Fae magic?"

21

Joanna

Déjà vu is weird and fucked up.

Augustine's warm hand in mine grounds me as the elevator opens to the basement of the armoury. The fluorescent lights are the same, the damp smell still floating around the air. Nothing seems weird or different besides the fact that I am breaking into a job site on Saturday night instead of letting Augustine lull me to sleep and chase me through my dreams. My fingers flex against his as we stand in front of the door and wait.

Wednesday's conversation repeats in my head over and over again. Lines are being drawn towards dots, and a vague shape is taking form. Like the scaffolding surrounding the building, the structure is there, but I can't see what's inside. I can't figure out why I am being targeted or who is going through all this trouble for what feels like nothing.

My stomach twists with nerves and I jump when a low feminine voice suddenly calls out to us.

Heading towards us from the opposite end of the hallway is a tall, beefy woman who looks about forty years old. Her dark

JOANNA

hair is flecked with greys and piled up on top of her head and she is wearing a uniform from the Wild Woodlands Trust. I'm not sure how to feel about letting another stranger into the site office to begin with, but Augustine convinced me that if I wanted to make sure there was no magic left in the basement, the fucking fae queen would be the person to check. That is a whole different world that I am struggling to wrap my head around.

Monsters being a part of my world? Fine, apparently. I had seen proof of it, and facts are facts for a reason.

Other realms existing next to ours? That is just a step too far for me right now.

"Breathe, *mon abeille*," Augustine whispers against my cheek, and the knots in my stomach loosen with the heat rising in my cheeks. A tingling sensation behind my ear makes my blush stronger when I meet his gaze. One problem at a time, I remind myself. I can add Fae Realm to my list of topics to discuss with him later, after a game of hide and seek.

"Auggie." She smiles big and broad when she reaches us, flashing thin, razor-sharp teeth. Up close, I can see the high points of her ears and how her dark skin actually glitters under the fluorescent lights. "And you, what is your name?"

I gulp when her full attention is directed at me. "You may call me Jo," I say the practised phrase Augustine gave me.

She makes a friendly 'pft' noise and punches Augustine's shoulder. Sands from under the collar of his jacket slip out before she can make contact with him. Her gaze returns to me, and I see a twinkle in her eyes. "You may call me Nora, or my queen."

Augustine growls at Nora's flirting and my nerves crack with a big smile on my face. The fingers wrapped around mine become tipped with talons and the feeling behind my ear shifts. I knock my hip against his, and the urge to remind him to be nice is almost overwhelming. We want Nora's help. He can swallow his feelings for a bit so we can get this done with. I am his, and he knows it. He just wants to put on a show.

I put in my new PIN for the door lock and flick on the switch quickly. Just like the first night I was here, the switch from dark to light makes me flinch a little, but everything else is clear. No mess or masked men hiding in dark corners.

And Augustine is here, in this room. I am awake and his sands are covering my whole hand like a protective blanket. I take a deep breath and turn around to look at Nora. Her lips are pursed as she looks around. She drops the backpack she's carrying onto the floor and crouches down. She pulls something from her cargo trousers and then whispers to it. When it starts to glow, I see it's a little crystal and I have to contain my questions. I want to ask Nora a lot of stuff, but I hold my tongue. I don't know what's an appropriate question and I don't want to interrupt her work.

"This place will always fill me with shame."

I blink and look up at Augustine. His expression is pinched as he looks down at the floor. While I have vivid memories of what happened that night to a certain point, the whole after is black and Augustine gave me a scrubbed version of what happened with Deg'Doriel and Nash. I don't know how bad it was when they opened the door and Augustine saw everything.

"You did everything you could," I say, wishing I could make him feel how grateful I am that he was able to do what he did. If I hadn't been at the library that night, if he hadn't

JOANNA

followed me, I probably would have died. Those guys would have delivered their message and then gone on their merry way while I laid in the dark, alone and forgotten. My regret about that stems only from my desperation to do well at my job, to prove I could do it.

Augustine saved my life, and has given me a new one, an eternal one that I will get to spend with him until the world ends. He is my hero, my saviour. I don't want him to feel anything but my love for him. I want him to know that buzzing, sweet warmth that takes over me is because of him and only him. That he makes me feel alive and like a person who is allowed to take up all the space I need.

"I should have sensed them." His jaw clenches and I see his lips stretch. "There was no reason for it to have happened that way. I was not focused on you the way I should have been."

"Stop." I pull him down and kiss the corner of his mouth. The tickle behind my ears flutters for a moment and Augustine's shoulders slump slightly. "There was no reason to think there was anything wrong. I am alive because of you."

"Joanna," he whispers, something in his voice shaking, but I give him another kiss to distract him from what he is going to say. There is no point rehashing the events of that night. It won't do us any good at this point. Those guys are dead.

There is a loaded sigh from the far corner of the room.

"Goddess, you are cute. You sure you only want one mate?" Nora looks wistfully at us as she asks. Augustine sneers again and she snorts. "There is definitely still something here, but I'd have to take apart this whole room and probably even the wall to find it."

"You can't do that. Your majesty." I add quickly. Nora winks at me again and the blush rises in my cheeks. I run my hand over my face and blow out a heavy breath. "Okay, so what do we do now?"

"I mean, from my end, the magic still here won't cause side effects. Any non-humans you have working for you will probably be able to sense it, but it's not like it will hurt them. The magic here is *old*, old, but harmless."

Nora begins to pack up her bag, pocketing the small crystal that is no longer glowing. She pats her cargos and does a final sweep of the office to make sure she has everything. I do the same after grabbing a few binders from behind Gary's desk. I'll return them on Monday with any excuse for why I used my access code on a weekend. Augustine immediately takes them from my hand to tuck them under one arm before grabbing my hand with the other. Goodbyes are quick after that, and I am soon nestled into my chair in Augustine's office.

I have to fight the urge to chew on my nails. That is really not how I wanted that little meetup to go. Nora was supposed to confirm there was nothing, not there absolutely is something hidden in that office that could be setting some crazy shit off. Florals and honey fill the room as Augustine pours tea for us. He passes me a cup, a small chocolate-covered biscuit tucked against the saucer.

"Thank you," I say, unable to keep from frowning. "I know what you are going to say."

"And what is that?"

"This is not something my queen should lower herself to, *mon abeille*. You are above this menial office work. They should be so lucky to have had you for as long as they have. You are better than those plebeians. I hate Lance." My nose scrunches up as I play up Augustine's French accent.

He rolls his eyes with an indulgent smile that sets me at ease.

JOANNA

I sigh into my tea before taking a sip. Augustine leans against his desk and stares at me, his teacup balanced easily on his finger.

We are complete opposites.

While I feel like a tight bundle of nerves and anxiety and guilt for something I can't even place, he appears languid and at ease. I am average and forgettable and Augustine extraordinary and commanding. His very presence demands acknowledgement. He is always so in control, collected in his thoughts and actions, while I am drowning in even the most basic of tasks and barely able to keep my head screwed on straight.

"You are thinking too hard, mon abeille. Tell me what has you so sour?"

"You are perfect, and I don't know how you ever looked twice at me," I confess.

"Mmm, well I did not," he shrugs. "I looked once and was blinded by the truly opulent nature of you. Golden, burning, and honey sweet, your dreams were a drug I could not resist."

Heat rushes to my cheek and I take another sip of my tea. Augustine inhales deeply and an over-large smile grows on his cheeks.

"Spun sugar that teases my senses all the more now that we are bound for eternity."

I take a deep breath as my belly somersaults. I don't think I will ever get over his own sweetness.

"Can you explain the magic shit to me again?"

"Such vulgar words from sweet lips." He clicks his tongue and gives me a pointed look before continuing. "The Fae magic that Nora was sensing is from her predecessors. At the first rustling of war with the South, the last monarch reached out to Deg'Doriel to make a bargain. In exchange for moving their gateways to safety, our local militia would be protected from death."

"Yeah, but why not just move anywhere? Why bargain?"

"I cannot say. I was in London at the time assisting with the beginnings of a society similar to our group forming."

"So they made a deal, got magicked up, but then post-war didn't clear shit up?" I asked.

"It would appear that some more advantageous humans were able to hide away their Fae gifts, and now someone is out to get their hands on it."

"Are all monsters ancient?"

"No," Augustine scoffs like the very idea offends him. "Different species, different lifespans."

"You're being snooty," I say, looking at him with my own pointed expression.

"As one of the oldest, it is my right." He smiles, finishing his tea. "But I wouldn't be surprised if one of your new hires is a young monster looking for a longer life and they are willing to do whatever it takes to get it. Harming humans will mean nothing to them."

"So you think it is a monster?"

"Definitely," he asserts. "Humans are greedy, but stupid-"

"Rude."

"And they cannot tell normal from paranormal, so they are not a risk."

"I'm still upset with how this has all turned out." I slump deeper into my chair and kick off my trainers. "It was supposed to be an easy win for me to show Patrick I am actually good at my job."

"Joanna."

JOANNA

Augustine stands abruptly and grips my chin with clawed fingers. Pin pricks of pain make my soft skin tingle and my bottom lip juts out in a pout. For a moment, he is distracted looking at my lips, licking his own slowly before he turns the heat of his gaze full onto me. I swallow slowly.

"You are doing the best you can. Forces outside of your control are working against you. If those imbeciles cannot see how integral your work is, they do not deserve you."

My shoulders slump. I have heard this speech many times, but it never gets rid of all the feelings or thoughts trapped in my head. That is something that will take time, and I have plenty of it now.

"You are doing exceptionally well, mon abeille," Augustine continues, his grip loosening just enough for me to bite my lip. Another blush spreads across my cheek at the praise. "Don't ever doubt that."

He pulls me in for a kiss and it tastes like reassurance. The flavours of Augustine and comfort coat my tongue as I press harder into his lips, searching and craving more of him. He indulges me by letting me lead this kiss, stroking my tongue against his until my lips tingle and my thoughts start to slow.

"So sweet," he murmurs against my lips. "Now, shall we go home so I may show you just how exceptional I believe you are?"

22

Augustine

35 days

I spent the rest of the weekend trying to convince Joanna her job is not worth it, that she should allow me to spoil, ravish, and worship her endlessly. Still, she insists on proving to Patrick that she is not going to back down from his threats, even if it is putting her in danger by staying. Which it absolutely is. I could taste the treacherous disdain in that office when I collected her for lunch today. Patrick stared daggers into my chest the moment I walked into that office to take *mon abeille* away for the *full* hour of her lunch. I am not sure what has poisoned him against me exactly, but I do not care. He is a parasite sucking the life from my queen and I will remove him before he drains her.

Monday was subtly different. There was a flavour in the air that made my sands roil with hunger. It is not the employees' fear or Joanna's exhaustion that she believes she is hiding from me. It is dark and murderous. There is definitely some form of creature in that office, but Joanna never allows me to linger in anyone's company. She believes I am going to cause some sort of scene if any of those silly drones approach me.

She is probably correct in that assumption, but I would never, will never, embarrass her in such a way.

At our usual table in the small French cafe, Joanna shows me the file of a man who looked exceedingly average, and perhaps a tad grumpy.

"He knew about the sh-stuff," she whispers before taking a large bite of her pain au chocolat, crumbs falling onto the small plate tucked under her chin. "He worked a couple of jobs for us last summer, but he's got a big scar on his face this summer."

"Scar withstanding," I say, drinking my weak chai latte. "I would need to meet and speak with them to be able to tell you what they are."

"I will see what I can do, but I think it's this guy causing problems and getting humans killed for it."

"And you are sure Patrick is not..." I wave my fingers around instead of saying the exact words I wish to say. To me, it makes perfect sense for the mastermind behind all this to be Joanna's boss, who has recently returned from a midlife crisis. He also has the funds and security to ruin his own venture if the results are worth it.

"I-" Joanna stops herself and takes a drink of her sugary coffee, thinking about that. Her fingers drift my bond mark, the subtle shining dots turning pink under the pressure of her fingertips. Something primal inside of me threatens to rumble out as she seeks comfort in my mark on her throat. I recross my legs and lean back subtly in my chair to ease the growing ache between them. "I think he is just human."

Even through the haze of aromas and auras in the cafe, I catch a hint of something tart from my mate and quickly change the subject to plans for Thursday evening to attend the theatre again. Joanna's cheeks burst into a deep shade of red and I cannot hide the smug satisfaction it brings me.

The sooner she leaves this job, which she has insisted she will not do until she has a new role in place, the better. Perhaps Kragnash has something with the city that would fit her specialities. It would be easy enough to secure her an interview, or maybe I could simply convince her to work with me at the library. Then we could spend our days together, recreating her dreams and making new ones. I only want for her to taste of sweetness and pleasure if I can help it.

"Orthia."

Nora sounds like she is about to cry when the sea witch walks into the room, interrupting the meeting. She looks on edge, avoiding my gaze as she stands in the doorway. She smells of the docks and her aura is as dark as ever. I would be pleased to see her if it were not for the woman clutching her hand like it was anchoring her to reality. As I stare at the new woman, her eyes firmly looking just over the heads of everyone, I swear I see them go milky white. Her aura glows a soft, subtle pink around her that is almost imperceptible. She tastes of sea salt and rage, just like Orthia though. I make a note of both of them in my notebook.

"You're late," Deg'Doriel growls.

A vicious sneer crosses his face as he looks at the two women. Unphased as if he already knows who this new human is, our demon's tail flicks with light agitation. Another note in my book, double underlining the need to have a private meeting with Deg'Doriel once again to discuss keeping the group updates noted fully.

"We aren't staying," Orthia says. "I won't return until I know that he has righted the wrong he has committed."

"Witch." My eye roll is barely contained as I stare down Orthia. "My mate is perfectly content-"

My phone ringing cuts through my speech, Joanna's cheeky grin over a mug flashing across the screen. I hold my expression, but I am nearly overjoyed to have a reason to skip this discussion with Orthia. While I have no desire to explain my actions to the witch, I will in order to avoid ruining Orthia's return to the group. I excuse myself quickly, breezing past the two women and turning down the hall to obtain a level of privacy. The door to the meeting shuts behind them quietly and cuts me off from the group's emotions and scents.

"Impeccable timing, mon abeille. Is everything alright?"

"Yeah, just walking out the building, so I thought I'd call while I walk to the house. Is the meeting over?"

"Not exactly, but you know I am more than happy for you to interrupt me."

"Augustine," she chastises me, and it feels glorious. "I'm hanging up. I'll text when I get home, go participate, or whatever."

"Fine, fine, fine. I need to stop by my office to collect a few books, and then I shall be home as well."

"Good, see you at *home*."

She hangs up and my sands are in a riot. *Home.* She admits that my house is her home.

I have a new goal, to singularly rip every update from the creatures in that room so I can rush to my mate's side. Tonight, I am going to worship her and make her forget her name before she falls asleep in my arms so I can do it all over again in her dreams. My sands beneath my skin ripple and I blink to keep my eyes clear. The meeting must continue.

I am actually smiling when I walk back into the room.

Orthia and her human are gone, and the meeting has resumed. A succubus discusses having to take a client to the hospital after a feeding got out of hand during their session.

"I saved that fucker's life. The least he could do is buy me a new dildo."

With a sigh, I pick up my notebook and make a note of the near miss. This demoness is getting very close to having an intervention or removal. But even as I think of upcoming schedules, I cannot stop thinking about what Joanna would want to do this summer. Could I convince her to take a week or two off? Maybe even go to the seaside, re-enact one of her little dreams.

The meeting goes on and I am lost in thought for nearly all of it. Only when Deg'Doriel does his final wrap-up do I look at my phone to check the time and for Joanna's message. Except she is not at home. *Going to armoury. Security called about an issue.*

Sands explode from my hand and shatter the phone. Arlo jumps nearly a foot in the air, and Ramón hisses. Nora looks like she is about to say something, but I am already rising from my chair.

"What the fuck, Ravenscroft?" Deg'Doriel demands.

I shove my notebook into my satchel and tug my arms through my jacket. "I must go. Leave a message at the library if you need me."

I storm out of the church and into the courtyard. I do not even know how long ago that message was sent. My control had snapped like brittle China before I noted the timestamp.

What was she thinking? Of all of the places to go to alone. For Christ's sake, does my human have a death wish? Does she?

I bound down the pavement with one clear motivation. Find my mate and force her to see the error in this course of action. I have made my feelings about her returning to that place alone clear as crystal. Even if Nora is certain the lingering magic is harmless, Joanna is not to go there alone.

The scaffolding comes into view quickly. As my boots slap against cracked concrete with each hurried step, something in my chest tightens in a way I do not understand. My claws dig into my palms as I rush into the lobby and pass the security guard at the desk without a second glance. If he tries to stop me, I will kill him. I will not be slowed. My sands pulse erratically under my flesh. They push out of my pores before boring back inside my skin.

My eyes burn and my sharpened teeth grind together. Every ounce of control I have is slipping from my grasp as the lift takes me into the basement. I will not fail Joanna again. That night will not repeat itself. I will get to my human on time, my mate, my queen.

The door to the site office is closed when I round the corner in the darkened hallway, but I can hear the low rumble of arguing. The voices are silent when I wrap my fingers around the handle, waiting to hear how many people will die tonight. A yelp, high and familiar, vibrates through the door. I do not even think. I ram the door with my full strength. Joanna lies on the floor as Lance towers over her. The scarred man stands next to him, bulging arms crossed and a scowl on his face. When he meets my gaze, I see it, the shift in his eyes and how he bristles in my presence. The overwhelming taste of anger in the air cannot douse the recognition of this man's scent. He's a monster, a predator, but he has been cornered by a bigger threat.

"Jameson." He growls and unfolds his arms, claws catching in the light. "Lance, back the fuck up."

Lance finally tears his eyes away from my queen, and I see the mania on his face, the way it twists his lips and furrows his brows. Even if the Fae magic left lingering in these walls is harmless, something else has sunk its teeth into Lance Jameson. Or perhaps he has always been this way. His greying hair is mussed and the shadow of hair on his jaw only ages him further. He reeks of desperation and nothing more– nothing is altering the whipping red aura around him except his own emotions trying to claw their way out of him.

When he looks at me, I see the blood drain from his face.

"You," he seethes. "How the fuck-"

Lance's question cuts into a screech when I look down at Joanna. Her right cheek is stained red and tears shine in her eyes. If I had control before, it vanishes now. My spines burst through my jacket, hardening and flexing against my skin as my body morphs. Finally, he will get to see the monster. No more control, only hunger.

I stalk over him, sands lashing out at his limbs. I lift him off the ground, sands racing from my grip to his skin.

"Drop him, Sandman, or she gets it."

The other being. So quickly, I forgot he existed when I saw my chance to destroy this repugnant excuse of a man. My Joanna whimpers, her heart racing and the terror rotting away her sweetness nearly brings me to my knees. He grips her throat, claws pricking the delicate skin so close to my mark. I sneer and throw Lance into the shelves on the other side of the room. His body crumbles in such a gloriously satisfying way.

My chest aches as I wait to see what he will do now. Joanna's aura flickers in and out of my vision as I stare down the monster. Sands pour from my body as I watch him shift, bones cracking and skin moulting enough for me to recognise what he truly is, a Gnoll.

"This Fae shit ain't worth dying over." His voice is rougher. "You're gonna let me leave, or I tear her fucking throat out."

"She does not leave this room."

"I'm not a fucking idiot. She reeks of you, Sandman. You want her alive, she stays with me until…"

His voice trails off as my sands penetrate his pointed ears. His body jerks, muscles tensing and shaking as he tries to fight me, but the savoury burn of his emotions, his soul, seeps into me as my sands take from him. Fear spikes in the room and I see the blood on Joanna's neck. My sands rush from me and the dead man's arm tears from his body. Blood coats my mate as she collapses onto the floor. The dead Gnoll falls to the side as I race to Joanna's side.

"Mon abeille." I cup her cheek and pull her face to me. I need to know she is with me, that she is alive and well. "Mon abeille, speak to me please. Are you okay?"

"He's fucking lost it, Augustine. He's, he's, he's-"

A crack explodes. Joanna screams and it's the last thing I hear before everything goes dark.

The library is dark, low candlelight guides me back into my domain. I take note of each shelf. All of my books are in place, and it looks like the maid has been keeping up with the growing collection well. Not a speck of dust to ruin the paper in sight. My shoulders relax. I should feel at ease when I sit down behind my desk. The tea on my desk wafts with steam and I can smell the smoky aroma of the Lapsang Souchong.

Something is not right here. I survey my office. The coat rack is in the correct spot, the correspondence from Deg'Doriel is on the side table. The candelabra burns just as I left it. My belongings are in place, just as they should be.

I look over at my reading chair. That is what is making me feel uneasy. There is something missing from that spot. I round my desk and look at the leather wingback. The embroidered cushion is in place. The book I was reading before I had to leave for something is still resting on the arm. I wrack my brain, staring down at the piece of furniture trying to figure out why this is not correct. There is something about the leather, it's missing something. Did the maid clean my chair? A stain used to be on the seat, but how did I stain the seat?

"Augustine? Can you hear me?" someone shouts, their voice echoing around my domain. "Augustine."

The longer I hear the voice, the more the chair before me seems to be missing something very important. My sands reach out and brush over the cushion. By the gods, by magic, by my own sheer will, a golden thread appears around my black sands. It grows and pulls at my sands and I see something, someone, forming in my chair.

I am struck with the scent of honey.

Mon abeille.

AUGUSTINE

"Augustine, holy shit!" Joanna rushes me, her soft form wrapping around mine before I can raise my arm. Her terror rises with each breath she takes. "Holy shit, you're alive."

"Of course, I am alive," I soothe her, pulling away to cup her cheeks. "How did you do that?"

This space has always been my sanctuary; it is my own resting point amongst the dream realm. It is simply me and the souls I have acquired through all of time. Now Joanna is here, and everything is as it should be. I cannot see a more perfect place for us. Here for eternity, where I can keep her safe and provide for her everything she may need.

"Fuck, you're alive." Tears leak from her eyes as she touches my face. Her fingers weave into my hair, ruining the styling and pulling me closer to her lips. "You need to wake up, please. Please, Augustine, wake up. I need you."

Everything burns. My head is on fire and I can barely feel my extremities. I cannot open my eyes.

"You, you really did. This is your fault. You just couldn't-"

"Lance, please-"

"Lance, Lance, Lance, do you know how your voice grates? My ears bleed every time you say my name. Jesus Christ."

There is rustling to my right, I taste the mania in the air, the fear, and the panic that mixes into it as well. My eyes crack open just enough to see Joanna. She is taped to a cheap folding chair. She shakes as Lance paces just behind her. When he kicks a box that has fallen on the ground Joanna nearly jumps out of her skin. My sands pulse with life, tasting the terror in her. Her delicious fear morphing into something rotten and foul on my tongue.

"Please just let us go, I-I am going to quit. I won't tell anyone, promise-"

"I don't believe you. You didn't get the message the first time. I even had to risk Patrick flying back." He grabs her shoulders and I swear I am going to rip his hands from his body first. How dare he touch my queen.

"I don't understand."

"No, because you are too fucking stupid to get it. You should've left it all alone, but you couldn't. First with the accounts, then when I thought I had found the jackpot you stole it."

"No, I didn't, they aren't he-here-" A tear leaks down her cheek as she tries to think and I am forced to watch her panic and stutter as my sands, my body, refuse to operate at my will. I cannot protect her. I cannot save her.

I *have* to save her.

"Then where are the pins? You were here on Saturday. Where did you fucking stash them."

"I don't-"

"Yes, you fucking do," Lance shouts and grabs Joanna by the hair, forcing her neck back to look at him. "Yes, you do, Jo, you have that fucking fae magic shit. You haven't been the same since your little *sick leave*."

"I don't," she insists, her voice cracking. "I don't, Lance. There are no pins or any shit, I swear."

"Don't fucking lie to me." His screech makes even my ear hurt. "I am not leaving here empty-handed, you selfish bitch. Where'd you put them?"

"They aren't-" Lance twists her hair tighter and Joanna cries out. My sands vibrate and quake beneath my skin, trying to get closer to my mate, my Joanna.

"Yes, they are real. You can't lie to me any more. That freak of a dead boyfriend proves it. Does he have them?" He shoves her head forward hard and the chair teeters. Metal flashes under the fluorescents and a gun points directly at me.

Joanna's sharp cry echoes in my pounding skull. I desperately try to push my sands towards her, but they will not leave me. Useless, I am useless. Until my body has healed, or my sands have reformed my missing parts, I am forced to watch the horror scene play out before me.

"I know you were here on Saturday. A dirty jerk off in the johns and David from IT showed me everything. You two and that weird crystal bitch found the last of those fucking pins." Lance seethes, his chaotic anger making my gut roll. "I really thought after last week, with Gary on this fucking project, he'd make sure you got fired so you wouldn't get in my way again. I really did. I don't know what you said to that fucker, but Patrick had no clue about the security breach."

"I buried legal's report," Joanna admits, tears dripping off her chin.

"You what?"

"Gary submitted the report to legal about the breach so they could record it in case of an incident, but I hid it so he wouldn't see it. I can't-"

Joanna's confession breaks off into a harsh sob when Lance shoves the small handgun into her cheek.

"Joanna finally has to pay for her fuck ups, and you fucking do this, huh? Can't risk people seeing how useless you really are." Lance shoves the barrel harder into her cheek and the chair crumbles.

Joanna's face bounces off the floor. My body jerks. Every grain of sand I can take control of pushes out of me. I have to protect her. I have to save her. She gasps, sobs wrack her prone body as she tries to breathe, but I cannot reach her. I cannot comfort her. Her eyes meet mine, a flicker of something in her iris, but it is just as quickly gone when she blinks away tears.

"Piece of shit." Lance pulls his foot back to kick her.

"Don't," I groan. My tongue forms the words and forces them through my sharp teeth. "Don't you-"

"Shit." He jumps and almost drops the gun. "What the fuck are you?"

Distracted at last, he steps away from my Joanna. He must have shot me in the head to make my recovery this slow. And now he has that damnable thing pointed at my chest again. He cocks the gun and shoots. His aim is poor. The bullet pierces my shoulder. Sands dribble from the hole, forcing the bullet out of me. My ichor cools quickly against my shirt.

"Your," I roll over onto my stomach, "worst nightmare."

My body jolts as another round crashes through my spines, but I force myself up. I move my body, swaying on my feet as I stand. My fingers move to my face and the crusted ichor that sticks to my hair. That is an amount that will take me time to recuperate, the grains of my sand still slipping from the wound.

Another shot is fired at me and I stumble back. My knee gives out and I fall back down.

"Augustine," Joanna whimpers.

"Do not worry, *mon abeille*," I say. "This is nothing."

My sands are pouring from holes in my body and pooling lifelessly below me. Certainly not the worst scrape I have ever gotten into, but Joanna does not know that. I can taste her despair in the air. It burns, like ammonia being forced underneath my nose to wake me from a faint. I cannot escape the scent.

Lance cocks the gun again, and I brace for another shot. A plan is already forming in my head, how I am going to torture and torment his soul for eternity, twisting his dream into nightmare tales for all time. When my sands are alive again, Lance will die. He just needs to shoot me again, empty that stupid weapon into me and then it will be all over for him.

"Do it," I command him through grit teeth. *"Fucking snake."*

Vile, stupid snake.

He shoots me again. The bullet pierces my stomach, and it takes everything I have to hold myself up. My spines tremble before sinking back into my body. The sands suddenly become too much and I choke. It rushes through my head, filling the empty space and making my thoughts scramble. I collapse on my side.

"Augustine!" Joanna screeches, and I see the gold thread again.

It floats through the air in a slow pattern, like a lost bumblebee searching for a flower. I look at my human and see a true shine in her eyes I have never seen before. Honey gold eyes meet mine as a second thread flies and dances with the first. They both land on Lance's hand, the gun jerking in his hold.

"Shit, get off. What the fuck?" The panic in his voice rises to match his flavour. It tastes herbal and savoury on my tongue and I crave more. I am losing what little grip on this realm I have left, but I need to stay awake. I will not leave my mate.

23

Joanna

"Augustine," I scream.

He's not moving. The dark sands around my lover are lifeless, and my body aches to touch him, comfort him, pull him back together so he won't leave me. My bond mark burns like it's being erased from my skin, my very soul being cut off from his.

Lance scrapes at the golden sand wrapped around his wrist, but it keeps wrapping around him. With every wave of the gun in his hand, I flinch. He's going to shoot me next. I know it. Whatever has happened to him, his mind is broken. The Lance who used to sit next to my desk and tell me bad jokes about hard hats is gone. He isn't my friend any more. He hasn't been my friend for months, maybe years.

"I had it all, the wife, the money. God the money! It was so easy until you had to go sticking your nose in places it didn't belong."

His words echo in my head over and over again. Lance has been embezzling money from the company. That was why my budgets never came up right. That was why he was always so willing to help and review my work. He needed to make

JOANNA

sure I didn't see it. It's why Patrick was furious with me. Fuck knows how much he has taken. Who fucking cares at this point?

And it still wasn't enough for his ex-wife to stay with him. They left him, and he thinks more money, a longer life, and magic will save their relationship? Greed isn't going to fix his wife leaving him.

I know what it is like to be left behind. He is trying to desperately hold onto something that he will never be able to get back.

After everything he has done, there is no going back to how things used to be. He can't buy his wife's love back; he can't forget all the hurt he has caused. Whatever he was going to do with those pins– keep them to live longer or sell them to the highest bidder, it's pointless. They are as lost as Lance's sanity.

I am barely able to breathe, the tape constricting my body too tightly. My pulse pounds in my skull and my muscles ache. I am losing feeling in my fingers, everywhere. That part of me that hasn't been alive for years is consuming my every thought.

I am going to die.

Tears cloud my vision as my thoughts spiral further and further into the darkness, the loneliness, the fear. My gut aches with a bottomless pit consuming my insides. I pull at the tape, the sticky bonds yanking the hair from my arms. They twist and twist, but I can't rip them. I am not strong enough. The broken chair digs into my back as a sob racks through my body.

Another sob echoes around the office. This one is deeper, filled with anguish.

"Fuck," Lance cries. "Oh god. What's wrong with me? What have you done?"

His ruddy face looks at me so openly, eyes wide with tears staining his cheeks. Fluttery gold sands creep across his neck. I am transfixed as the man before me sobs. He falls to his knees, shoving the heel of his palms into his eye sockets.

The gun is still in his hand, dangling across his face, and I can't take my eyes off it. I can't. That stupid thing is what stands between me living, saving Augustine from whatever the fuck is happening to him and dying right in this fucking hell site.

"Joanna," Lance moans. "I feel so empty, why am I so empty? Do I even deserve to live?"

My gaze flicks to the black sands surrounding Augustine; they haven't moved. There is a line of it trying to reach me. I can just make that out through my tears, but they aren't reaching for Lance. The only thing touching Lance is the gold sands. The grains seep into his ear the longer I stare at him. My stomach rolls at the sight and Lance gags. He grabs his stomach and wretches like he has lost control of himself.

The acrid smell makes me want to throw up all the more and as my stomach and chest riot, I feel like I am choking all over again. Even as he vomits across the floor, Lance claws at his chest, his throat. His fingers slip through the sands like water and he can't stop gagging.

His shaking, weeping form matches my own. As I struggle to breathe, to stay present enough to see Augustine's fingers twitch and his chest slowly rises up, Lance breaks down between us. Golden sands drip from his eyes and mouth, coated in tears. They look almost like honey. He can't stop it. Every swipe at his face he makes only smears it across his skin until he is glittering gold.

"I'm sorry, I'm sorry, I'm sorry," he cries over and over again, smashing the side of the gun into his temple. More of the gold sand leaks from his mouth, but now blood drips from his temples. The sense of unease that ripples through me is so whole and violent.

"Lance, you have to calm down," I say, voice straining as my lungs fight for air. "Please, let me help you for once. I- I- I will find the pins or find you something new. I have a lot of friends."

"NO, no, no you won't, you won't, you won't. Joanna." He draws out my name in such a long whine that it turns into a blood-curdling scream.

I want to cover my ears, to run away, but there is nothing I can do to escape his wailing. The tortured sounds that rip from his throat sicken me, make the nausea buzzing around my insides ratchet up higher. Lance shakes as he continues to scrub at the mess falling from his lips and slithering back up his body. The golden sands that leak from him cycle through his body endlessly, uncontrollably, and the more I stare at the horror of it, the more hypnotised I become by the sight of it.

Finally, when I look away, I turn to my boogeyman, my lover. Augustine's chest is barely moving, but his sands have started to come back to him. The mess of black around his body is shrinking the longer he lies there. His ichor stains his clothes and the floor beneath him as the sands disappear. I need him. I need him to survive and wake up, even if it is just long enough for us to run away. I look at him again, how his chest shudders as it rises and the bee pinned to his lapel catches the light.

"LANCE!" I shout his name as loud as I can, my voice

straining and echoing around the room. "It's there."

For a moment, he stops shaking, even as the gold sands nearly coat his body.

"It's there. It's- his- pin on his-" My words are frantic as my jumbled-together plan tries to spew from my lips. Fuck, I just need him to believe this lie, hope that his brain will fucking understand what I am saying. Lance looks up and I see gold sands covering all of his eyes now. Something like hope flashes over his features before he scrambles to Augustine. The gun is tossed across the room, the metal scraping across the linoleum, setting my teeth on edge.

His fingers tear apart Augustine's jacket, fumbling and gripping and shaking until the pin is in his hands. I hate it. Seeing him touch Augustine makes my blood burn, but I can't do anything from this chair. I just have to get Lance away. I will lie to save us for now.

"It won't work." I start, my throat seizing violently as I cough.

"Why not?" Lance's voice sounds almost small, desperate and wet from crying. "Why won't it work? It has to work."

I draw in a ragged breath. "You have to take it to him. Bless it."

There is no *him*, there isn't anybody. As far as I know, that is just an accessory that Augustine likes to wear. From what I have gleaned from him as well, there is no being who gives blessings away, it is always a transaction.

As frantic as Lance was on Augustine, he is more frantic when he grabs onto me. He rips the tape from my body, and I scream. My skin burns, but air rushes through my body and makes my head swim all the more. I slump harder into the floor.

JOANNA

"Take me. Take me to him now. You owe me."

Lance doesn't give me a choice. Grunting, he pulls me up. My aching arm is tossed over his shoulder, and the sands surround me. They're warm, so soft and gentle on my skin it is almost soothing. Lance half drags me to the door, my knees buckling every time I try to step forward.

"That way." I point him in the opposite direction of the lifts, and he doesn't even question it. I am taking us to that tunnel because I don't know what else to do. I know that is how Nora got into the building, so maybe Lance will get lost in there long enough that Augustine will find me. The further away from him get, the more my bond mark aches. I don't want to leave him alone, but I have to keep him safe.

It takes a while for us to get to the storage room. Every few moments, we stop because my legs have given out or because Lance attempts to wipe away the golden sands still trying to take over his body. I feel like I am going to pass out again by the time we get there. My head is pounding and my vision blurs and focuses at random.

"There's nothing here," Lance groans, his own knees beginning to shake.

I blink, trying to clear my vision and orient myself. It is exactly like Augustine said it would be. An overcrowded room of shelves and broken computers and office furniture. My head falls forward as I try to think where the tunnel is, what shelf it's behind. Picturing the buildings above us makes my head throb, but I do it. Finally, I point my finger in a direction.

"Behind the shelf, tunnel." My words slur and I can barely string my instructions together.

Lance drops me. I crash into the hard floor and it's almost a relief. Pain radiates up from my hips and down from my shoulder, but I am alone. Metal screeches across the floor suddenly and then all is quiet again. He doesn't move the shelf back, he doesn't say goodbye, he doesn't need me any more. Lance stumbles into the darkened tunnel while I lay here, forgotten.

Gold fills my vision slowly. The sands that once covered Lance are now coming for me. I shake as they softly cover me, warmth radiating from them like the first sunny day of spring. There is nothing I can do but wait, and as if my brain knows what I really need, my eyelids droop.

This isn't my dream. Something about this version of the library screams it isn't built for me. The curtains seem heavier, and the art of the walls looms more, darker and quieter. The only light here seeps out from under a shut door. As I approach it, I see the thin brass plaque that says "The Librarian" in a stamped font. My knock echoes around the vast expanse of the library, off the towering shelves and into the great depths I can't even see.

"Enter." Augustine's voice is quiet, yet booms through his library and vibrates my whole being.

As I turn the handle and enter the room, fabric rustles around me and I feel the weight of what I am wearing. I look down and see lush, vibrant green chiffon and silk draped across my body in a style I can't place but know it's Augustine's doing. Even with the unwieldy train behind I can't help but smile when I look up.

My monster, my boogeyman sits behind his desk, with a cup

of tea in one hand and a book in the other. Another steaming cup sits across from him in front of a sturdy chair. He hasn't looked up from his book yet, his brow set in a hard line that tells me he is trying to solve a puzzle that is truly stumping him. Carefully, I take my seat and wait for him. The tea in front of me smells like flowers and honey, and the smile on my face stretches even wider.

This feels so right and normal, like this is where I am supposed to be. My chest flutters and fresh tears well up behind my eyes. I want to spend eternity with Augustine, watching him, surrounded by him. Everything about this is perfect.

"Mon abeille," Augustine sighs, setting his teacup down. "I am sorry to keep you waiting, but I am trying to understand why this book arrived at my library. I have not taken this soul, yet here it sits."

"Whose is it?" I ask, picking up the biscuit on my saucer.

"Well, I do not know. I cannot see a name attributed to this-this action man thriller? Gods, is this what modern men read now?" He gesticulates, the paperback flopping his hand before he tosses it down.

The cover looks like something from an airport or that would be promoted at the checkout aisles of a grocery store. It's over-saturated but still dark and has big, bold letters on it. There isn't a title, but clear as day on the cover is the author, the soul whose story is told in this book.

Lance Jameson

I choke on crumbs in my mouth. Guilt swells in my stomach as I try to swallow down all the other feelings churning inside me. He's dead. Lance had been a friend, or a mentor at least, and he is dead now. It... it's my fault. It has to be, right?

On instinct, I pick up the book, ready to flip it all the way to the end of it. The moment my hand touches the cover, gold sands burst from my fingers. They buzz and dance across the cover of the book until the font is gilded and the cover designed anew. A classic noir mystery novel with a darkened character on the cover holding a smoking gun and walking into a tunnel. A book I would have devoured as a teenager when I had the time and will.

"Fuck."

My heart pounds against my chest. I drop the book back on the desk, my empty hand reaching for my throat, my mark, but when they get close to my skin, I panic. What if the gold sands come for me? They know I don't belong too. They are gonna turn me into something else.

"*Mon abeille*," Augustine whispers.

"I can explain, I can," I say, really not sure how I can explain what the fuck just happened.

"You are truly a goddess among men, my queen." An awe-filled smile stretches across his face as he stands.

He rounds the desk as I flounder, trying to remember what happened before I entered the library. Where had I come from, what I was doing, how the fuck I got here again. As he kneels at my feet, Augustine grips my hands, pins them together until my shaking fingers are still at last. Hazel eyes meet mine and my world collapses around me, tears dripping off my cheek. I can't bear the look of adoration on his face, everything in me folding in on itself.

"Joanna," His fingers brush across my cheek, and he turns my face in his direction. "What are these tears for? Why does your scent sour with guilt?"

Blinking away the tears, I say, "I-I don't know what happened, Augustine. He just walked into the tunnel. He-he was covered in all this gold stuff and screaming and crying and you were just lying on the floor-"

My voice cracks as a sob strangles my throat.

He looks at me with confusion and then it dawns on him. His expression softens, a soft coo vibrating his throat as he pulls me onto the floor with him. My knees sink into the plush rug. I can't stop the guilt from clutching tighter around my heart. I am the reason he is gone. Lance was going to kill me, I had no other choice, and yet I still chose.

"You did what you had to do," he murmurs, kissing my hair like I deserve comfort. "You are alive, you belong, you are mine. You will never be apart from me. Nothing you do or want will scare me away, Joanna."

"You don't understand," I cry. "Lance walked down that tunnel because I told him he would find what he was looking for there. I didn't know. I just needed time for you to wake up."

My voice cracks as another sob takes over me, and I can't force out the right words. Augustine holds me tighter, his fingers digging into my sore flesh the least I deserve.

"You did what you had to do to survive a nightmare," he tells me. *"Mon abeille*, he was going to die."

"How do you know that?"

"He was going to end up in this library one way or another, your hand or mine. Lance was going to die tonight, no matter what. If anything, you gave him a much easier demise than I would have."

"I-I could feel his emotions, or he was feeling mine, I don't know. It's all mixed up, and I just had to get him away."

"You did the right thing."

"It feels so wrong, Augustine. I feel wrong."

"It will fade, in this life or the next," Augustine says with such certainty it makes me feel even worse. How can I ever move past what I have done?

"If it doesn't?"

"Then I will remind you, every day, for the rest of our lives, how much you are worth to me and the world, alive and well and in my arms."

Augustine's spines emerge from his back and slowly, the black sands surround us, encompassing all of us in a blissful darkness. My fingers dig into his jacket. I am desperate to hold onto him, desperate to hold on to the darkness I know rather than one that is trying to consume me whole. Even with my face buried against Augustine's shoulder, there is still too much light. I blink and blink away tears, trying to make the dots and colours go away, but they won't.

"Mon abeille," he whispers, lips stretched and pressed against my mark. With everything churning inside of me, I miss the silly feeling behind my ear. I miss the bond that flows between the two of us until I am overwhelmed with a sense of awe and adoration. "Do not hide away in the dark when you are the light."

Fingers dig into my hair until I am pulled away from his shoulder. I blink away tears, scrubbing the heel of my hand into my cheek. The long sleeves of my tea gown are ruined with tears and snot, but when I can finally see, I can't bring myself to care. Surrounding our beautiful dark sands are dots of gold. They float and dance around, landing on the thin branches formed from Augustine's sands.

"These are yours, Joanna, my honey bee, my queen," Augustine says, the conviction of his words bringing more tears to my eyes.

They don't make the guilt go away, they don't change what has happened or what will happen, but they settle me into this new world that I am officially a part of now. The darkness that surrounds Augustine, the choices he makes and the ones I will undoubtedly have to make again weigh on my shoulders, press into my chest until it is hard to breathe, but I don't fight it. Augustine lets me cry into his shoulder until my tears have dried up and my soul is as tired as my body feels.

"It's time to wake up so we can go home, *mon abeille,*" Augustine whispers.

I shake my head, content to never open my eyes again, but I can already feel this dream slipping away. My sands pull and pull all the way back into my being as I slowly awaken.

Epilogue

56 days

I pour boiling water into a cracked ceramic mug, watching the mass-manufactured tea bag bloat and expand. While it steeps, I pour a cup of coffee into another mug, adding two spoons of sugar and a splash of the new creamer bottle that arrived tonight. When that is done, I toss the tea bag from my mug into the trash and set the spoon aside to be washed. Chemical sweeteners assault my senses as the steam from the mugs in my hands wafts into my face. I do not pull a look, but if I were the type to do such a thing, it would be one of disgust.

The sea witch still has not returned from her summer holiday. Her Love has been feeding, though. A body washed up on the riverbank last week with all the signatures of one of Orthia's predilections… although this is the first time we have ever seen one in the city. If they wash ashore at all, it is usually in winter when they have had a few months amongst the fishes, as it were.

As I take a seat, setting the mugs on either side of my chair, I pull out my notebook and make a note to get more information from Deg'Doriel about her companion.

Ramón, smoking a large cigar and with his shirt mostly

unbuttoned, saunters up to the vacant wooden chair next to me. The sewer rat eyes the seat, eyes the mug next to it and grins at me. Something on his scales catches the light and as his tail swishes back and forth, I catch a whiff of something that isn't his normal stench.

"If you so much as touch that chair, I will end you, Ramón." I do not even bother to look up from my notebook.

"So pissy all the damn time, Auggie, the ball and chain not-"

"Ray, c'mon now."

Arlo's intervention is the only thing that saves that vile lizard. Ramón knows exactly how to push my buttons, that bloodthirsty buffoon. He is lucky to have monsters as gentle as the ghoul around. Who has begun to look sallow again, his skin lacklustre and his hair greying at the temples. Even though he will deny his hunger, his true nature, Arlo must feed like the rest of us. It seems that there have not been so many accidents as of late. While he may have the highest count of us, having never actually killed anyone, he has expressed concerns about what happens when he goes too long without a proper meal.

Still, he is supposed to hear back about an interview at St. George's any day now, so I will wait to have a tête-à-tête with him.

Nora is not here. An envoy from the fae realm, a coquettish little beast, has taken her place. They prance from one lesser monster to the next, absorbing as much information about them and what they do as they can. I even see them taking notes. At one point, I think I hear them say a name, which is practically against fae law, but I do not make a note of it. They are simply flirting their way through a group of new people. This one must still be green to not understand the mortal realm's full goings.

Deg'Doriel is his same cheerful self. With the upcoming arrival of his new skin bag, the demon is on high alert. I do not want to know why. Perhaps he has looked the monk up online, or perhaps Margie Lawson is trying to drive him into a murderous rampage, but our fearless leader has been cagey, to say the least. Or perhaps even more so, he is still furious he was outvoted by the group.

The demon has always been one to hold a grudge for petty things.

I take a sip of my tea to avoid looking at my watch. Lesser monsters begin to take their seats, and Deg'Doriel looks pointedly at me.

"*Mon abeille* will-"

As if speaking her into existence, the door to the basement room creaks open. Joanna's shoulders hunch, and she makes some pathetically human gesture of apology before taking the empty seat next to me. I watch my mate settle into the wood back of the chair, her shoulders softening even though Ramón picks Arlo off his chair to sit next to her. She is not oblivious to the lizard, but she has already turned towards me while I hand her the coffee I have prepared for her.

The way she smiles, her cheeks flushed from running here, make my sands ripple under my skin. Thin tendrils reach out for her, to taste her gentle, sweet scent. It is not until Deg'Doriel aggressively clears his throat that I break eye contact with her.

"Jo, this is your first time here." His grin is cruel as he looks at her, and I can feel the wavering in her emotions. "You can go first, though I'm not sure Augustine'll need to take notes."

"For Christ's sake, Deg," I say, waiting for him to turn his

EPILOGUE

surly mood on me. I know not to speak of that person in his company, but I cannot find it in myself to care when it comes to easing my mate's comfort.

"It's no problem, Deg'Doriel," Joanna smiles, but it is a bit wobbly.

She stands and turns to face the group of twenty or so monsters in the room. Her fingers dig into the handle of her coffee mug, and I feel her anxiety, the almost fungal taste it brings to her sweetness. I control myself, keeping my sands away from her. This is her moment; she can do this. I believe in her.

"Uh, hi everyone, I'm Jo."

The crowd parrots back, as they are all transfixed. *Mon abeille* is still mostly human. Her scent, her aura, her soul, they are still a part of her. The delicate gold sands that dance from her fingers tip are the small part of me that she has taken on. While we have not discussed the possibility that she may obtain some of my abilities, I do not think she would care either way. Her constant reminder to me, *you make me feel alive*, rings in my ears as I taste the hunger in the air. The sharks think they smell blood.

"I am officially unemployed as of today." Joanna tucks some of her hair behind her ear and lets her fingers run over the bond mark on her neck. I watch, my sands threatening to rip through my shirt, as she presses into the raised scar. My lips stretch fully across my face as we make eye contact, and the blush deepens on her cheeks. "Um, I turn thirty soon, which I think if you had asked me at the start of the year how I felt about that, I would have said anxious and surprised. But uh, now I feel kinda ambivalent about the whole thing."

There is a snort from a vampire in the back who is about

Joanna's age in physical form but has been coming to our meetings for almost as long as she has been alive.

She pauses before she starts again. There is a tension in my jaw, Joanna's emotions in the bond turning from a slow drip to a steady bleed of guilt. She takes a sip of her coffee and swallows hard.

"And it's been fifty-six days since I last killed a human."

Thank you for reading!

What started out as a silly little novella idea with no plot really turned into something didn't it?

None of this would have been possible without the amazing help from generous and supportive people in my life. Thank you for never giving up on me.

Special shout out to-

- To Bex, Carolina, Allie, Kassie, and all the BWoY, who invited me into their group and helped me achieve this goal!
- To Emma and Orla for constantly being around to do sprints and cheer me on. We'll be tier 9 one day.
- To my developmental editor, Caitlin, who pushed me to make this story more fulfilling and real.
- To my beta team, I'm so sorry for all the typos, but your encouragement and kindness brings so much joy to my heart.
- To my editor, Angie at Lunar Rose Editing Services, it wasn't easy getting here, but you are a fucking super star. Thank you!

About the Author

Ash Raven is an indie author who specialises in spicy romances that make their mother equally proud and scandalised.

A mood writer who isn't afraid of biker gangs, shadowy monsters, or baseball coaches– their books focus on plus-size and LGBTQ+ leads who get the romance of a lifetime. When they are not writing, they are cuddling with their two orange cats and drinking oat mochas through a straw.

Born and raised in Indiana, they have been living their own insta-love romance in London, UK since 2015.

You can connect with me on:
- https://www.authorashraven.com
- https://www.tiktok.com/@authorashraven
- https://www.instagram.com/authorashraven

Subscribe to my newsletter:
- https://www.authorashraven.com/subscribe

Made in the USA
Las Vegas, NV
10 September 2023